SAS
OPERATION

Days of the Dead

DAVID MONNERY

HARPER

Harper
An imprint of HarperCollins*Publishers*
1 London Bridge Street,
London SE1 9GF
www.harpercollins.co.uk

This paperback edition 2016
1

First published by 22 Books/Bloomsbury Publishing plc 1996

A catalogue record for this book
is available from the British Library

ISBN: 978 0 00 815551 3

Set in Sabon by Born Group using Atomik ePublisher from Easypress

Printed and bound in Great Britain

MIX
Paper from
responsible sources
FSC **FSC˚ C007454**
www.fsc.org

1

Placida Guzmán shifted her swollen body on the twin bed, trying to ease the cramping pain in her lower abdomen. She was dressed only in T-shirt and knickers, but the erratic swish of the air-conditioner seemed devoid of any power to cool, and the heat of the day still clung damply to her skin.

She manoeuvred herself on to her elbows, wincing at the pain. On the street outside the level of conversation seemed to be rising, and in the distance several sources of music were competing for attention. After a few moments she recognized Selena's voice among the throng.

The patch of sunlight had almost finished its climb up the peeling wall and perhaps a breeze would soon be blowing in from the sea. It would be so nice to go out for a walk on the famous beach, just a simple walk in the sand, just to feel free again.

She sank back on to the bed, knocking a couple of empty laxative packets on to a floor already littered with them, and gently massaged her stomach with her palms. Fifteen months they had been on the island, fifteen months at his beck and call. And the call had come often. He had told her more than once that she was the most beautiful of the five, and it had sounded like a life sentence. She would still be there now if she hadn't got pregnant.

But that was all in the past. Him, the island, the shame. She just had to get through this, and a new life was waiting.

Another wave of pain ran through her body and for a few seconds she had trouble breathing. Where was Victoria? She'd been gone for what seemed like hours. Placida hoped to God her friend hadn't got lost in the strange city. It shouldn't be that difficult to find a drugstore, but something had snapped inside Victoria during one of the nights with Bazua's men, making her behaviour difficult to predict. Sometimes she seemed just like her old self, but at others it was like talking to a small child.

The first thing they should do after this was over was to get help for her. But how and where? On Providencia all the girls had dreamt of going home, but once off the island, once away from him, Placida had found that the thought of returning to Cartagena, to the familiar streets and familiar faces of family and friends, seemed not only unreal but also, in some strange way, the ultimate surrender. It was as if the past could only be buried as a single entity; if she was ever to be happy again the slate had to be wiped completely clean.

She wondered if they would receive the money they had been promised. The man had been angry last night, and she supposed he would be again if nothing had happened, but what else could she do? If he refused to pay them then who could they complain to?

She grimaced, and felt another knot tightening in her gut.

It was almost dark now, and maybe the air was cooler, but the thought of trying to open the window was too daunting. Victoria could do it when she came back. If she came back.

Where the hell had she got to? Surely the obviousness of her condition would have saved her from being hassled in the street.

Placida thought about the baby growing inside her own belly. For the child's sake she knew she should go back to Cartagena, where her family could certainly offer him or her a better start in life than she could manage on her own. She herself had been happy enough in the house in La Matuna, and the garden with its sweet-smelling hibiscus flowers. Maybe it had been different at the time but she found it hard to remember having a care in the world as she grew up, at least not until Rogelio came into her life, and her father's discovery, not that much later, that she was no longer a virgin.

She laughed at the sheer absurdity of it all, and felt something shift inside her. It wasn't a cramp like the others and for one delightful moment she thought it must be the baby's first kick, but then a hot white light seemed to explode inside her, so sweet and so painful, and her heart seemed to thunder in her head. Her back arched once, and as she slumped back down on to the bed the darkness fell across her brain like a swirling black sheet.

A couple of blocks down Miami Beach's Washington Avenue, Victoria Marín was looking in vain for a street sign. It had taken her much longer than she'd expected to find a drugstore and now, clasping the bag containing the new supply of laxatives, she couldn't seem to find the hotel again. The pavements had seemed to suddenly fill up once the sun went down, and with all the non-stop motion and incessant noise she was finding it hard to think.

It had to be that way, she thought, staring hopefully down the neon-drenched street. That building in the distance might be the hotel. It looked white, and its shape seemed familiar.

As she started to walk a hand suddenly grasped her around the waist. 'And how much would you be?' the man asked in

Cuban-accented Spanish, his hand working its way up her T-shirt towards a breast.

She stopped and looked at him, tears erupting from her eyes.

His leer gave way to surprise, and then the hand was gone, and she had a fleeting glimpse of his angry face as he turned away. Why was he angry? she wondered. What had she done?

Several people were staring at her, she realized. She hurried on, passing through the aromatic clouds which hung like advertising hoardings outside the restaurants. She was hungry, she thought, and there was only forty cents left in her pocket. They would have to ask the man for some money when he returned that evening.

She reached the building she thought she'd recognized, but even up close she couldn't be sure – they all looked alike, and she hadn't thought to check the name when she went out. But the fat woman behind the reception desk was familiar, and so was the look of contempt she threw Victoria's way.

She thinks we're whores, Victoria thought, and remembered, clear as if it had been yesterday, Marysa shouting at Placida that 'whores got paid', that the five of them were slaves, not whores. 'Slaves have no choice!' she had yelled, eyes glittering with angry tears. 'None of this is our fault! None of it!'

It had been a comforting thought then, and it still was. Victoria started to climb the stairs, taking it slowly. Even though the pellets had all come safely through, her body still felt strange. It was like a country after invaders had been expelled, she thought – it would take time to get back to normal.

She remembered sifting through her shit for the condom-wrapped pellets and shuddered involuntarily, even as her mind thought how strange it was, getting upset about something like that after all they'd been through.

4

She stopped on a landing, and tried to remember how many flights she'd climbed. Through a window she could see a fat crescent moon setting behind the city, and she stood there for several minutes staring at it, lost in a thoughtless reverie.

Eventually she turned away, and again there were tears in her eyes – these days she couldn't seem to stop crying. But at least she was on the right floor, and it took only a few moments to reach the door with the badly painted number 314.

'I'm back,' she said cheerfully as she walked in, and it was several seconds before her mind accepted the information her eyes were passing on. Placida was lying on her back, one leg raised, its foot twisted inwards. Her eyes were wide open and seemed full of surprise.

Her skin was still warm to the touch, but there was no doubting that she was dead. Victoria sank to her knees, her arms on the bed, like a child about to say her bedtime prayers. This time the tears didn't come, just a soft mewling sound, which seemed to be seeping out of some crack in the night, but which she knew was emanating from her own mouth.

She would never know how long she stayed in that position. The next thing she remembered she was gathering her few things together and, on a sudden impulse, taking Placida's passport as well as her own. She crossed her friend's arms, closed her eyes and mouth, straightened her legs and covered her to the neck with one of the hotel's grimy sheets. Then, after one long and despairing look back from the doorway, she fled the hotel.

Jesús Barbosa walked jauntily across Washington Avenue and through the front door of the Grant Hotel. He was carrying a calfskin briefcase and wearing an open-necked white shirt, freshly pressed cream chinos and a new pair of alligator-skin shoes. A large gold earring in the shape of a fire-breathing dragon hung from one ear, and the smile he offered the fat lady behind the desk reflected, literally, the fifteen hundred dollars he'd just spent on cosmetic dental work. In the words of the last detective who'd found reason to question him, he gave the impression of someone who'd seen one too many *Miami Vice* reruns.

He took the stairs two at a time, hoping that the bitch had finally got herself on the pot. He didn't like making unnecessary journeys, not in heat like this. It was days like these which made him nostalgic for the mountains he had grown up in, where the heat was dry, there was always a breeze and in the evening the temperature dropped more than a couple of degrees. The trouble was, there was nothing to do in those mountains – no music, no cars, not enough women.

Barbosa reached the third floor and walked down the short corridor to the women's room. Normally he would treat himself to the female mules, but this pair were too obviously pregnant for his taste, though he could see that they'd both been lookers before. He didn't bother to knock on the door, just turned the handle and stepped inside to find the body laid out beneath its shroud.

'Shit!' he muttered angrily, ripping the sheet aside. 'Shit,' he repeated with rather less vehemence, and looked at his watch. He was meeting the *gringa* in an hour and a half, and he didn't want to turn up smelling of corpses. But there was close to half a million dollars' worth of heroin inside this one, and no *puta* was worth that. He sighed, unclipped the mobile from his belt and ordered some transport.

That done, he plucked the six-inch blade from its sheath on his right calf, ripped away the dead girl's clothes, made a rough twelve-inch slit in her abdomen and began searching

6

through her innards for the sixty-nine pellets of heroin that she had swallowed on Providencia.

Half an hour later he had recovered sixty-six, which, with the one that had burst, left two unaccounted for.

It was enough. He wrapped the mutilated body in a sheet, washed his hands and was just looking at his watch when the rap sounded on the door. In the corridor Miguel and Roberto were standing on either side of the small refrigerator, breathing heavily. Once they had carried it into the room he helped them cram the still-flexible body inside – in heat like this rigor mortis took a long time to kick in. Then he followed as they wheezed their way back down to the truck, which was parked in the alley beside the hotel.

They drove off, headed for one of the usual dumping spots in Dade County, and Barbosa, his briefcase now two pounds heavier, hailed a taxi. With any luck he still had time to store the merchandise and take a shower at his fitness centre before his assignation with the Pamela Anderson look-alike.

It was almost midnight when the cops found Victoria Marín on the moonlit beach. At first they assumed she was help-lessly drunk, but there was no smell of liquor on her breath. They searched the canvas shopping bag for drugs but found only two Colombian passports and a few cosmetics. She apparently had no money.

Throughout this process Victoria refused to speak, and it was only by exercising enormous will-power that she refrained from screaming when one of the cops took her arm to lead her to the car.

She couldn't stop herself from crying. She didn't think she ever would.

2

The road arrowed into the distance across the flat Pampas countryside. Farmland stretched away to either side, the farms themselves mostly pinpoints of light on the low horizon. In the vast sky a full moon was playing hide-and-seek with an armada of clouds.

They couldn't be much more than forty kilometres from the outskirts of Buenos Aires, Jamie Docherty reckoned, and soon he would be able to see a red glow in the sky above the highway. He remembered nights as a young man driving back down from Loch Lomond to Glasgow – a close friend had always insisted that the glow was nature's way of warning people that cities were bad for their souls.

Docherty took a glance in the rear-view mirror. Both nine-year-old Marie and seven-year-old Ricardo were fast asleep, which wasn't exactly surprising. Between them, he and Isabel had driven nearly eight hundred kilometres that day, and over four hundred and fifty the day before. The two children had certainly started out hyperactive, but they just hadn't been able to stay the course.

Beside him Isabel was also more than half asleep. She was in her mid-forties, a couple of years younger than he was, but she seemed just as beautiful as the day they had met, more than fifteen years ago.

Docherty smiled to himself as he remembered the first time he'd seen her, striding in through the doors of a hotel in the southern Argentinian town of Rio Gallegos. It had been at the height of the Falklands War – in the immediate aftermath of the landing at San Carlos – and Docherty had been leading one of two four-man SAS patrols which had been secretly airlifted on to the Argentinian mainland for the purpose of observing enemy activity at the Rio Gallegos and Rio Grande airfields. Having done everything which was required of it, his patrol had been on the point of heading for the Chilean hills when a complication arose. Two members of the other patrol had been captured, and there were fears that they would be tortured into revealing the name of MI6's only agent in the area, an Argentinian woman based in Rio Gallegos. So someone had to warn her of the danger.

Docherty had taken the task upon himself, and changed his life in the process. The two of them had ended up escaping together across the mountains and falling in love along the way.

Now here they both were, driving towards Buenos Aires on a warm winter evening. It wasn't the first time they had been across the Andes since setting up home in Chile two years before, but it still felt vaguely akin to putting their heads in the jaws of a lion. Of course, as far as the Argentinian authorities were concerned, Docherty was just a retired English soldier who happened to be married to an Argentinian national. And though his wife had once been exiled for involvement in terrorist activities, that had been long ago, in the time of the 'Dirty War', which nearly everyone but the still-active 'Mothers of the Disappeared' was so keen to put behind them. No one in authority had any inkling that husband and wife had met on Argentinian soil, midway through a military action which had probably helped to swing the Falklands War decisively in Britain's favour.

After Docherty's retirement from the Army they could even have settled in Argentina if they had wanted, but neither of them had. There were too many painful memories for Isabel, and Docherty preferred Chile. There wasn't much to choose between the behaviour of the two armies in recent decades, but he found the people west of the Andes more friendly – more Celtic in spirit than the Anglo-German-oriented Argentinians. The climate was better too, and the mountains, lakes and islands of the south were like Scotland revisited.

Isabel still had friends and relations in her homeland. Her father had died during her exile in England, and her mother had cut all ties, but there were a couple of her father's sisters with whom she still kept in touch and one cousin to whom she had always been close. Rosa lived with her academic husband and three children in a large, rambling house in Recoleta, and it was she who had invited them to the capital. Just for a holiday, she had said, but the two women had known each other a long time and Isabel suspected an ulterior motive. She had told Docherty as much, but neither of them had any idea what it might be.

Maybe she wanted Isabel's help with her elder daughter, who seemed to have inherited her wider family's interest in left-wing politics. The country might be run by a president more interested in cars and women than politics, but the same bastards as always lurked in the shadows.

It could be anything, Docherty thought, as a Mendoza bus blared by in the opposite direction. A holiday was a holiday, and any excuse to take time away from the damn word processor and his wretched memoirs was more than welcome.

He'd been working on them on and off for over a year, and on a more or less nine-to-five basis for several months, but he didn't have much more to show for his efforts than a huge pile of handwritten notes. When he tried actually writing it never seemed to come out the way he intended, leaving him to mutter 'you had to be there' at the annoyingly unresponsive screen. And when he had finally managed to put together a coherent chapter on the Bosnian business his publishers in London had come back with a long list of suggestions for alterations, most of which seemed designed to either obviate the risk of Her Majesty's Government taking exception to Docherty's version of events or to encourage Jean-Claude Van Damme to accept the movie part.

Docherty was well aware that a Van Damme movie might make him rich, but the thought of faking his own life story didn't sit too well. If he was going to write the damn thing, he wanted it to tell the truth. He wanted his children to see him as a man who knew he had lived and worked on a moral tightrope, not as some glib action hero pumped up with either Hollywood cynicism or gung-ho fascism. A month had passed since Docherty and Isabel had seen Mel Gibson's Oscar-winning *Braveheart*, and he still felt angry about how bad it was.

Well, at least he didn't have to think about any of that for another week. And the sky was growing red above the highway ahead. He leant over to nudge his wife awake, as she'd asked him to. 'Not far now,' he said.

Isabel yawned and reached for the tube of mints on the dashboard. 'I wonder what Rosa really wants,' she murmured.

In the Colombian city of Cartagena it was almost five-thirty in the afternoon and the lengthening shadows were throwing the crenellated walls of the old fortifications into dramatic relief. Carmen Salcedo, who had just finished her spiel on the era of piratical sackings and let her tour party loose to explore the walls on their own, watched the mostly American tourists happily ambling away, camcorders whirring, cameras poised.

It was certainly a beautiful evening. She stood leaning against one of the abutments, enjoying the blues of sea and sky, the gold-flecked waves and the buildings of the old city glowing in the evening sun. For all its problems – which ranged from drug traffickers through political corruption to air pollution – Cartagena was still a magical city.

Carmen had lived there for all of her twenty-six years. Her parents still lived in the hills behind the city, but she now shared a two-bedroom flat with Pinar, a fellow tour guide. They were going to the cinema that evening, she remembered, and looked at her watch. She should have given her charges twenty minutes, not half an hour.

But it was too late to worry about that now, and so far this group had proved more reliable than most. She walked back across to the bus and found Mariano squinting at a sex comic which he was holding only a few inches away from his eyes.

'Getting short-sighted?' she asked sweetly, making him almost jump out of his seat.

'Don't do that!' he half shouted, glaring at her.

She didn't think he had ever quite forgiven her for turning down the offer of a date, but he was a good driver, and on the streets of Cartagena that was no small matter. 'Sorry,' she said with a smile.

He huffed and puffed, then went back to the comic.

The Pearsons, an American couple in their sixties who had commandeered the front seats of the minibus on day one and, despite several heavy hints, never surrendered them to anyone else, had left a Miami newspaper to guard their precious space. It was almost a week old, but better than nothing, and Carmen sat down to improve her already near-perfect English.

She read the entertainment section first, hoping for a preview of the films which she would be able to see later that year in Cartagena, but they all seemed to be the same old boring hi-tech thrillers. She hadn't heard of any of the bands mentioned in the music section, and if their music bore any relationship to the way they looked in their photographs she doubted if she was missing much.

She ignored the sports section, and was just skipping through the local news when she saw the headline 'COLOMBIAN GIRL KILLED BY DRUGS'. Underneath it the sub-head claimed that 'Traffickers cut her open to reclaim shipment'. Jesus, she thought, and then the two names stopped her in her tracks, and she could suddenly hear her own heart beating. She read the whole paragraph:

'Another girl, whose Colombian passport identified her as Victoria Marín, was taken into custody by police last night. She was carrying a second passport, which enabled police to identify the dead girl as Placida Guzmán, but was either unwilling or unable to further help the Miami Beach PD with their investigation.'

She read on, but there was nothing else, no mention of the other three, no mention of her sister.

'Could you take a picture of us, dear?' someone asked, disturbing her reverie. It was one of the Englishwomen, with her husband hovering behind her. Carmen nodded dumbly, climbed down from the bus, pointed the camera and pressed the button, still in a state of shock.

'Are you all right, dear?' the woman asked, a concerned look on her face.

'Yes, I'm fine,' Carmen replied, smiling. 'It's been a long day.'

'Well, you'll soon be rid of us for the night,' the woman said with a twinkle.

Carmen smiled again, and looked at her watch. Ten minutes more.

They went slowly, but everyone was on time. On the drive back to the hotel she went through the next day's itinerary – they were visiting the nearby Corales del Rosario National Park – and then asked the Pearsons if she could borrow their newspaper for the evening to help brush up her English.

Mr Pearson seemed a bit reluctant, but his wife was only too happy, probably seeing it as a down payment on their continued tenure of the best seats. At the hotel she counted them all out, remembered to re-check the next morning's pick-up time with Mariano, then headed for a phone. Pinar was upset that their evening at the cinema was off, but she could tell from Carmen's voice that something serious had happened. 'I'll tell you later,' Carmen explained, and rang her parents' home. Her mother answered.

'I'm coming up,' Carmen told her. 'I have to talk to you both.'

'But we're going out at eight . . .'

'Just wait for me,' Carmen insisted. 'It's about Marysa.'

'What about her?' her mother asked, sounding almost angry.

'I'll tell you when I get there.'

It was an hour's journey on the bus, maybe even more at that time of day, so she decided on the luxury of a cab, as much for the privacy as the gain in speed. It had seemed the most natural thing in the world to immediately ring her parents, but the tone of her mother's voice had given Carmen cause to wonder. Should she have sat on this information for a few hours, thought about what she wanted to do with it, before putting herself at the mercy of her father's stubbornness and her mother's selfishness? What were they going to say to this? The last time she'd raised the issue with them they'd both been really angry with her, as if somehow it was her fault that their other daughter had been taken from them.

The trouble was, their instinctive approach to anything potentially disturbing was to ignore it, in the hope that it would go away. And it worked for them, or at least it did in the sense that they managed to avoid most of the disturbance which other people called living. But it had never worked for Carmen.

The traffic seemed worse than ever, but shortly after seven the taxi deposited her at the foot of the bougainvillea-bordered drive. Her parents were fairly rich by legal Colombian standards, her father having inherited the family footwear business. It was the combination of this wealth and the lack of a ransom demand which had eventually convinced them all to accept the police investigator's conclusion that Marysa was dead.

They had likewise assumed that Placida Guzmán and Victoria Marín were dead. And Irma. And Rosalita.

Carmen let herself in through the front door, and a few moments later found her parents putting the finishing touches to their evening's apparel in the enormous bedroom.

'Oh, I wish you wouldn't tie your hair back like that,' were her mother's words of greeting. 'Can't you afford a proper styling?'

'I don't want a proper styling,' Carmen said, running a hand over her severely pinned black mane.

Her mother just looked at her.

Carmen laid the newspaper out in front of her on the dressing table. 'Read that,' she ordered, pointing out the item with a finger.

Her mother sighed and started reading, still fiddling with her earrings as she did so. Then her hand suddenly stilled, leaving the filigree ornament swaying in mid-air. 'Oh, my God,' she said softly.

'What is it?' her husband asked, leaning over her shoulder to read.

'Guzmán and Marín are common names,' Carmen's mother said in a small voice, as if she was arguing with herself.

'Not that common,' Carmen said gently. 'And Victoria Marín and Placida Guzmán together – it's too much of a coincidence. It even says that Victoria is twenty-three, which would be right.' She looked at her parents, both of whom seemed to have been suddenly aged by the news. 'Don't you understand?' she said. 'This means there's hope.'

'We understand,' her father said, and the look in his eyes seemed to add: we've lost her once and now we'll get the chance to lose her all over again.

Carmen felt like slapping them both. 'So what are you going to do?' she asked her father abruptly.

He looked at her for a moment. 'Talk to the Chief of Police, I suppose, and get him to contact the police in Miami.'

'Don't you think you should go there yourself? I'll come with you,' she added – his English had never been good.

He shook his head. 'The police in Miami are more likely to listen to a fellow-officer than a Colombian civilian.'

Which might well be true, she thought. 'So will you call now?'

He smiled wryly. 'He won't be in his office.'

'His home then.'

'I don't have his home number, and even if I did . . . Carmen, the newspaper article is a week old. Putting the man's back up to save a few hours is not worth it.'

'And we're going to be late,' his wife added, earrings finally in place.

'You're still going out?'

'What do you expect us to do – spend the evening wringing our hands?' her mother asked.

'No, I suppose not, but . . . You will ring first thing in the morning?'

'I'll go and talk to him in person.'

'Good.' She felt relieved.

'There's food in the kitchen if you want some,' her mother told her, and once they'd gone she toyed with a plate of warmed-up fish risotto for a while before deciding to head back into town.

On the bus she found her mind running through the events of that fateful August. The five young women, all from good families, all in their last year at college, had taken a picnic a few miles down the coast, in an area which had always hitherto been considered safe. In the early afternoon they had been seen by several other picnickers, as well as joggers and courting couples, but after four o'clock the record of sightings came to an end, and the party had not returned to the college that evening.

No suspicious groups or vehicles had been seen in the area, but when after several days the women had still failed to reappear the assumption had grown that a new guerrilla group must be holding them to ransom. Once two weeks had passed without any demand for money being received, the betting had shifted in favour of either some catastrophic and completely unfathomable accident or what seemed an equally improbable mass rape and murder.

Now it seemed likely that they had been in the hands of drug traffickers all this time. Placida was dead and Victoria was 'unable to help', whatever that might mean. Where were the other three, and what had their lives been like for the last two years?

The answer to the last question was too horrific to contemplate.

Victoria would know, Carmen thought, and she was more likely to talk to a friend than a gringo policeman. If her father didn't get anywhere with his contacts, she decided, then she would go to Miami herself, with or without her parents' blessing, and find out what had happened to Marysa.

Docherty and Isabel didn't discover the reason for Rosa's summons until three days after their arrival in Buenos Aires. On that Tuesday Docherty and Rosa's husband, Giorgio, a second-generation immigrant of Italian descent, had driven to the university, where the media unit's satellite link-up was being put to good use, showing England's final group game against Holland in Euro 96. England outplayed the Dutch and Docherty, a true Scot, duly lamented the Auld Enemy's victory. But as they drove home to Recoleta he had to admit that England seemed to be playing football these days, rather than just kicking it upfield and running after it like headless chickens.

The two men arrived back to find the children running riot in the house while their wives were preparing the ingredients for a barbecue on the patio. Rosa gave the task of igniting the charcoal to Giorgio, collected a bottle of chilled white wine from the fridge and poured glasses for the four of them on the patio table. 'A toast,' she said. 'The future.'

They all drank. Here it comes, Docherty thought.

'Though it's the past I want to talk to you about,' Rosa began carefully. Behind her the evening sun glinted on the waters of the River Plate estuary, and the panorama of Recoleta's famous brightly coloured houses seemed like a child's drawing. 'I have something to ask you – you, Jamie, though of course it concerns Isabel too.' She sighed. 'I don't even know if I should ask you, but I promised I would. And you can always say no.'

His SAS bosses used to say that, Docherty thought.

'Do you remember Gustavo and Eva Macías?' Rosa asked Isabel.

'I don't think so.'

'Gustavo was a close friend of my father. He and his family used to visit us quite often when I was a child.'

'I do remember one friend of your father's,' Isabel said. 'A tall man, stood very straight. He had a beard, I think.'

'That's him. He and Eva had three children – two daughters and one son. The son's name was Guillermo – he was about three years younger than us, I think. I probably didn't pay much attention to him, but I seem to remember he was nice enough.' She took another sip of wine. 'He was arrested by the Army in 1976 – he was a student at the university in Rosario – and never seen again. He wasn't interested in politics, apparently, and no one knows why they took him away.'

'Except the Army,' her husband said drily.

'True. But I'll leave Gustavo and Eva to tell you the details, if you're willing to talk to them.'

'Why now?' Docherty asked. 'After so long.'

'Two reasons, as far as I can see,' Rosa said. 'Are you two aware of what's been going on here the past couple of years? With the Disappeared, I mean.'

'Only vaguely.'

'Well, basically, when Menem became President he made a few noises and sat back to wait for the whole business to just fade away. But it didn't, the Mothers were still at his gates, and then for reasons best known to themselves, a few of the beasts broke ranks and started talking. The old Navy commander not only admitted that up to two thousand people

20

had been dropped in the Atlantic, but even went into details – how those who'd been weakened by torture had to be helped on to the aircraft, and were then given sedatives by Navy doctors before being stripped and thrown out. A little while later the Head of the Armed Forces actually admitted responsibility for human rights abuses in the late 70s and early 80s, although of course no individuals were called to account, and the files have still not been produced.'

'They've probably lost them,' Isabel said scornfully.

'I doubt it,' Giorgio said. 'They may not be very good at fighting other soldiers, but they know how to keep records.'

'The Eichmann syndrome,' Docherty murmured.

'Something like that. A lot of people have claimed that the military kept meticulous records of each and every person they tortured and killed.'

They all sat silent for a few seconds. All these years on, it was still hard to accept the enormity of what had happened.

'Anyway,' Rosa said, 'the other thing that happened was that the graves started coming to light. A group of young people calling themselves forensic anthropologists have started digging in many of the rumoured locations, and they've already found several mass graves. One of them was outside Rosario, and I think that was what set Gustavo off. From what I can gather, both he and Eva have been busy pretending that they never had a son for most of the past twenty years, but the discovery of that grave . . .' She sighed. 'And then there's the fact that he's dying himself. Some sort of cancer, and I don't think he's expected to last many more months.' She ran a hand through her hair. 'But whatever his reasons – mostly guilt, I suppose – he seems hell bent on making up for lost time. Over the last year – and much to his daughters' annoyance, I might add – he's spent a small fortune trying to find out why Guillermo was arrested and what happened to him. It's become an obsession. He has to know.'

Docherty looked at Isabel, whose face in the shadows seemed drawn with pain, and he knew that she was reliving the traumas of her own arrest and torture, the loss of so many friends. For her sake he wanted to leave the surface of the past undisturbed. 'Death will heal the man's need to know,' he said, the words sounding harsher than he intended.

Isabel looked up at him. 'What does he want from Jamie?' she asked.

'I think he has the name of a man, an Argentinian living in Mexico. I'm not sure, but I think he wants someone to go and talk to this man.'

'Why Jamie?' Isabel persisted.

'Gustavo is convinced this man will not talk to another Argentinian. But Jamie – he is both a foreigner and a soldier, someone both safe and *simpático*, yes? This man might be willing to talk to him, just man to man.'

'Macho to macho,' Docherty murmured.

Rosa rolled her eyes in exasperation.

'We should at least talk to Gustavo,' Isabel interjected.

It was Docherty's turn to look at her. The word 'Mexico' had taken him back to a buried chapter of his own life, one that came before Isabel. 'OK,' he said quietly. 'But no promises.' He knew Isabel still had nightmares about her time in the Naval Mechanical School – he had been shot into wakefulness on enough occasions by her sudden screams – and if it looked like this was going to upset her, there was no way he was touching it.

But there was always the chance it might have the opposite effect, he realized. Maybe something like this would help Isabel to finally exorcize her past.

He was probably grasping at straws, rationalizing his own desire to see Mexico again. Or even worse, just grabbing at any excuse to leave the cursed word processor behind.

The following morning, once Rosa had rung to make certain that Gustavo was well enough to receive them, Isabel and Docherty took the long drive across the city to the Macíases' house in Devoto. 'House' was actually something of a misnomer – 'mansion' would have been a better choice. There was obviously quite a lot left for the daughters to inherit.

Eva Macías, a handsome, white-haired woman in her seventies, greeted them and led them out to the conservatory, where her husband was soaking up the tropical humidity, rather like General Sternwood in the opening chapter of Chandler's *The Big Sleep*. The General had also wanted to know the fate of a missing young man, though in his case the man in question was assumed to be still in the land of the living.

Gustavo Macías was obviously not long for this world himself, but there was still life in the eyes and in the force with which he clenched his gnarled hands. It had taken him a year and a half, he told them, but he now had two names. Major Lazaro Toscono had supervised the operations of the arrest squads in Rosario for all of 1976 and most of 1977. Colonel Angel Bazua had commanded the Army base just outside the city, which served as both detention centre and place of executions, from late 1975 to mid-1978.

Bazua was two years into a five-year prison term for drug trafficking, and would probably be impossible to reach, but Toscono was now an ostensibly legitimate businessman in Mexico City. His business was doubtless a front, but there was nothing to stop anyone knocking on his office door, and Docherty could name his price for doing so. 'Just go and see him,' the old man said. 'Ask him about my son. He will remember. They always remember the names, because they know no other way of telling people apart.'

Docherty looked at Isabel, then at Macías. 'He may just refuse to speak to me, and you will have paid my fare for nothing.'

'When I started this,' the old man said, 'I put half my wealth to one side for Eva – more than she could ever spend. Now money means nothing to me. I will pay you twenty thousand US dollars to make the journey, a hundred thousand if you bring me back the answer. And, of course, any expenses you incur. If you need more, just tell me.'

Docherty was silent for a moment. They didn't exactly need the money, but twenty thousand dollars would certainly come in handy, and all he had to do was travel to a country already etched deep in his heart and ask someone for a consequence-free conversation. It seemed a no-brainer, but . . .

'He'll go,' Isabel answered for him.

Docherty shrugged his acquiescence.

In the car outside, still sweating from their immersion in the conservatory steam bath, Docherty and Isabel sat in silence for a few moments. The quiet street, with its luxurious mansions, perfectly coiffured lawns and ornamental palms, seemed far removed from torture chambers and mass graves, but both knew it for the illusion it was. The torturers might have come from all sections of Argentinian society, but the men who had delivered up their victims had come from streets like this one.

'You're not doing this for my sake, are you?' Isabel asked.

'No. And if this is going to be hard for you I won't do it. We don't need the money that much.'

'I know.' She sighed. 'Sometimes it seems so long ago,' she murmured. And sometimes it seems like yesterday, she thought.

'Some wounds take a long time to heal.'

She grimaced. 'I'll be fine. As long as you look after yourself. You're not in the SAS now. If this pig Toscono refuses to talk to you, that's it.'

'As long as he refuses nicely,' Docherty said with a grin.

She wasn't amused. 'We need you back.'

'Aye,' he said, leaning across and cradling her head in his arms. 'I love you too.'

The 727 from Cartagena touched down in Miami in the middle of the afternoon. Her parents had acquaintances in the city who would happily put her up, but the thought of explaining the reason for her visit to strangers was too daunting, and Carmen had already decided to ignore the list of telephone numbers her mother had written out. The money her father had given her would probably be enough for several nights in a cheap hotel, and if not she had a little of her own to fall back on.

Her parents would be appalled, of course. Carmen knew they hadn't really wanted her to come, though she was far from sure why. They had said they were worried for her – that losing one daughter was bad enough – but they obviously hadn't been worried enough to accompany her. It was hard to believe that they weren't desperate to know what had happened to their other daughter, but . . . Carmen shook her head and turned her attention to the business of disembarkation. She had come. Her parents' feelings – or lack of them – were neither here nor there.

She had changed planes in Miami on all of her three trips to the United States, but the airport had never seemed quite so vast before. Immigration and Customs seemed to take for ever – no doubt flights from Colombia merited special attention.

She had half expected the humiliation of a strip-search, but the officials were obviously as tired of the queue as its occupants and she was asked only a few cursory questions, her bag not even opened. With the aid of her guidebook she sought out the elevated Metrorail station just in time to catch an inbound train, and sat watching the sunlight reflect on the looming clutch of windowed towers which marked the city's downtown.

Beneath these towers she had a glimpse of an older and more elegant Miami, but it was getting dark and she had no time to explore. A local woman helped her find the right bus stop for Miami Beach, and when the bus arrived she was amused to see an English-speaking passenger trying, and failing, to communicate with the Spanish-speaking driver. It was like her friend Miguel had said: Florida, California and Texas had been taken from Spain by the gringos, and now the gringos were having to give them back.

The bus drove east across a long causeway, giving Carmen her first views of the Miami which *Miami Vice* had made famous, and sooner than she expected they were driving up through the faded pastel splendours of Miami Beach. She had picked three hotels out of the guidebook, and struck lucky at the first attempt, finding a room that was clean, spacious and cheaper than the book had led her to expect. She showered, changed and sat on the bed, rereading the copy of the report which the Miami police had faxed to Cartagena, and which the local police chief had passed on to her father. The only new fact it contained was the name of the Miami Beach lieutenant in charge of the investigation, and she had an appointment with him the following morning.

There was a small balcony to the room, and she stood out on it for a few minutes, looking down at the busy street, her nose twitching to the aromas of cooking food. She was hungry, she realized, and ten minutes later she was ordering Orange Chicken in a Chinese restaurant recommended by the hotel receptionist. After eating she walked down to the beach, but in the darkness it looked more scary than inviting, so she made her way back to the hotel. She flicked through channels on the TV for a while but then decided it was time for bed, despite the earliness of the hour. She was exhausted, and with any luck tomorrow would turn into a big day.

She was woken by the barely risen sun shining through the window, and after showering and dressing she made her way down to the empty beach and walked along it, a few feet from the gently breaking waves. She felt apprehensive about her meeting with the American police, but really glad that she had come. Whatever had happened to Marysa, she told herself, life was better than death.

The small Cuban café which she chose for breakfast served the best coffee she had ever tasted, which had to be a good omen.

Back at the hotel she smartened herself up, checked the directions she'd been given and set out for the police station. The walk took ten minutes, and once inside the incongruously modern building she was kept waiting for only a couple of minutes before being shown into Lieutenant Trammell's office. He was a harassed-looking man well into middle age, with an argumentative jaw, big mouth and thinning grey hair. His greeting was warm enough, but he seemed to be having trouble keeping his faded blue eyes open. Fortunately, he was not personally in charge of the case – that honour belonged to Detective José Peña, whose overflowing desk in the squad room was her next port of call.

Detective Peña also seemed harassed, but at least he was looking at her with wide-open eyes. 'Coffee?' he asked, once the introductions had been made and Trammell was back in his office.

'Yes, thank you,' she said.

'Cream and sugar?' He was speaking Spanish now.

'Just one sugar,' she answered in the same language, and examined him as he programmed the machine. He was in his early thirties, she guessed, with short, wavy hair and a face that managed to be both handsome and friendly. The photo of a woman and two children on his desk suggested he was also married.

He presented her with the plastic cup of coffee, and she took a token sip. Pretty good, she thought – in two hours she'd had the best and worst coffee of her life.

'Dreadful, isn't it?' he said with a smile.

'Yes,' she agreed.

They stared at each other for a couple of seconds. 'So what is it you want to know?' he asked.

'Everything,' she said shortly. 'All I know is what was in the newspaper – that Placida was carrying drugs – inside her – and that one of the packets burst and killed her. And that you found out who she was from Victoria . . . How is Victoria?'

He shook his head. 'It's hard to say. I've tried talking to her several times and sometimes she's almost lucid, sometimes she just stares at me as if she can't understand a word I'm saying, sometimes she just can't stop crying.' He looked up at her, and she could see in his eyes that he'd found the experience a more than usually distressing one. 'Whatever they did to her,' he added, 'it wasn't pretty.'

'Where is she now?' Carmen asked.

'She's in a hospital. She's pregnant too,' he added. 'So was Placida Guzmán.'

Carmen bowed her head, then lifted it again. 'Can I see her?'

28

He shrugged. 'I don't see why not.'

'I want to take her back to Cartagena with me. Her parents are both dead, but she has an aunt who's willing to look after her.'

Peña looked doubtful. 'I don't know when that will be possible,' he said slowly. 'I'm not sure what the legal situation is right now.'

'What do you mean?' she said, both surprised and alarmed.

'She has admitted to bringing in about half a million dollars' worth of heroin,' he said mildly.

Carmen was appalled. 'But she can't have been acting willingly,' she said angrily.

He sighed. 'I know,' he said, 'and I'm on her side. But she and the Guzmán girl had been in Miami for three days before they were found. Even if they had been forced to ingest the drugs there was nothing to stop them telling the officials at the airport what had happened. If they had, both of them would have received immediate medical treatment, and Placida Guzmán would probably still be alive.'

'They were probably too frightened.'

'Probably. And don't quote me on this, but I expect something can be worked out. It should be obvious to anyone that the girl needs help, not a jail cell.'

Carmen took a deep breath. 'Has she said anything about who did this to them? Or where they came from?' And where my sister may still be, she thought.

'Not yet. The plane they arrived on came from Bogotá via Panama City, but there's no record of them getting on at either place. And whenever I've asked her about either place, or anything about the time before she arrived, she just started to cry. She was crying when the uniform found her on the beach,' he added.

29

'She told you where Placida was?'

'Not exactly. "In the hotel," she said, but she couldn't remember which one. So we just started with the closest, worked our way outwards, and found the place the next day. Placida wasn't there, but there was a lot of blood and . . .'

He stopped for a moment, and she could see that he was picturing the scene.

'The body was found in a canal about twenty miles away – they hadn't done a very good job of weighting it down.'

'In the hotel room, weren't there any clues to where they'd come from?'

'He'd cleared it out. Jesús, he told them his name was – Victoria remembered that in one of her lucid moments. He was young, Hispanic, medium height – one of a million.'

'What about the passports?' she asked.

'The only stamps were ours. But the passports themselves are probably forged anyway.'

She felt disappointed with the information she had gathered, but could think of nothing else to ask. 'Maybe Victoria will find it easier talking to me,' she said, mostly to bolster her own spirits.

'Did you know her before?'

'Only by sight. My sister was – is, I hope – five years younger than me, and we didn't have the same friends.'

'Well, I'll try and arrange a visit for tomorrow, OK?'

She managed a thin smile of gratitude. 'I have no other reason to be here.'

3

John Dudley took his eyes off the lighted windows of the timber-yard office and turned to his partner. 'Anything?' he asked.

'They just took a corner,' Martin Insley told him from the armchair. 'Seaman caught it.'

'But how's it going?'

'Sounds pretty even so far. But you never know with Spain.'

'He should have given Fowler a game,' Dudley muttered as he put his eye back to the mounted telescope. Through the open window he could hear traces of the match playing on several TV sets, and over the gabled roofs to the south-west he thought he could make out the faint glow in the sky above Wembley Stadium. Everyone in London seemed to be watching the damn game – everyone but him and Insley. If only the damn boat had come in a day later.

It had docked at Tilbury soon after dawn that morning and had begun unloading almost immediately. The four thousand logs of tropical hardwood from Venezuela had been one of the first shipments ashore and after a cursory customs examination the importers had been cleared to reload them on the waiting fleet of trailers. A thorough search would probably have resulted in the seizure of a large haul of Colombian heroin, but the British authorities were hoping for more than drugs to burn. MI5 and the Drugs Squad were eager to break the new and highly ominous distribution link-up between the Colombians and the local Turkish mafia, while MI6 were more interested in the foreign end of the pipeline, and the man who ran it.

The logs had all been delivered to the timber yard in north-east London by mid-afternoon, no small feat considering the state of the capital's traffic, and had been stacked in no apparent order in the open-sided shed. Since then Dudley and Insley had been watching them from the upstairs room of an empty terraced house some seventy yards away.

'We've got another corner,' Insley reported.

Dudley took one last look at the lighted windows, and walked across to grab the proffered earpiece.

'It was a good save,' Insley explained, as they waited for Anderton to take it.

At that moment they were beeped.

'Fuck,' Dudley growled, grabbing the handset.

'The fax is coming in,' a voice told him.

There was a pause, and in the background Dudley could hear the groan of the crowd. They were even listening in the communications room!

'Five names,' the voice said. 'They all look Turkish. Beeper numbers and times. Amounts. Christ, there must be about two tons of the stuff in those logs.'

'Did Six get their source?' Dudley asked out of curiosity.

'Yeah. The one they were expecting.'

'Well, that should cheer the bastards up.'

* * *

In the suite occupied by the British Consulate on the fourth floor of the Swissbank building in Panama City the English contingent were gathered round a borrowed portable, willing the half-time whistle to blow. David Shepreth was probably the least involved of the spectators, and it was with no great reluctance that he deserted the TV to take the incoming message from London. It was brief and to the point, containing nothing more than the source number of the fax which had just been received by the London timber-yard office.

He placed it on the desk in front of him and punched out a number on the phone. Somehow he doubted whether the American Embassy would have closed down for Euro 96.

It hadn't, and a few seconds later he was talking to Neil Sadler, the head of the US Drug Enforcement Agency's Panama Field Office. He didn't know Sadler anything like as well as his opposite number in Mexico City, but they had a relationship of sorts and Shepreth was curious to see what reasons the other man would eventually come up with for refusing his request.

'Hi, David,' the DEA man said cheerfully enough. 'And what can we do for the British Empire today?'

'I need an address to go with a fax number,' Shepreth told him, then read the number off the paper in front of him.

'No problem,' Sadler said. 'It'll probably take me a couple of hours. I'll call you back.'

'Great, thanks,' Shepreth said, and hung up, thinking that anyone who believed the Americans no longer ran Panama was living in a dream. Their only real challenger had been Manuel Noriega – 'Old Pineapple Face' as the media had less than affectionately dubbed him – and the General had been rather too assiduous in promoting his country's number-one industry – the import and export of drugs. Involvement in itself might not have condemned him, but he had compounded his crime by giving Uncle Sam the proverbial finger, and for that he was now languishing in a Florida jail.

He was not exactly missed by his fellow-Panamanians. Like everyone else, the Americans occasionally did the right thing for all the wrong reasons.

Shepreth stood by the window for a few moments, staring out at the square of blue Pacific which filled the space between the two high-rise buildings on the other side of the Via España. As usual a breeze was ruffling the palms which lined the wide avenue; Panama City was not the steamy hell of legend, though in just about every other respect it qualified as a major-league modern dump. The city's business was business, and if Orson Welles had ever done a Central American version of *The Third Man* he could easily have substituted Panama for Switzerland in Harry Lime's famous speech about what makes civilization tick.

The second half had started in the room next door, and Shepreth walked through to join the others. England were not playing half as well as they had against the Dutch, and another Spanish near-miss had the Embassy officials chewing their lips in agitation. Even the two secretaries – both local girls – seemed caught up in the anxiety of the moment. Both of them had lovely legs, Shepreth thought, and wondered why he hadn't noticed before.

He supposed he didn't come to Panama that often, or at least not lately. Large quantities of cocaine and heroin still passed through the country, but the focus of the drug trade had moved north in the past couple of years, and nowadays Shepreth spent most of his time in Mexico City.

His real employer was MI6, that arm of British Intelligence which dealt with external threats to the security of the United

Kingdom. Up until the end of the Cold War its principal occupation had been counter-espionage, but now that spies had either gone the way of the dodo or signed up with one of the corporations for non-political duties, MI6 had been forced into grabbing a share of the war against the unofficial corporations of international crime. These included the Sicilian, Russian, West African and Turkish Mafias, the Chinese Triads, Japanese Yakuza and Colombian drug cartels. With the exception of the Triads, most of these organizations had few soldiers on the ground in the UK itself, and sticking spokes in their collective wheels could only be done on foreign soil.

The other EC intelligence services had a presence in Central America and the Caribbean, but for obvious reasons the principal sharers of Shepreth's patch were the various over-lapping American agencies – the US Customs Service, Coast Guard, Drug Enforcement Agency, Justice Department, FBI and CIA. Originally Shepreth's relations with these American agencies had seemed better than those they had with each other, but over the past couple of years this situation had deteriorated somewhat. The Americans' decision to adopt a 'kingpin strategy', whereby all their resources were committed to bringing down a selected few of the biggest drug barons, took little or no account of British and European interests. And when this most-wanted list was finally shared with America's allies it was found to omit the one man the British most wanted included.

It would of course be difficult to put Angel Bazua in prison – he was already in one. It had been specially constructed for him and his 'business associates' on the Colombian island of Providencia, and was said to contain all the comforts of home and a few others besides. Everything that Bazua needed to continue running his billion-dollar business had been thoughtfully provided by the Colombian authorities, from mobile phones and computers to an impressive boardroom table. It was even rumoured that a commodious shelter had been dug beneath the jail, as protection against a bombing raid by competitors.

Elements of the Colombian military and civil administrations were obviously armpit-deep in the necessary corruption, but Bazua himself was not a Colombian – he was an Argentinian. And herein lay the other compelling reason for MI6's interest in him. Bazua had been one of the leading protagonists of the Argentinian Army's 'Dirty War' against its own people, and one of the prime movers behind the attempted liberation of the Malvinas. His son had been killed at Goose Green, further deepening his lifelong hatred of the English, and after the military's reluctant abdication of power he had gone into exile rather than face a potential investigation into his activities during the Dirty War.

By this time the fortune he had accumulated – most of it stolen in one way or another from his hundreds of victims – was considerable, and with the help of old Colombian contacts from his years at the US-sponsored anti-subversion school in Panama, he had bought himself a slice of the Cali drug cartel's international action. In the late 80s, as the star of the Medellín cartel had fallen, his had risen with that of his Cali partners, and even the inconvenience of a prison term had done nothing to slow his enrichment. Most of the returning dollars went into Colombian banks to earn legitimate interest, but Bazua had not forgotten his own country or his hatred, and it was his deepest wish that the two new boats riding at anchor off his Providencia prison would soon be ferrying another invasion force to the Malvinas. Once such a force was ashore the liberal government in Buenos Aires would have no choice but to support the invasion, particularly since it would soon become apparent that this time the British were incapable of transporting a force large enough to dislodge it.

This was not a welcome prospect in London, but British efforts to interest the Americans in action against Bazua had proved ineffective. Washington wouldn't even countenance ganging up on the discredited Samper regime in Bogotá, much less direct action against the centre of operations on Providencia. Bazua was not one of their targeted kingpins, the British were told. There was no real evidence against him. And in any case, there could be no sanctioning of military action on the sovereign territory of Colombia.

This of course was pure bullshit – Grenada and Panama should have been so lucky – but there was no shaking Washington's resolve, even when their own DEA people in the field supported the British. Increasingly, Shepreth and his superiors in London had been left with the feeling that as far as Bazua was concerned the Americans had a hidden agenda.

This idea received further confirmation when Neil Sadler rang back, seconds after the final whistle. The cheerfulness in his voice was gone – now there was an uneasy mixture of resentment and embarrassment.

'No luck, I'm afraid,' the American told him. 'Are you sure this is the right number?' He repeated the one which Shepreth had told him.

'Yes,' the Englishman said, slightly amused by the pantomime.

'Well, it's not listed. Sorry.'

'OK. Thanks for trying,' Shepreth said coolly.

'Any time.'

Shepreth put the phone down. He'd have to check it out in person, which shouldn't be too difficult – the fax machine in question was almost certainly in the office on Calle 35, the one to which he had trailed the freighter captain earlier that month.

He would pay it a visit later, once the Panamanian evening got into its undeniable swing. Then Whitehall would get its t's crossed, and there would be more proof for the Americans to ignore.

In the other room the celebration of a penalty shoot-out win had already begun, and while HM's Consul waxed eloquent about Sheringham's intelligence – 'He thinks before he kicks the ball,' he gushed, slurping his G&T – his number two seemed to be contemplating another goal altogether, his eyes locked on, like heat-seeking missiles, to the valley between the younger secretary's ample breasts.

Victoria looked healthier than Carmen had expected, and very obviously pregnant. If it weren't for the eyes, which seemed to be watching from a great distance, she would have found it hard to believe that the young woman in front of her had gone through a succession of terrible experiences.

The institution in which she was housed seemed more true to type; situated in one of Miami's less salubrious inner suburbs, it felt more like a prison than the hospital it supposedly was. Closed-circuit cameras had watched Carmen all the way to this fourth-floor room, and the nurses all seemed cold-faced and unsmiling. Detective Peña, who had driven her out here in his lunch hour, had warned her it wasn't exactly a rest home, and he'd been right. Victoria's room contained a bed, a basin and a single chair. The door was locked from the outside at all times.

For her part, Victoria eyed this new visitor with more trepidation than warmth. She might look vaguely familiar, but she would probably want to ask questions, like the police detective who had been to see her several times. He'd been quite nice, but she knew he hadn't believed that she couldn't remember anything. And of course he was a man. At least this one was a woman. And maybe she wouldn't stay long – it was so wonderful being alone.

'Victoria, do you remember me?' Carmen asked her, and could tell from the look of alarm that she didn't. 'I'm Carmen, Marysa's sister.'

Tears formed in Victoria's eyes and started rolling down her cheek. She was beginning to think she would dehydrate herself.

'How are you?' Carmen asked. 'How do you feel? Are the people here good to you?'

'Oh yes. They're good to me. They leave me alone.'

Carmen ignored the reproachful look which went with the last statement, and sat down on the bed beside the other woman. 'Do you remember Cartagena?' she asked gently, half expecting the flow of tears to increase. 'The college?'

Victoria gave her a strange look. 'What does it look like?' she asked.

'The college?' Carmen asked, surprised. 'It's a park full of white buildings, with a hill behind it. There . . .'

'Can you see the sea from it?' Victoria asked.

'Yes, you remember . . .'

Victoria shook her head. 'No, but I have dreamt about this place.'

Carmen waited for her to continue but she didn't. 'Do you remember the dream?' she asked.

'Oh yes.'

'What happens?'

Victoria tilted her head to one side, and Carmen could see what Detective Peña had meant about a six-year-old. 'Nothing happens really,' she said. 'I am eating and walking and reading a book and looking at the sea – things like that.'

'Are you alone?'

'No, I have friends. Marysa is there,' she said, and smiled at Carmen, as if she had finally realized who her visitor was.

Carmen took a chance. 'Do you ever dream of going on a picnic?'

Victoria's eyes first widened with surprise and then darkened. 'That's a bad dream. How did you know about it?'

'I don't know. Why don't you tell me about it? Then maybe it won't seem so bad.' Victoria looked at her – almost hopefully, Carmen thought. 'Tell me what happens,' she said again.

'It's a bad dream,' Victoria repeated. 'We're having a lovely time, swimming and sunbathing and talking. We have some wine and Placida is pouring it into the paper cups and the men come out of the trees and they have guns. We have to go with them in their cars and then the car turns into a plane and we're in the sky above this island, looking down. And the plane comes down to land and the wheels hit the runway and there's a big jolt which wakes me up. It always wake me up, and then I feel better, knowing it's just a dream.'

As if in contradiction of the words, the tears were flowing once more.

Carmen wanted to take the other woman in her arms, but she pressed on relentlessly. 'The island in your dream – is it big?'

'I don't know. It's not small. There's a mountain in the middle and little towns by the sea. It's shaped like an egg. And there's another island – much smaller – at one end, with a bridge between them.'

It was a good description, Carmen thought triumphantly. There couldn't be many islands in the Caribbean which fitted it. Victoria was looking at her expectantly, but Carmen had no idea what she was expecting. 'Do you remember any other dreams?' she asked.

Victoria seemed to retract her limbs, to pull her body closer together. 'Yes, but they are evil dreams.'

'Evil . . . You don't have to tell me if you don't want to.'

Her voice apart, Victoria seemed turned to stone. 'I am with men. They are doing things to me.'

'Who are they?'

'They're his men.'

'Who is he?'

She looked straight at Carmen. 'He told me he was the Angel of Death, but he laughed when he said it.'

'Is he the father of your child?'

It was the wrong question. Victoria shook her head violently, and started crying again. Carmen took her in her arms, held her close, and slowly felt the tension in the younger woman's body begin to lessen.

'Is Marysa in these evil dreams?' Carmen asked after a while.

'Sometimes,' Victoria admitted. 'But I don't want to talk about my dreams any more,' she added.

'All right,' Carmen agreed. She'd thought she was ready to hear the worst, but she'd been wrong. 'So what shall we talk about?' she asked.

'Nothing,' the other woman said. 'Let's just be quiet together.'

And for the next twenty minutes they sat next to each other on the bed, with Victoria's head cradled on Carmen's shoulder. At the end of that time the younger woman made no attempt to deter Carmen from leaving, but she did seem at least slightly pleased by the prospect of another visit the following day.

Carmen had intended to talk to the doctor in charge about Victoria's prospects, but decided to leave that until her next visit – she felt too distressed herself to fight for her sister's friend. Instead she just stumbled out on to the street and started walking, and it was only after a couple of cruising drivers had slowed to offer her remuneration for services to be rendered that she realized what sort of neighbourhood she was in. Luckily a crowded bus stop soon presented itself, and half an hour later she was back downtown. There she walked into the first bar she came to, stonewalled the hopeful greetings of the male clientele and ordered a large tequila.

In a dimly lit booth she thought about what Victoria had told her.

An island. A recognizable island.

Her drink finished, she asked the barman directions to the nearest bookshop. He looked at her blankly, as if the idea of buying a book had not occurred to him before, and she had to be rescued by one of the men she had ignored. He gave her directions to a shop two blocks distant.

She walked down the palm-lined street and found it. An assistant showed her the atlases and hovered beside her until another customer pulled him away. She found the right page, and pushed her finger northwards across the blue Caribbean from the Colombian coast. The first island it reached was San Andrés, the second Providencia – both of them Colombian. The former was long and thin, the latter could have been egg-shaped. She needed a bigger map, and found it in a guidebook to her native country. Providencia was egg-shaped, with a mountain at its heart. And, she noticed triumphantly, there was a small adjoining island at its northern end. A bridge ran between them.

At around a quarter to nine the taxi deposited Shepreth by the sea-front monument to Balboa, and after a few minutes' contemplation of the dark ocean he crossed the busy main road and headed inland up Calle 35. The building he wanted was a couple of hundred metres up on the left – a nondescript modern construction, six storeys of steel and glass. Through the glass doors he could see a liveried guard reading something at his otherwise bare desk.

It was a porn comic – Shepreth had a fleeting glimpse of the usual giantess straddling the usual giant before the guard innocently slipped it under the desk.

'I've got an appointment with someone at Azul Travel,' Shepreth told him. 'My name's Bates,' he added.

The guard picked up his phone to confirm it, and after a few words with someone nodded Shepreth in the direction of the lift. 'Fifth floor,' he said grudgingly, reaching for his comic.

It seemed unlikely that he'd be watching the lighted floor numbers above the lift, but Shepreth went all the way to five just in case. On his way to the stairs he passed the door of the travel agency, with whom he had earlier arranged the necessary appointment. He hoped they would wait at least ten minutes before phoning down to find out what had happened to him.

The office he was interested in was on the third floor. There was no writing on the glass door, and he didn't expect to find a happy bunch of workers inside. Certainly, whoever was renting the space hadn't taken much trouble to protect any contents – the door yielded to Shepreth's lock-picking expertise with almost insulting ease.

The room proved even emptier than he had expected. The fluorescent light revealed no desk, no chairs, no filing cabinets – just a fax machine and a shredder floating on an ocean of burgundy-coloured carpet. 'Snap,' Shepreth murmured as he read the fax's number.

Now all they needed was evidence linking this office with the prison on Providencia. Which wouldn't be easy. Presumably each missive from the island was consigned to the shredder the moment it had been read. He would have to try to set up an intercept of some sort, Americans or no . . .

As if in answer to a prayer the fax clicked into life. Shepreth stood over it, hoping it wouldn't be someone trying to sell Bazua double glazing for his prison.

It wasn't. The fax, emanating from a number which Shepreth recognized as including the prefix for Colombia's two Caribbean islands, contained the usual list of buyers, together with amounts, beeper numbers and instructions for onward transmission to the organization's cell head in northern Mexico. The Americans wouldn't be able to ignore this, Shepreth thought. They would either have to add Bazua to their precious list of kingpins or come up with an honest reason for refusing.

He detached the sheet from the machine, folded it twice and put it in his back pocket, then headed for the door. He listened for a moment before inching it open. The corridor was empty. Relocking the door seemed more difficult than unlocking it had been, and he was still struggling to engage the catch when the lift doors suddenly opened behind him and two men emerged, guns in hand. He had no time to do anything but stare sheepishly at them.

'Looking for Azul Travel?' one of the men asked. He was probably in his mid-thirties, with a pencil moustache and uneven teeth.

The other man, who was younger and wearing tinted glasses above his pitted cheeks, sniggered.

They advanced, one man pushing into the unlocked office while the other kept him covered.

Shepreth just stared at him, willing his mind to keep on working through the fear that was threatening to choke it off. If it didn't his chances of living past midnight were remote.

Even if he stayed James Bond-cool they were less than good. The thought plunged him further into shock – in eight years of working for MI6 he had not often found himself at the mercy of people with so little interest in his living and so little fear that they would have to pay for his death.

The one with the moustache pushed Shepreth into the office, closing the door behind himself, and then stood with his gun in the Englishman's ear while his partner did the frisking. This didn't take long. Pitted Cheeks stepped back, shoved Shepreth's automatic into his waistband, unfolded and read the stolen fax, then examined the wallet.

'You're a long way from home, English,' he said in conversational Spanish.

'So are you,' Shepreth replied in the same language, recognizing the man's Colombian accent. He wondered if his voice sounded as brittle to them as it did to him.

'Panama used to be a part of Colombia,' Moustache told him.

'It still is,' his partner said, and both men laughed.

Shepreth said nothing.

'You have probably come to Panama to see the Canal, yes?' Pitted Cheeks asked playfully.

'I've seen it,' Shepreth said.

'Not from underwater,' Moustache said almost perfunctorily, leaving Shepreth with the stomach-sinking realization that the two of them had been through this particular sketch several times before.

Pitted Cheeks, meanwhile, was picking out a number on the phone. 'I need to speak to the Chief,' he said when someone answered, and a few moments later, smiling all the while at Shepreth, he was reporting what had happened. He then listened for a while before signing off and putting the phone back down on the carpet. 'The Chief has a few questions for you,' he said.

Shepreth found himself taking a deep breath of relief.

'But not too many,' Pitted Cheeks added, reading his mind. 'We'll probably still have time to show you the Canal tonight.'

The ludicrous thought flashed through Shepreth's mind that he would never know who won Euro 96. Get a grip, he told himself. This was life and death.

They led him down the deserted stairs and out into an empty alley, and Moustache kept a gun on him while Pitted Cheeks went off, presumably to collect their car. This might be his only chance, Shepreth thought, but really it was no chance at all. Moustache was too far away for a lunge and there was no reason to suppose the Colombian would do anything other than put a bullet in Shepreth's kneecap if he tried. And then he'd never get another chance.

Despite the training, despite what his head told him, it all seemed unreal somehow, standing there so helplessly in an alley in Panama City, with a man who'd more or less promised that he'd never see another dawn. The sounds of the city were all around them, but strangely distant, as if the alley was enclosed in thick but invisible glass.

The Colombians' car bumped its way towards them, shattering the spell.

Pitted Cheeks got out and the two of them discussed whether or not to put him in the boot. They decided against, reasoning that if they knocked him out the questioning might be delayed, but if they didn't he might drum on the lid at the wrong moment. They both clearly enjoyed this discussion – such attention to detail, Shepreth realized, was their proof of professionalism. These men might be lacking in humanity, but not in job satisfaction.

He was ordered into the wide back seat of the car, a black Toyota Camry, and Moustache climbed in beside him, eyes watchful, careful to keep a couple of feet between prisoner and gun.

Pitted Cheeks got in behind the wheel and started the car rolling forward. They turned left out of the alley on to Calle 36 and purred uphill towards Avenida 3, now jostling with people out for their evening stroll through the shopping district. Shepreth thought of lunging for the door, but knew it would be fatal – Moustache's eyes had not left him for a second since they entered the car.

They crossed Avenida 3 and headed up towards the next big crossroads. In ten minutes they might be out of the city altogether, Shepreth thought. If he was going to do anything, it had to be soon. But what? He felt paralysed. Moustache smirked at him, as if he knew exactly what was going on in his prisoner's mind.

As Pitted Cheeks waited to turn right on to the busy Avenida 2 a bus first lurched forward and then abruptly pulled up again as the lights changed. This motion not only fooled Pitted Cheeks, who paused for a second before pulling out, but also a taxi coming up on the blind side of the stalled bus, which was through the red light before the driver had realized his mistake. His emergency stop would have pleased his original instructor, but there was no way he could avoid making contact with the side of the Toyota.

The crash was louder than it felt, and Moustache's gun hardly seemed to waver, but the taxi driver was already out on the street and hundreds of eyes were turned their way. Two of them, Shepreth realized with sudden hope, belonged to a traffic cop who was now walking their way.

Moustache had seen him too, and the gun was now in his pocket, albeit still obviously aimed in Shepreth's direction.

Pitted Cheeks climbed reluctantly out of the Toyota, just as the cop arrived to take charge. As he looked into the car Shepreth deliberately reached for the door handle, opened the door and climbed out on to the street. No bullets gouged into him.

He smiled at the cop and leant against the car's roof for a moment until the man's attention was back on the two drivers. There had to be about two hundred people standing around enjoying the show, and the cop was obviously going to milk the spotlight for all he could. A cacophony of horns was rising from the stranded traffic.

'I'll see you later,' Shepreth told Moustache, and began walking away. Ten steps later he was through the first line of watchers, and looking back he could see that neither of the Colombians was making any attempt to follow him. He walked on along the crowded pavement, his heart thumping in his chest, hardly daring to believe his luck.

From Avenida 2 he took a taxi to his hotel, tipping the driver with a generosity which the man appreciated better than he understood. It took Shepreth three minutes to clear his room and check out; fifteen minutes later he was registering at another hotel under another name, using the alternative identification he carried for such emergencies. He didn't think the Colombians would come looking for him – the risks seemed to outweigh the potential benefits – but he spent most of the night dozing in a chair, fingers wrapped round the butt of his other gun.

4

With an hour-long stopover in Quito, Docherty's journey from Santiago de Chile to Mexico City took just over ten hours. For almost all of the first flight he was able to stare out of his window at the majestic Andes, but most of the second was over water, and the choice of entertainment came down to either Arnie Schwarzenegger or his own thoughts.

Five days had passed since he and Isabel had visited the Macíases in Devoto, two since their return home from Buenos Aires. He had watched out for signs that his wife was regretting her decision to approve the trip, but, natural anxieties apart, there had been none that he could see, and on the eve of his departure, after they'd made love on a bed still strewn with his packing, she had made her feelings clear. 'If it wasn't for the children,' she had told him, 'I'd be coming with you. In fact, there's one voice inside me says I should be going instead of you. These are the people I've been fighting all my life. The people who killed my friends.'

Sitting in the plane, Docherty could see her face on the pillow, the same mingling of determination and anxiety in her dark eyes, and he could remember that moment in the car outside Rio Gallegos in 1982, when the rest of the SAS patrol had been captured and she'd refused to head for the border alone. 'I could cross ten borders and never leave this war behind,' she had said at the time.

But what was his excuse? Terrible things had been done in Argentina, but the same could be said of many other countries, and though he had more than a vague attachment to old-fashioned notions of justice, Docherty had no desire to take on the mantle of a one-man crusade. The money would be nice, of course, but that wasn't the reason for his presence on this flight either – in fact he wasn't at all sure what his motivation was. He hoped it was more than an older man's attempt to relive his youth. 'But I wouldn't bet money on it,' he murmured to himself.

He shook the doubts aside, and picked up the guide to Mexico City which Isabel had bought for him the previous day. In his two stays there in 1977 he had found the place oppressive, but that was hardly surprising – during the first he had still been crazy with grief and by the time of the second he had the rest of the country to compare it with. In nearly five months of travelling he had fallen in love with Mexico, its people and its churches, its mountains and its beaches.

A part of him had always meant to go back, but another part had feared that for him the country would always be entangled with memories of Chrissie. It was her senseless death on a zebra crossing just six months after their marriage which had driven him abroad in the first place, and fate had decreed that Mexico should be the place which brought him back to life. The life he had given to the SAS and his family, and not necessarily in that order.

He turned his attention to the present. If Gustavo Macías was right, and Lazaro Toscono's business in Mexico City was just a drug-trade front, then he would have to be careful about how he approached the man. It would not do to start hammering on the bastard's front door before he found out what was behind it. As one of his old SAS instructors had put it: a few hours of observation is worth a thousand stun grenades.

It was a pity he had no local contacts – he'd made friends in Mexico, but none in the capital. It suddenly occurred to Docherty that he might be able to pick up some intelligence from the Embassy if he used his contacts in Hereford, but then he remembered that Barney Davies had finally stepped down as SAS CO, and been replaced by someone whom he barely knew.

In any case, he thought, that would be like using a sledge-hammer to crack a nut. Or a general to run a country, as they said in Chile.

The plane was losing altitude now, and he spent the next fifteen minutes yawning to unblock his ears, watching as the yellow-browns and greens of the central plateau grew more distinct. Then they were flying down through either thin clouds or dense smog, re-emerging less than a kilometre above an overcrowded multi-lane highway that was snaking its way through shanty-covered hills.

The airport seemed three times as big as he remembered it, but he had no trouble getting through Immigration or Customs. Noticing the Hertz sign, he thought about hiring a car, but decided against it – there was no point in leaving such an obvious trail for an enemy. Instead he fought his way on to the modern Metro, remembering as he did so a recent traveller's comment that its off-peak crowds would pass for a rush hour anywhere else. Two changes and several buffet-ings later, he emerged from the Zócalo station, no more than a stone's throw away from the great square at the heart of the old city.

This seemed unchanged from nearly twenty years before, and he realized with a grin that he had arrived just in time to witness the six o'clock flag-changing ceremony – one of the world's longest-running farces. The troop of a dozen soldiers was already halfway from the Palacio Nacional to the flagpole in the centre of the square, and by the time Docherty had joined the circle of spectators the drums were echoing, the national colours on their way down. A kind of baroque minuet followed, whereby the huge flag was folded to the size of a small tablecloth and then carried, with stunning reverence, back into the palace.

The crowd was now filtering away, the sun almost gone, its rays touching only the highest reaches of the cathedral on the square's northern side. The sound of more drumming – rhythmic, distinctly unmilitary drumming – was coming from the corner to the right, and he walked across to find a circle of dancers whirling around a single drummer. They looked like Indians, and their speed and agility were amazing.

This was Mexico, Docherty thought. Mayan feet on Spanish stone, the past entwined with the present, drunkenness and death, farce and tragedy. After Chrissie's death everything had seemed grey, but this country kept hitting you in the face with the whole damn palette.

He smiled to himself and resumed walking, heading up Cinco de Mayo towards the hotel he had stayed in nineteen years before. It was still there, but either his standards had risen or the hotel's had dropped, and a cursory look at one room was enough to send him back on to the street. A few yards further on he found one of the places the guidebook recommended. The room he was shown seemed clean and the hotel itself seemed suitably anonymous. He checked in, left his bag in the room and continued on up Cinco de Mayo in search of something to eat.

The old city seemed seedier than he remembered, and not so lively; he supposed a lot of the night-life must have moved to the Zona Rosa a couple of miles to the east, where the streets would doubtless look much like modern streets did everywhere else. No matter, he told himself – he'd get the business with Toscono out of the way and then spend a few days in the real Mexico. He'd take the overnight train to Oaxaca, drink mescal sours in the main square, and see the world spread out beneath his feet on Monte Alban.

Sir Christopher Hanson was only a few minutes late arriving at his club for lunch, but his guest was already there, skimming through one of the hunting magazines with an amused expression on his face.

'These'll be like porn soon,' Manny Salewicz said as he got up, flourishing the magazine.

'What?' Hanson asked, taken aback.

'The way we hear it,' the American said, 'banning blood sports will be the only thing a new Labour government can give its activists which doesn't cost anything. And then the nobility will have to hide magazines like this under their four-posters.'

The MI6 chief smiled despite himself. Since their first meeting a couple of years earlier Salewicz's observations had often had that effect – the CIA man had a refreshing, and sometimes alarming, habit of cutting gleefully through the crap. The last time they'd had lunch together Hanson had been requesting American help for an SBS mission to Azerbaijan, and Salewicz had taken great pleasure in pointing out all the potential pitfalls before agreeing to provide it.

Now, as then, they spent the actual lunch in small talk. Salewicz was fascinated by Euro 96, mainly because the game itself left him completely cold. 'What's so great about a sport where you can't use your hands?' he demanded of Hanson, who could only shrug sympathetically. They then talked about President Clinton's problems with Whitewater, the Queen's with her children, and the Russian election. 'You know what they say about globalization?' Salewicz asked between mouthfuls of roast lamb and mint sauce. 'The only thing worse than its failure would be its success.'

It was only when they were nursing large glasses of port in the members' lounge that Hanson brought up business. 'I want to talk to you about Angel Bazua,' he told the American.

Salewicz raised a quizzical eyebrow.

'In the last week we've connected him to a large heroin shipment,' Hanson went on. He told the American about the timber yard, the hollowed-out logs packed with the stuff, the arrests of the local wholesalers and their Turkish distribution ring. 'We traced the list of buyers back to a fax machine in a Panama City office, and in that office one of our people intercepted an incoming fax from Providencia. There's no room for doubt here,' Hanson said, pulling a file from his briefcase and handing it to the CIA man, 'the trail leads right to Bazua's door. His prison door,' he added with evident disgust.

Salewicz was rifling through the file, playing for time. He'd suspected that Bazua would come up, but his bosses in Washington hadn't given him many cards to play. 'There's no copy of a fax from Providencia here,' he said, looking up.

'It was taken from him.'

The CIA man gave Hanson a hurt look. 'No proof?' he asked.

'He saw it. He'll tell the President he saw it if you like.'

Salewicz shook his head. 'If you want us to get heavy with the Colombians we need real proof, cast-iron, irrefutable, on-paper proof.'

Hanson took a deep breath. 'In there,' he said, indicating the file, 'you'll find documented evidence that Bazua is stockpiling weapons. In a prison! He already has two boats, both of which could transport a couple of hundred men. In Argentina his people are openly advertising for "patriotic soldiers of the motherland".'

'We know. But two boats? Give me a break.'

'When Castro and Guevara set out from Mexico in 1957 they only had eighty men in one boat, and by the time they reached the mountains there were only twelve of them. Who's ruling Cuba now?'

'It's not the same.'

'No, but it's not that different either. We can't afford to leave our garrison on the Falklands for ever, and I wouldn't be at all surprised if a Labour government doesn't bring it home sooner rather than later. A force of highly motivated mercenaries would be hard to dislodge with what's there now, and who knows? – if Bazua picks his moment the government in Buenos Aires may find it easier to back him up than wash their hands of him. The man has to be stopped.'

Salewicz raised both hands in surrender. 'OK, I get it – he's one of the bad guys. But what can we actually do – invade Colombia?'

'You've used special forces against the drug labs on the mainland.'

'Maybe, but not against a prison.'

'It's not a prison – it's a luxury fortress. And if your people don't do something, then I'm afraid we shall have to.'

'All that beef's gone to your head,' Salewicz said jokingly, but he could see that Hanson wasn't amused. The English were certainly in a kick-ass mood these days, what with beef and their goddam football tournament. Even the reference to Cuba had probably been deliberate – all the Europeans were pissed off about Washington trying to tell them who to trade with. 'Look,' he said, 'just hold your horses for a few days. I'll let Langley know how strong your feelings are on this one, OK? I can't promise anything, but . . .' He raised his hands again.

Hanson smiled at him. 'That would be most useful,' he said.

I doubt it, Salewicz thought, taking another sip of port. But maybe he'd find out what his own people's aversion to taking on Bazua was based on, and then convince the Brits accordingly. He certainly couldn't see Washington giving the Brits a green light to go rampaging in the Caribbean.

Docherty woke up feeling good, without any real idea why. Don't fight it, he told himself, and after winning a long battle with a recalcitrant shower, he felt even better. A café a few doors down supplied a Mexican egg sandwich – complete with avocados, onions and peppers – a papaya shake and coffee, and for the first time in several years he had a hankering for a cigarette. It was the city, he decided. It remembered that he used to smoke.

The streets were a lot fuller than the night before, and not only with milling pedestrians and honking traffic – goods for sale now seemed to cover most of the pavements. He walked back to the hotel intending to call one of the car-hire firms, but decided to ask the receptionist instead. And yes, of course he could get their English guest a car, especially if cash or traveller's cheques were involved. A short phone call to a relative confirmed as much – a brand-new VW Golf would be there in half an hour.

Docherty then spent a couple of minutes with the hotel's city directory, which confirmed the two numbers Gustavo Macías had given him. Toscono's business address was on Balderas, a street running south from the Paseo de la Reforma; his home was in the rich man's suburb of Las Lomas de Chapultepec. Docherty returned the directory to the receptionist, walked out to the bank of public phones he had noticed on his way back from breakfast, and called the home address.

A woman answered, which surprised him. 'Can I speak to Señor Toscono?' he asked.

'He is not here,' she said, and if the tone of her voice was any clue she didn't seem too upset by the fact. 'Who is this?' she asked, as if she'd suddenly remembered the correct procedure.

Docherty hung up and walked back across the street to the hotel. By the time he'd returned from his room the hire car was waiting for him. 'Brand-new' was perhaps something of an exaggeration but at least it started, and the furry breasts hanging alongside the Virgin Mary seemed a typically local touch. He drove west until he reached the Paseo, then turned south down the wide boulevard with its towering palms, over-the-top monuments and modern skyscrapers. One new building which caught his eye looked like a giant Stanley knife, the tip of its blade poised to scratch the low-hanging smog.

In 1977 it had nearly always been possible to see Popocatepetl and Ixtaccihuatl, the two volcanoes which loomed over the city, but Docherty sensed that such clarity was gone for ever. 'Progress,' he murmured to himself.

He followed the Paseo as it swung west along the northern edge of the vast Chapultepec Park, and five minutes later he was entering the suburb from which the park derived its name. 'Hill of the locust' was the translation, he remembered, and the name seemed appropriate enough – the people who lived around here probably hadn't noticed Mexico's economic crisis, much less suffered from it.

Las Lomas de Chapultepec, a few kilometres further out, seemed even richer, and its shady avenues seemed depressingly free of traffic. He was going to stick out like a sore thumb, Docherty thought, not least because nearly every car he saw seemed to be a BMW or a Mercedes.

He found Toscono's house without difficulty and immediately noticed the coils of razor wire interwoven with the tumbling bougainvillea. Driving on up the hill, he found a small park, and from this relatively innocent vantage-point he was able to get a good idea of the compound's layout and take a sneak shot with his Polaroid. The camera's definition might not be that good, but it was quick, and there was no need to involve a processing firm.

The place didn't look any more inviting on the way down. He had seen no sign of dogs but that didn't mean much; the wire was crossable but the neighbourhood was far too quiet, and probably well watched – in countries like Mexico the police had a clearer idea of who paid their wages. There had to be better ways of getting to Toscono than over that wall.

Docherty drove thoughtfully back into the centre of the city, trying to ignore the rattling noise somewhere beneath him. On the edge of the Zona Rosa he found an outdoor café which put together a passable chicken *torta*, and then sat in La Ciudadela square for an hour or more by way of a siesta. At about three he walked up Balderas to Toscono's office address, which turned out to be a ten-storey glass tower. He waited outside until the lobby receptionist was busy with someone else's query, then walked in and examined the plaques on the wall behind him. As far as he could tell, Malvinas Import-Export was the sole occupant of the fifth floor.

He walked back outside and circled the building, noting the entrance to the underground car park. A car was just going in, and it seemed that the only entry requirement was money. Docherty strolled down Balderas, collected the Golf and drove back to the office building. The man in the booth at the entrance to the underground park took his pesos without even looking up from his newspaper, and he was in.

There were two levels and he examined them both before parking on the upper, along one of the side walls with a good view of the lift doors. Then he settled down to wait, wishing he'd had the sense to bring a magazine or book with them. The car's radio worked after a fashion, but there seemed to be only an unrelenting diet of Latino pop on offer, and he would rather have listened to country music. Well, maybe that was a bit of an exaggeration.

Between four-thirty and five the car park began to empty, and Docherty became worried that only his and Toscono's cars would be left, always assuming that the Argentinian was in his office. After all, he could be at the races, at a casino, or even, to judge from the tone of the woman on the telephone, in the arms of a mistress.

And then there he was – the slightly plump, slightly balding, impeccably dressed man from Gustavo's photograph. The man with him looked and acted like a bodyguard, and as they walked straight towards the Golf, Docherty slowly lowered his head below the level of the dashboard.

He didn't lift it again until he heard the sound of a car starting up. It was the big white BMW about twenty metres to his left, and Toscono himself was in the driving seat, looking pleased with himself. The other man, who was almost a head taller, seemed to be scowling at the world. It was probably something he had picked up at bodyguard school.

Carmen was a few minutes late arriving at the restaurant, but Detective Peña had phoned to say he would be later still. The table he had booked was beside a window, and she sat there with a glass of chilled white wine, thinking about him. In other circumstances, she thought, it was possible that something might have happened between them. Possible but not probable; he might be attracted to her but he was also happily enough married not to act on the attraction.

She had visited Victoria four times now, and each time it had been painful for both of them. Victoria might seem the less affected on the surface, but the fact that she was still hiding in the fiction of dreams suggested a degree of psychological damage which Carmen found almost as distressing as the story which was emerging between the lines of those dreams.

No real names had emerged, either of the people concerned or the place of the girls' imprisonment. 'He' was the 'Angel of Death', the men were 'his men', the island was just that. The details that emerged – the squelch of a water-bed, the stuttering fan, birdsong through a window – seemed rooted in evasion; they were like a condemned man's musings on the beauty of rope.

And yet sometimes there was clarity. 'We all used to play cards in our room,' Victoria suddenly said in one of their sessions. 'I can remember Marysa making a joke about him and we all laughed so much . . .'

Obviously not every moment had been nightmarish, but then they never were. Marysa had always made good jokes, Carmen thought, and found a tear rolling down her own cheek. Seeing Detective Peña zigzagging through the table towards her, she quickly dabbed it away.

'Sorry I'm late,' he said, 'but I've got good news. The charges against Victoria are going to be dropped.'

'That's wonderful!' Carmen said.

'She'll be deported – just formally,' he added, seeing Carmen's eyes turn angry – 'and your government's already agreed to pick up the tab for everything. You can take her home to Cartagena. That's good news, isn't it?' he asked, noticing that the smile hadn't returned to her face.

She tried to give him one. 'Yes, yes, it has to be. I'm just afraid that my country will not be able to give her the sort of help she needs. I don't know . . .'

The waiter arrived to take their order. 'On expenses,' he said, but she had the feeling he intended paying out of his own pocket. She ordered one of the set lunches – she had never had Vietnamese food before – and another glass of white wine.

'It will take time,' he said, resuming the conversation.

'I know.'

'What will you do next? About your sister and the others, I mean.'

She shrugged. 'I don't know what I can do. What is happening here? Is no one interested in what Victoria has told me?'

'Everything she told you is being passed on to the DEA. But if you're right, and the island she talks about is the one you think it is . . .' It was his turn to shrug. 'It's foreign soil – no US agency could intervene physically. The best they could do would be to make representations to the Colombian government.'

'I understand that,' she said. 'But it's not foreign soil to me,' she added simply.

He almost dropped his chopsticks. 'You're not thinking of going there?'

'I don't know what to do,' she said. 'I don't think you under-stand what life is like in my country – it is not like here – I can't go to the police and expect that they will prove trustworthy.'

'I know that.'

'Well,' she said, forgetting her food for the moment, 'if I tell the police in Cartagena that I think my sister is a prisoner on Providencia, what will happen? First they will look for reasons not to believe me, and they will say I have only the word of a sick person. If they do believe me and are honest enough to do something about it, I expect there will be queries to Bogotá and the police on Providencia itself. If by some miracle there are honest policemen on the island the only result will be that the kidnappers will have to kill Marysa and the others to hide their crime.'

Peña looked at her with new respect. 'You've thought this through,' he murmured.

'It is not difficult,' she replied, resuming her eating.

'You said your father and the Cartagena police chief are on good terms, so they at least could talk the matter through in private.'

'Maybe,' she agreed. So far she had just passed on the bare outlines of Victoria's story to her parents – giving them the unexpurgated version was going to be a nightmare.

'How big is this island?' Peña asked.

'About twelve kilometres long and six wide.'

'That's a lot of ground to search. And even if you found the place . . .'

'I might be able to take a photograph, get some evidence that no one could talk their way out of.'

She might be right, he thought, but he shuddered to think of her being caught by whoever it was had broken Victoria Marín. 'Talk to your father first,' he urged her.

'I will. But if nothing happens, I can't just leave it. Could you, if it was your brother?'

'No, I suppose I couldn't. But getting myself killed or caught wouldn't help him,' he added.

She smiled ruefully. 'I know.' They looked at each other. 'And thank you for all your help,' she said.

'It's been a pleasure,' he replied, and meant it.

5

Lazaro Toscono left for the city centre shortly before eight o'clock in the morning. As on the previous evening, he was driving himself, the tall bodyguard in the seat beside him. Docherty, who had watched their departure from the small park above the villa, didn't bother to tail the BMW, but simply followed at the snail's pace allowed by the rush-hour traffic. At ten to nine he found a parking space a few blocks from the office building on Balderas, and went in search of somewhere to drink coffee and think through his approach to Toscono. He soon found a pleasant café, its pavement tables shaded from the already bright sun by the branches of a tall eucalyptus.

For a while he sat enjoying his coffee, watching the office latecomers hurrying by. He found it fascinating but not surprising that Toscono worked a nine-to-five day – these days the pull of convention was obviously just as strong for drug traffickers as it was for insurance salesmen. He remembered reading an article about how the Colombian drug lords were all sending their children to the best schools and colleges, then giving themselves up to the government in return for the legalization of their fortunes, which their well-educated children could then use to become legitimate business leaders.

It was all a bit pathetic, somehow.

Docherty had never lost much sleep over the drug trade. As long as there was a demand there would be suppliers – a point so transparently obvious that only the politicians could have missed it. But of course they hadn't really – it was just a lot easier to demonize the suppliers than to work out why the demand kept rising. Drugs had been in use in one form or another for almost as long as fire, from the Native Americans' use of peyote in their ceremonies to Celtic fans' use of lager in theirs, and Docherty, who at times in his life had slipped perilously close to alcoholism, was less inclined than most to see their use as an aberration. People needed to let off steam, relax their own inhibitions, simply have a good time, and there was no doubt that some drugs did the job.

Even so, drugs like heroin didn't do much for the gaiety of nations, and others, like crack and methamphetamine, tended to turn a good proportion of their users into decidedly unpleasant, often dangerous, neighbours. All of which begged the question: why did people want such drugs in the first place? No doubt a hundred people could come up with a hundred different reasons, but as far as Docherty was concerned they all came back to one – this was a world which, for all its surface excitement and technological wizardry, offered less and less to the human heart, and drugs were one of the easiest ways of sidestepping that reality.

Since this process was unlikely to be reversed, and since there seemed little prospect of legalizing soft drugs, Docherty had no problem with locking up the dealers of hard drugs. He just didn't feel that ridding the world of their presence should be a moral crusade – they were crooks, not devils, and in their pursuit of money and influence they probably caused far fewer casualties than their legitimate brethren in the arms trade.

Lazaro Toscono, though, was a different matter. He was not just a drug dealer – he was also a soldier responsible for several thousand civilian deaths. According to conventional wisdom it took two sides to make a 'dirty war', but from what Docherty had read – and what his admittedly biased wife had told him – this had not been the case in Argentina. The military there had not been under any real attack, but had gone about the business of setting up a network of torturers with enthusiasm – child bullies might pull the wings off insects, but these men pulled the limbs off people. And then, unable to accept any responsibility for their actions, they had disposed of the evidence in unmarked graves or the South Atlantic, and left thousands of families like the Macíases in the agony of not knowing what had happened to their siblings and children.

How people lived with themselves after being part of something like that was beyond Docherty's comprehension. He had killed people when his own or a comrade's life was at stake, and he knew what it felt like to be angry enough to want to really hurt someone, but he couldn't begin to understand how a man could countenance the infliction of pain on people he had never met, day in and day out, for years on end.

All of which, he realized, probably put him at something of a disadvantage when it came to dealing with scum like Toscono. What was there to appeal to? Guilt? Making the career move from death squad to drug trafficker hardly suggested a working conscience. Much the same could be said of an appeal to the kindness of Toscono's heart – if he had one, it was presumably available for use only by his nearest and dearest.

The man's sense of honour, perhaps, for military men everywhere, and Latin Americans in particular, often had an exaggerated respect for such notions. If he combined such an appeal with a convincing promise that any revelations would be for the ears of the Macías family only, then maybe Toscono would talk. Docherty doubted it – what was there in it for the drug dealer? – but the only other options were bribery and threats, and despite his desperate desire to know the truth of Guillermo's fate, Gustavo Macías had refused to countenance any payment to those who had taken his son. Docherty had already decided that he would try to scare the shit out of Toscono only when all else had failed.

He drained his cup and got to his feet. The deal with Gustavo required him just to ask, and he had promised Isabel he wouldn't take any real risks. He smiled to himself as he began walking towards the office building – he just knew that he wasn't going to like taking no for an answer from a man like Toscono.

But on this visit he would be polite. It wouldn't have been hard to get hold of a gun – the hotel receptionist would no doubt have a brother or an uncle who just happened to have one for sale – but carrying one into Toscono's den would be asking for trouble. He wouldn't get to see the head honcho without being frisked, and, should they decide for some reason to shoot him, a gun would simplify the task of convincing the local police that they had killed the gringo in self-defence.

He pushed through the glass doors into the air-conditioned lobby and walked confidently up to the attendant. 'I am here to see Señor Toscono on a personal matter,' he said, hoping the Argentinian's curiosity would get the better of him. 'My name is James Docherty, and I have travelled here from Chile to see him.'

So what? the attendant's eyes said, but he picked up the internal phone and relayed the message. 'Fifth floor,' he said briefly, nodding towards the lift.

Docherty walked in, pressed the button, and allowed himself to be carried skyward. So far, so good, he thought. He'd already got further than he'd expected.

The lift doors slid open to reveal a reception area and several doorways leading into the rest of a richly carpeted suite. The waiting bodyguard ran professional hands over Docherty's arms, legs and back, then led him into what looked like a doctor's waiting room. There were several paintings on the wall, all of flowers, and a framed front page of an Argentinian newspaper celebrating the sinking of HMS *Sheffield*, which took Docherty back to the night he'd heard the news himself, pissed half out of his mind in a Glasgow pub.

The door to Toscono's office opened and the bodyguard gestured him in. The man himself was sitting behind his desk in shirtsleeves; through the large window behind him the roofs stretched away towards the fuzzy green line of Chapultepec Park.

'What can I do for you?' Toscono asked as Docherty sat down. He had not offered to shake hands, and his voice was decidedly cool.

'It is a delicate matter,' Docherty began. 'A family matter.'

'You are English, yes?'

'Scottish. And I am married to an Argentinian. This matter has to do with her family,' he went on, stretching the truth somewhat. 'Her uncle had a son, who was a student in Rosario in the late 1970s.'

At the mention of Rosario, Toscono's face seemed to congeal. 'This conversation is over,' he said, getting up.

Docherty remained seated. 'My wife's uncle is dying,' he continued. 'He just wants to know what happened to his son.'

'I expect he died,' Toscono said coldly, his eyes catching the bodyguard's.

Docherty stood up as the man towered over him, and the temptation to take him out was almost overwhelming. But Toscono would probably have a gun in his desk and there were probably other people in the suite, so a demonstration of SAS unarmed-combat skills would be more satisfying than wise. He turned to leave, then stopped at the door. 'Why would you refuse to comfort a dying man?' he asked, but Toscono didn't even bother to look up, the bodyguard grabbed an arm, and a few seconds later he was being bundled into the lift.

'Don't come back,' the man said, speaking for the first time and displaying a row of gold teeth which Docherty could have combed his hair with. He emerged into the lobby and walked out on to the street, telling himself that he'd been wise not to fight back. If he was going to get anything from Toscono he would need to get him alone, and it would be much easier taking out a bodyguard who underestimated him.

He stopped at a convenient bar for a drink and reminded himself that he'd just earned $20,000, but he still felt angry. He told himself it was a childish kind of anger, but that didn't make it go away. He needed to put Toscono on the back-burner and regain his ability to think clearly.

A walk in the park, he thought, and then he remembered one of the things he'd planned to do once his business here was done. In 1977, during his last couple of days in the country, he'd set out to visit two famous houses in the southern suburb of Coyoacán, but both had been closed for refurbishment. He could visit them now, spend a few hours allowing his anger with Toscono to subside, then put his mind to the business of their next meeting. He already knew there'd be one – he might have satisfied the conditions of his deal with Gustavo Macías, but he hadn't satisfied himself.

The thought of driving ten kilometres and back through the capital's traffic was not a pleasant one, so he took the Golf back to the hotel, recovered the guidebook from his room and took the Metro south. A pleasant walk through shaded streets brought him to the last home of the Russian revolutionary Leon Trotsky, whose politics had obviously not prevented him from living in an upmarket neighbourhood. The house itself was not big, but it had a lovely cloistered garden. The rooms had supposedly been left exactly as they were on the day Stalin's agent stuck an ice-pick in Trotsky's skull, and the latter's broken glasses were still lying on the desk where they had fallen.

Docherty found himself wishing his father had been here to see this. The old man, who had been a shop steward on the Clyde most of his life, had often announced his admiration for the man who'd lived and died in this house. If Trotsky rather than Stalin had followed Lenin, he'd been fond of saying, it would all have been different. Docherty doubted it, but seeing these rooms and the hammer-and-sickle-draped grave in the garden, he felt moved just the same.

After sitting for a while he got up and left, walking the couple of blocks to the Frida Kahlo Museum. She had lived in this house with fellow-Mexican painter Diego Rivera, and both had been friendly with Trotsky. Isabel liked her paintings a lot, and seeing them here in all their vibrancy Docherty could better appreciate why. Looking out into the well-tended back garden he could imagine her, Rivera and Trotsky sitting round the wrought-iron table drinking coffee in the late 30s, lamenting the fact that the rest of the world was sliding inexorably into war.

He ate lunch in an overpriced Coyoacán restaurant, then headed back north on the packed Metro, still wondering what to do about Toscono.

David Shepreth had been back in London only two days but already he felt at a loose end. On impulse he rang his father to suggest a visit, and almost instantly regretted it. His father's words were welcoming enough, but the tone wasn't, and the final 'of course, I'll be watching the football' effectively guaranteed one more evening of non-communication in a relationship already burdened with too many.

Feeling depressed, Shepreth steered the Escort in the direction of Barnsbury and his father's basement flat. The kick-off in the German game had to be imminent but half the fans still seemed to be in central London, or maybe it was just that the whole country had gone mad. As he swerved to avoid one flag-waving pedestrian in Kingsway it occurred to him that it was almost impossible to serve MI6 in the field and maintain any level of patriotic fervour. If you lived out there in the world it was impossible to ignore the fact that everyone else had a point of view. In these days of international travel only the Americans were still clinging to the childlike belief that theirs was the greatest country on earth – everyone else had grown up and accepted relativity. True, most people were fondest of their own homeland, but that didn't stop them realizing that many other countries had just as much to offer.

As far as MI6 was concerned, this was a two-edged sword. Their agents were working for one country and one country only, but if they were any good at their job they acquired a knowledge of the way the world worked which was completely at odds with any simple notion of 'my country, right or wrong'. The end-result, as Shepreth knew only too well, was a thoroughgoing cynicism, sometimes worn like a badge, at others hidden beneath the mask of a cold professionalism. Everything became impersonal.

And I'm sick of it, he thought, as he waited at the King's Cross lights. He wanted it to be personal. The two goons in Panama with their 'B'-movie dialogue, they hadn't thought of killing him as anything personal, and if he allowed the curtain of his profession's cynicism to close behind him then he was no better than they were – just a player of violent games. Like a Len Deighton, he thought. Game, Set and Match. Hook, Line and Sinker. Egg, Beans and Chips.

Well, he'd already laid an egg in Panama, and Mexico seemed typecast for beans. It only remained to see where he'd cash in his chips.

The thought gave Shepreth his first real smile of the day, but his father's offhand welcome – they hadn't seen each other for six months – soon put paid to it. The game had already been on for about half an hour, and by some miracle England were a goal up. Shepreth took the other end of the sofa and tried to watch, but soon found his mind beginning to wander. Looking round the room at his father's things from Spain he felt himself drawn, as always, back into the past, to the school holiday visits to his parents in Madrid, which had always promised so much more than they actually delivered. Looking back now it was easy to see that both his parents – his journalist father and highly social mother – had been busy people and that even if either of them had been really interested in their only child, they would have acted little differently. But at the time he had felt alternately abandoned and ignored, and deep down he knew that his life was still ruled by the consequences, that he was torn between conflicting compulsions to hide and to prove his worth to the world.

Why did I come? he asked himself. He tried to take an interest in the game, but found himself wondering once more at how easily his parents had got used to living without each other. His father had taken early retirement and announced that he was returning to England; his mother had said fine, but she would be staying in Spain. Five years later she was still in Madrid and he was still here, and they didn't seem to miss each other at all. Twenty years ago their desire to spend every minute together had caused him to be sent off to boarding school, and now they didn't even bother to call each other.

'How are you doing?' his father asked, and Shepreth noticed that the half-time whistle had been blown.

'OK,' he said. 'How are you?'

His father grinned. 'Pretty good. I've got quite a lot of stuff in the pipeline, and the novel's coming on. Want a beer, glass of wine?' he asked, getting up.

'Beer,' Shepreth said.

By the time his father came back with it the second half was about to start. The old man wasn't as steady on his feet as usual, but he was probably into his fifth or sixth beer by now. There was something vaguely pathetic about him these days. Shepreth thought. He was fifty-seven, but rather than realize the dreams of his youth he seemed to have just carried them through middle age. In his thirties he could often be heard on the radio reporting on events in Spain, and several newspapers had been happy to print his articles, but there had been no advance from that position – he was still writing the odd article, doing the odd piece of translation, talking about the novel which no one else expected would be written. He was a classic under-achiever.

Am I the same? Shepreth asked himself. He lived in hotels, had no real home. His love life was non-existent, his sex life almost so. He was neither enough of a cynic nor enough of a believer to fit in, which didn't augur well for his career prospects.

'Fuck,' his father said, and Shepreth realized that the Germans had equalized. Even he had expected that to happen.

The rest of the game passed slowly by, through the ninety minutes and another non-existent 'golden goal' to the penalty showdown. When Southgate finally missed his father couldn't even manage a curse; he just turned off the TV with a look of disgust and indifferently asked his son if he was staying the night.

Shepreth had meant to, but now he couldn't face it. He felt like screaming at his father, but he simply took his leave and drove back across London to the studio flat which was this year's apology for a home.

Docherty got back to his hotel around five, to find both the receptionist and his room key missing from reception. Perhaps the room was being cleaned, he thought. Perhaps the receptionist was out distributing alms to the poor.

He stealthily climbed the stairs and edged along the corridor towards his room. The door was wide open, and one man in uniform was going through his bag while another leant indolently against the wall smoking a cigarette.

'This is a non-smoker,' Docherty told him as he walked through the door. 'And what the fuck are you doing?' he asked the one elbow deep in his bag.

The arm came out like a shot, but then the policeman remembered who was supposed to be giving the orders. 'Identification,' he demanded, holding out a palm.

Docherty handed over his British passport. The other policeman, he was pleased to see, had ground out his cigarette. Little victories, he told himself.

'You must come with us, Señor Docherty,' the first policeman said, shoving the passport into his tunic pocket.

'Where?' Docherty asked.

'To the police station. It is not far.'

'Why? Am I being arrested?'

'You are required to answer some questions.'

'About what?'

'That will be explained to you at the station.'

The policeman's patience was obviously wearing thin, but Docherty was damned if he was going to get into a car with two armed men he didn't know from Adam. 'I need to see your identification,' he said firmly.

The policeman looked at his partner, shrugged and pulled out a crumpled card.

As Docherty handed it back he said, 'And I want to phone your station to verify that you are who this says you are.'

'We do not have the time for such . . .'

'If I'm not allowed to make that call, you'll have to carry me out,' Docherty said, hoping they wouldn't take him up on it.

They didn't, and he made the call from the empty reception desk downstairs. The two policemen were genuine, for what that was worth in Mexico.

Their car was unmarked, which explained why he hadn't noticed it coming in. One man sat in the back with him while the other broke every rule of the road on their drive to the police station. It was almost dark now and by the time they arrived Docherty had only a vague idea of where he was.

The two men left him in a large, stuffy room and disappeared. He lay down on the long wooden bench lining one wall and stared up at the peeling paint on the ceiling. The fan, having shed one of its four blades, had apparently lost the will to turn.

The minutes went by, then an hour, then two. He could hear feet above his head and the occasional voices of passers-by but not much else. He wondered if they were just wasting his time or deliberately trying to scare him.

Another hour went by. He thought about Isabel and the children in Santiago – she would be putting them to bed about this time, maybe telling Ricardo a story. He wondered what they'd think if they could see him now.

Still, his only problem so far was thirst. His mouth was as dry as the Mexican dust he'd been swallowing all day, and he was beginning to get a headache. He could no doubt bang on the door and demand water, but in the unlikely event that some was brought it would not be bottled, and he'd rather be thirsty than spend the next week suffering Montezuma's famous revenge.

It was nearly nine o'clock when the door finally opened. Two uniformed men escorted him down one corridor, up a flight of steps and down another corridor, before ushering him into a much better-decorated room than the one he'd just left. Another man in uniform – this one in his forties or early fifties, with a balding head, moustache and rotund frame – was sitting behind a huge desk. 'Sit down, Señor Docherty,' he said in English.

'And who might you be?' Docherty asked.

'I am Lieutenant Colonel Orantes.'

'Police or Army?' Docherty asked. He had considered refusing to answer any questions until he was allowed to contact the British Embassy, but had decided that such a move might needlessly complicate matters. If Orantes was only going to slap him lightly on the wrist . . .

'Federal Police,' Orantes answered. 'It has . . .'

'So why am I here?' Docherty interrupted.

'You don't know?'

'If I did, I wouldn't be asking.'

Orantes raised an eyebrow. 'This morning you visited the offices of Señor Toscono, did you not?'

'I did.'

'Where you threatened him with violence . . .'

'I did not threaten him – he threatened me. I merely asked him about one of his victims in the Dirty War.'

'What happened in Argentina twenty years ago is not the business of the Mexican police. Threats against a prominent citizen – and Señor Toscono is a citizen of this country now – are our business.'

'I made no threats.'

'That is not what he and his employees say.'

'They are lying.'

Orantes smiled. 'And whose word should I take – a prominent Mexican citizen or an Englishman passing through?'

Docherty smiled back. 'I expect you'll believe the man who pays you to.'

Orantes, rather than getting angry, simply laughed. Once his amusement had subsided he fixed Docherty with his eyes, pointed a finger at him and said, 'Do not try to contact Señor Toscono again. If you do, I promise that you will regret it.'

Docherty returned the stare. 'Have you considered a career in films?' he asked.

That did seem to strike home. 'You may go,' Orantes said coldly, breaking eye contact. 'Enjoy your stay in Mexico,' he added sarcastically as the uniformed man led Docherty away.

A minute later he was out on the dark street, and after taking a look in both directions – neither of which seemed particularly inviting – he decided that either was better than standing still. Orantes might be finished with him, or the interview might have been a prelude to something else – like one more unsolved robbery and murder on Mexico City's mean streets. There was a hint of brighter light in one direction, so he started out that way, upping his pace from a walk to a jog, then a fast trot. It was probably unnecessary, but better to be safe than sorry.

No threatening figures emerged from the shadows, and as he ran the bright glow came slowly into focus. It was the Avenida Mosqueta, which distant memory told him ran past the main railway station.

Feeling relatively safe once more, he walked east, wondering why Toscono had gone to all this trouble. The Argentinian had hardly been ambivalent that morning, so why labour the point? It seemed gratuitous, even insulting, which was maybe the point. Either that or Toscono was an anal retentive who couldn't sleep until he'd covered every conceivable angle.

Outside the station Docherty found a cab. He gave the driver the name of his hotel, but halfway down Tacuba he changed his mind and told the man to drop him off in the Zócalo. There was a small protest demonstration going on in the middle of the square, which reminded him of the Day of the Dead in 1977, when a reproachful cross of flowers and burning candles over fifty metres long had been laid across the stones, pointing straight at the President's door.

In the far corner a drummer was beating out a rhythm, and he walked towards the sound. The dancers were different tonight, but every bit as good. He watched, enjoying the spectacle as his brain worked on the problem of Toscono. When the drum fell silent he realized his mind was made up.

Sir Christopher Hanson switched on his office TV for the news, but the only thing anyone seemed able to talk about was the wretched football match. He was almost glad that Germany had beaten England – at least now the fever would begin to subside and they could get back to a normal civilized summer of tennis and cricket. But he couldn't quite make the emotional leap – even fifty years after the war it was hard for most people of his generation to wish anything good for the Germans. Only the previous week a bout of insomnia had caused him to watch a film which followed a group of gypsies from pre-war Poland to Auschwitz. These were not crimes that could be forgotten in a hurry.

Would Angel Bazua have enjoyed the Third Reich? Hanson wondered, as he opened the bound printout once more. The light-brown hair and blue eyes suggested possible descent from the early German immigrants to Argentina, but there was no genealogical evidence. Bazua's father, Raul, had been a worker in the Buenos Aires cattle market, his mother, Steffia, a seamstress, but the names and occupations of their parents were unknown.

Bazua's track record suggested a Third Reich-friendly narrow-mindedness, not to mention an appetite for cruelty and pathological patriotism, but on balance Hanson decided the Argentinian would have found the discipline somewhat restrictive.

He read through the file for a second time, making sure he had imbibed all the relevant facts. The fifty-two-year-old Bazua had spent all his childhood years in Buenos Aires; his family, though poor, had never gone hungry, and by some miracle his parents had managed to put enough aside to send the boy to military school. From there he had won a scholarship to a prestigious academy, where he was implicated in a scandal concerning a maimed prostitute. There was no real explanation of how he had weathered this crisis – only a suggestion that blackmail had played a part – but he had graduated with honours a year later, and began the task of working his way up the Army's promotional ladder. He was soon active in extreme right-wing 'clubs' and in 1970–1 he spent a year at the US anti-insurgency school in Panama, where he made friends with like-minded officers from several other Latin American countries. As the war between Left and Right in Argentina escalated in the mid-70s the 'clubs' turned into semi-official death squads, bent on cleansing the nation of all opposition to the ruling coalition of big business and the military. Bazua had been in charge of operations in and around Rosario, a port city with nearly a million inhabitants two hundred and seventy kilometres north-west of the capital.

Some seven thousand people, most of them students or trade unionists, had disappeared during Bazua's reign of terror, but several hundred of those with the richest connections had subsequently turned up, presumably in return for substantial ransoms.

Bazua had not fought in the Falklands War, but his only son – the product of a short-lived marriage from his military academy years – had been killed at Goose Green, further deepening what seemed to have been a life-long hatred of the English. Defeat dealt a huge blow to the prestige of the military, and at the age of thirty-eight he had resigned his commission. Not enough was known about his activities over the next few years, but by the end of the 80s he had relocated to Cartagena on the north Colombian coast and emerged as a major player on the international drug-trafficking stage. He had not challenged the local cartels in the cocaine market, but had, from the beginning, concentrated on the refining, distribution and sale of his adopted country's burgeoning poppy crop. By the mid-90s Colombia had become second only to Burma in heroin production, and Bazua was profiting most from the growth.

He was not untouchable, of course, and by 1993 the need for a scapegoat had caused the Colombians to make a show of imprisoning their only non-indigenous drug baron. A whole new facility had been built on the Caribbean island of Providencia, largely, it seemed, to the chief prisoner's specifications. And the flow of heroin continued unabated. Or almost – the operation in London the previous week had doubtless caused a temporary shortfall in the British capital's supply.

Which would just raise the price and make the bastard a bigger profit on his next shipment, Hanson thought sourly. Some days he felt really nostalgic for the Cold War, and honest enemies.

Why were the Americans being so obstructive? Salewicz had phoned him back the previous evening with a list of rationales and excuses a mile long, but he hadn't even bothered to pretend that he believed any of them. Listen to the subtext, the CIA man had seemed to be saying – sometimes you just can't get what you want, and there's no point in wondering why.

Well, it wasn't good enough. He had given the Americans a chance to explain themselves, make their case, and they hadn't even tried. They might think that would be the end of it, but if Hanson had any say in the matter it wouldn't. Not many things made him angry these days – apart from his children, of course – but no one was going to finance a second invasion of the Falklands with profits from flooding Britain with heroin. One way or another, Bazua had to be stopped. The question was how.

Hanson stared out of his window. Somewhere in the distance there was shouting – it was probably football supporters. For all he knew, English and German fans were replaying yesterday's game in Trafalgar Square.

On his desk the ancient intercom crackled, as if it was clearing its throat. 'Mr Shepreth is here,' his new secretary announced.

'Send him in,' Hanson replied irritably. She always sounded like a dental receptionist.

Shepreth's tall frame loomed in the doorway. He looked bronzed from his three months in the field, Hanson noticed. 'David, how are you?' he asked.

The old man was in a bad mood, Shepreth thought, as he took the proffered seat. He hoped it had nothing to do with him. 'Fine, thank you,' he answered with more tact than truth. Thanks to his neighbours he had only managed about six hours' sleep in seventy-two. Someone across the street had played loud music for most of the night, and the Americans next door had thoughtfully erected a basketball hoop between the buildings, encouraging their son to bounce his ball through the hours of daylight.

'Good to have you back in one piece,' Hanson murmured, his eyes on the printout he had just rescued from a pile. 'I read your report. Did the Yanks in Panama give you any reason for not coming up with an address for the fax number?'

'I was told they didn't have one.'

'Which was nonsense, I presume?'

'I can't be sure – he might have been telling the truth.'

'But you didn't think so?'

'No,' Shepreth said, trying to recall why he hadn't thought so. 'I don't know Neil Sadler that well, but he sounded embarrassed to me. I don't think he knew why he'd been told to be unhelpful – but he had.'

Hanson leant back in his chair, twirling his pen between his fingers. 'I'm beginning to think this may be one of those stupid internal rivalries the Yanks seem to specialize in,' he said.

Like MI5 and Special Branch, Shepreth thought, but he didn't say so. His boss seemed unusually pent-up today – he couldn't remember him ever calling the Americans 'Yanks' before.

'OK,' Hanson said abruptly. 'I've got a pretty good idea of our current situation. Give me an update on how the Americans are doing in their war with the drug lords.'

'Not very well,' Shepreth said. 'As soon as they knock down one line of kingpins another one springs up. They'd hardly finished slapping themselves on the back for breaking the Medellín cartel when they realized the Cali cartel would probably have done it for them in a couple more years. And since 1992 the Cali people have been taking a beating – quite a few of them are trying to negotiate terms with the Colombian government now – but their old subsidiaries in Panama and Mexico have just struck out on their own. The Mexican traffickers are now the Americans' number-one targets.'

'We're still talking mostly about Peruvian and Bolivian coca, refined in Colombia and then sold on, yes?'

'Mostly. Though the Mexicans are now doing some refining of their own, and the Colombians have started growing poppies on a grand scale. The shipment we just intercepted was probably grown and refined in Colombia for Bazua's organization to move and distribute. More heroin's going north into the States as well, but at the moment the Americans are more worried by the way the trade in methamphetamines has suddenly taken off. They're just chemicals, so there's no need to grow anything – just get the ingredients to a small lab and cook them up. Thousands of these labs have been springing up all over Mexico.'

Hanson shook his head at the folly of it all. 'And what's the favourite mode of transport these days?' he asked drily.

'It changes from year to year. In the 80s they were sending convoys of planes all the way from Colombia to northern Mexico, but the interception rate got too high for comfort so they switched to small planes hopping their way north via Panama and Guatemala and into southern Mexico – often into territory controlled by insurgents – and from there they'd go north by road. The last bright idea – which was probably Bazua's – was to send jet liners into northern Mexico. They had fake identities painted over the old ones, radar transponders turned off, and they didn't file flight plans. They could carry huge shipments and they were fast enough to outrun anyone that saw them. But it wasn't something they could do too often – or at least not without giving the Americans the proof they wanted that the Colombian authorities were involved. A plane the size of a Caravelle can't take off from a jungle strip.'

'They don't try flying the stuff into the US itself?'

'Not in large quantities. Most of it goes across the border in containers and trucks, some of it inside human "mules". Each of the main crossover points – Tijuana, Ciudad Juárez, Matamoros – seems to be the personal fiefdom of one organization, and they each have their own links with the suppliers to the south and the distributors across the border. NAFTA – the trade treaty the US and Mexico signed a couple of years ago – has made things a lot easier for the traffickers. The volume of cross-border trade has shot up and there's no way the Americans can search more than one truck in twenty without effectively closing the border down. These days it's easier for the traffickers to get the drugs in than it is for them to get their money out.'

'How are the Americans getting along with the Mexican authorities?'

'Not as well as they'd like us to believe. The Mexicans have too many overlapping agencies, and none of them are completely clean. Traffickers have escaped pursuing Feds with help from an army helicopter. State police have come across Feds trying to bury a damaged jet liner in the desert.' Shepreth smiled ruefully. 'A couple of months ago one state's "policeman of the year" was arrested for trafficking.'

'I imagine the Americans are getting somewhat frustrated.'

'Of course. But the situation's not going to change. The Mexican police and army are paid abysmally, and their earnings on the side just about provide them with a living wage. The country as a whole is probably making about seven billion dollars a year from the drug trade, and it needs every penny of it.'

Hanson had opened the file in front of him. 'It was the DEA who pushed through the kingpin strategy, wasn't it?'

'Yes,' Shepreth replied, although the question was rhetorical.

'The National Security Council were in agreement, I think,' his boss went on. 'The Pentagon, the Coast Guard and the Customs Service were opposed. Where did the CIA stand?'

This time an answer was called for. 'With the National Security Council, I think,' Shepreth said. 'They usually pride themselves on being above such mundane matters as the drug trade.'

'Hmm. A more centralized DEA means less autonomy for the field offices, right?'

'The head of the field office in Mexico City has complained about nothing else for the last six months.'

'How do you know?' Hanson asked sharply.

'He's a friend,' Shepreth admitted. 'I mean I'm sure he doesn't tell me everything – he's a professional – but I do know he's as frustrated as we are that Bazua's not on the kingpin list. He may not be shifting the same volume through Mexico as some of the others, but he's not that far behind. And as I said, he was apparently the first one to have the idea of using the old jet liners to bring in huge quantities on a single flight. His organization on the ground in Mexico is said to be first-rate, with everyone from cabinet ministers to village cops on the payroll.'

Hanson thought for a moment. 'I want action against Bazua,' he said slowly. 'But the how and the what . . .' He looked up. 'I don't want to move against him until I know why the Americans are so reluctant to. Maybe they do have a good reason, and just can't be bothered to tell us what it is. If so . . . well, a good reason for them may not be a good reason for us – but either way I want to know. So go back to Mexico and see what you can find out. Try and get your DEA friend to tell you why he thinks his bosses are frustrating him.'

'Yes, sir,' Shepreth said. He didn't much like the idea of trading on his friendship with Ted Vaughan, but when all was said and done he knew that the American would love the idea of anyone taking a crack at Angel Bazua.

Carmen looked round the familiar room, but there was no psychological comfort to be had there. She had grown up in this house, and even after moving out she had thought of it as a safe haven from the troubles of the world, but that was not the case any more. Now it was just the place where her parents lived.

They were sitting together on the sofa, not touching or even looking at each other. Carmen had half-expected her father to rant and rage when she told him what she knew but instead of exploding he had seemed to crumple. Both of them had. In half an hour they had seemed to age about ten years.

She had explained about Victoria, trying to cushion the blow by emphasizing how unreliable the woman's testimony might be, but her father had not been fooled. 'You think it's true, don't you?' he had asked, begging her with his eyes to deny it. But she couldn't. The five women had been kidnapped, taken to the island of Providencia, and forced into sexual slavery by a convicted drug baron named Angel Bazua. When two of the women had become pregnant each had been forced to swallow about seventy condom-wrapped pellets of heroin and put on a plane for the United States. The other three were presumably still servicing Bazua and his men in their island prison. And there didn't seem to be a thing they could do about it.

Carmen had then explained to her shell-shocked parents why they couldn't just go to the police. Her father had tried to argue with her, but without a great deal of conviction. What was happening on Providencia might be outrageous, but it could only be happening with the tacit acceptance of law-enforcement agencies on the island. Giving the story to the press would probably get them more attention than an appeal to the police, but the closer they got to exposing Bazua and his cronies the more certain it seemed that he'd simply dispose of the evidence. The three women would just disappear into the sea.

'So what can we do?' her father asked numbly.

'I don't know,' she said. 'I thought about hiring someone – a private detective – but if we can't trust the real police why should we trust a man who works only for money?'

'There must be some honourable men doing that kind of work,' her father said hopefully.

'But how do we find out who they are?' She had been through this conversation more than once with herself, and her conclusion was always the same – the only person she could trust to ask questions on Providencia was herself. She knew it wouldn't be simple or easy – there was no way she was going to rescue her sister from a well-guarded prison – but if she could find out for certain that Marysa was alive that would at least be a start.

'I have to go myself,' she told her parents. An hour ago she would have expected an argument, but now they both just looked at her, fear and hope crowding their faces. 'I'll leave tomorrow,' she said, getting up.

Her father murmured something about paying for everything, but she was already halfway through the door which led out into the sunlit garden. The hammock was swaying gently in the breeze, and the sudden desire to simply lie down and close her eyes was almost overwhelming.

Instead she walked on through the trees, thinking that she would have to try to see Victoria again before she left. The aunt who had met the plane had seemed a kindly person, but Victoria had acted as if she was being abandoned, rather than passed into someone else's care.

Carmen reached the bottom of the garden and stared up at the distant hills, her heart weighed down with sadness, her stomach churning with fear.

6

Docherty sat on his haunches behind the white BMW, his back against the concrete wall. The car was one of only a dozen still awaiting collection in the cavernous car park, and that suited Docherty down to the ground – he didn't want an audience when Toscono came to claim his.

About fifty-five hours had passed since their first meeting, and by this time Toscono had probably forgotten he existed. Docherty had not been idle in the intervening period – he had spent most of the previous day searching out a suitable spot for a private tête-à-tête, and most of the evening shopping for the 9mm Walther PPK which was now stuffed inside his belt. He would have preferred one of the Browning High Powers he was used to, but the dealer he visited in Guadalupe said he hadn't seen one of those for months. Besides, Docherty had gained some experience with the Walther PPK during his first tour of duty in Northern Ireland. The fact that the gun came with a silencer was a big bonus – convincing people that you were prepared to use a gun was so much easier if it looked like no one else would notice.

Docherty tensed as the faint ping announced the opening of the lift doors, but the two men who emerged were not Toscono and his bodyguard. These two walked across his line of vision towards a dark Mercedes, their feet making a slapping sound on the concrete floor. The car's engine burst into life, sounding preternaturally loud in the subterranean space. It purred across the floor, smoothly accelerated up the exit ramp and disappeared from view, just as the lift doors opened again.

This time it was them. Toscono was carrying a briefcase on this occasion, which was all to the good – if he was armed it would slow down his reactions. Docherty's only movement as the footfalls drew nearer was to pull the Walther from his belt. His breathing sounded louder than it should but he knew that was just his imagination.

The slap of their footsteps turned from mono to stereo as the two men walked towards the doors on either side of the car, and the clunking sound told Docherty that Toscono had used his remote. He rose up from his crouch like a well-oiled jack-in-the-box, gun in hand. After a split second's hesitation the bodyguard started for his own weapon, but a perceptible shift in Docherty's aim and the sight of the silencer froze him in mid-motion.

'Both of you – hands on the roof,' the Scot snapped. 'And let the briefcase drop,' he told Toscono.

'You must be mad,' Toscono hissed, but both he and the bodyguard obeyed.

Docherty walked round the car until he was a few feet away from the latter, all the time keeping an eye on the man's boss. 'I can just as easily leave *you* dead on the floor,' he told the bodyguard. 'And if you move a muscle, I will.'

The man's mouth twitched, but he said nothing.

'On your knees,' Docherty told him, and when the man didn't move he pushed the snout of the silencer gently into his back. 'Now or never,' he added.

The man still didn't speak, but a whimper escaped his lips as he lowered himself to the ground. Taking his eyes off Toscono for no more than a second, Docherty crashed the butt of the Walther into the side of the bodyguard's head.

The man slumped forward, banging his forehead against the car door, and ended up curled in a foetal position half under the car. With his foot, Docherty dragged a stray leg out from under the wheel. 'Get in the car,' he told Toscono.

'No,' Toscono said shakily. His eyes were on the distant lift doors – no doubt he was praying they would suddenly disgorge a rescue force.

'Is that your final answer?' Docherty asked, aiming the PPK between the man's eyes and flexing his finger on the trigger.

Toscono got into the car.

Docherty climbed in beside him.

'There were thousands of prisoners at the Rosario base,' Toscono said petulantly. 'I can't remember all the ones I had dealings with, let alone all the others.'

'Shut up and drive,' Docherty told him.

Toscono looked at him.

'Drive,' he repeated.

Toscono drove.

'Smile at the man,' Docherty said as they approached the attendant's booth, but there was no one in it. 'Turn right on the street,' he added.

'Where are we going?' Toscono asked as they emerged on to Balderas.

'Head for the airport,' Docherty told him.

'The airport?'

'Don't worry – you won't be needing your passport,' he said, as the Argentinian slowed the car to join the long queue at the lights. The traffic might turn out to be a problem, Docherty realized – even with the tinted windows shut he didn't fancy holding a gun on Toscono for hours on end in the middle of a grid-locked street.

They crawled up Tacuba, but once past the Zócalo the crush thinned, Toscono was able to keep the car moving at a steady thirty and it seemed as if the worst was over. The Argentinian hadn't said a word since the car park, and his face now seemed set in a mask of cold fury. He had just about recovered from the shock, Docherty guessed, and was now rummaging through his brain for a way out of his predicament.

They turned left on to Puerto Aéreo Boulevard, and were soon passing under the thunderous flight path of an incoming American Airlines jet. 'We're not going into the airport,' Docherty said. 'Take the Texcoco road – it's about a kilometre beyond the entrance.'

Toscono said nothing, just gripped the wheel a bit tighter.

'If you drive into the airport, I shall just leave you dead in the car park and take the next plane out,' Docherty told him.

Toscono's shoulders seemed to sag. 'So where are we going?' he asked as the slip road went by.

'The Texcoco road,' Docherty repeated, and Toscono didn't ask again. They were about a kilometre down that road, the outlying areas of the airport receding to their right, when the small side road came into view. 'Turn off here,' Docherty ordered, and saw the flash of fear in the other man's eyes. 'If I'd just wanted to kill you I could have done it in the car park,' he said.

Toscono pulled the car off the main road and on to a bumpy dirt track which wound through the scrub for about half a kilometre before ending on the rim of a recently excavated crater some two hundred metres square and about thirty metres deep. 'It's for rubbish,' Docherty said drily.

The Argentinian stared out at the vast hole. A plane was taking off a few hundred metres beyond it, but as far as the rest of the world was concerned they might have been on the moon. The highway they'd turned off was an invisible murmur somewhere beyond the thick scrub, the city just a few distant towers beneath the smog.

'Guillermo Macías,' Docherty said softly. 'I want to know what happened.'

Toscono looked at him. He remembered both the name and the boy. Macías had been almost too good-looking, with an angelic face, soft, wavy hair, a colt-like grace. In his mind's eye Toscono could see the pale body on the table, arcing and bouncing under the electricity. It hadn't been necessary – he had offered the boy a way out, only to receive a faceful of spittle for his trouble.

He even remembered why he had been arrested. 'Macías was picked up with several other students,' he said out loud. 'They were found in possession of gummed labels with revolutionary slogans . . .'

'Labels?' Docherty asked incredulously.

'Yes. I was in command of the arrest squad. He was taken to the base for processing, and I don't know what happened to him after that. If he wasn't released I presume he ended up in either a grave or the River Plate.'

Docherty knew Toscono was lying, at least in part – his eyes and mouth seemed to be telling different stories. The gummed label part sounded sick enough to be true, and so did the choice of final resting-places, but Docherty was pretty sure the Argentinian knew more than he was saying about what had happened in between.

Did it matter? Gustavo Macías would at least know why his son had been arrested, and what parents wanted to know the details of how their child had been tortured? He had got what he needed from Toscono.

But not what he wanted. He wasn't even sure what that was, and the reasons he wanted it were no clearer – they might have something to do with old-fashioned right and wrong, or maybe with the fact that Isabel had been tortured by men like this one. At that moment he didn't care.

'That's not enough,' he said softly, as if it was a decision he'd reached reluctantly. He raised the Walther, supporting the wrist of his gun hand on the other, and hoped that an hour under the gun hadn't taken the edge off Toscono's fear.

'I can't tell you any more,' the Argentinian said. His voice was only slightly frayed at the edges, but the eyes were wide with terror.

'Who could?' Docherty asked.

'What do you mean?'

'Give me a name. Who was in command of the camp?'

Toscono thought quickly. Giving this mad Englishman Angel Bazua's name would be safe enough – there was no way anyone could get to *him*. 'Colonel Bazua was in command of the base,' he said.

That at least was the truth, Docherty thought.

'He's in prison in Colombia,' Toscono volunteered.

'I know where he is,' Docherty said coldly. 'What makes you think his memory is any better than yours?'

'It doesn't need . . .' Toscono began, then fell silent.

'This is the last question you'll have to answer,' Docherty told him. 'If I think you're telling the truth you can go and play in that big sandpit out there. If I think you're lying you'll need another couple of kneecaps. Understand?'

Toscono gave him a look of mingled fear and loathing. 'I understand.'

96

'So why doesn't Colonel Bazua need a memory?'

'Because he has the files,' Toscono said.

'The files?'

'The records of all the prisoners. Not just in Rosario – all the prisoners of the Army.'

Docherty believed him. He looked at his watch. 'It's been lovely talking to you, but I'm going to be late for my plane. So you can go now.' Once Toscono had climbed out he shifted over into the driving seat, put the BMW into reverse and accelerated back up the dirt road in the direction of the highway. By the rim of the crater Toscono had sunk to his knees and seemed to be praying to whatever God would listen.

Shepreth paid his money and paused just inside the doors of the Luz de la Luna, letting his eyes get used to the smoky gloom. A local band was doing a passable job on an old Clifford Brown tune and the jazz club's patrons were listening respectfully, toes and fingers tapping, heads nodding. As he'd expected, Theodore Vaughan was there, sitting alone at a table on the far side of the room, eyes closed in a smiling face. Jazz was the love of the DEA man's life, and this was far and away the best club in Mexico City.

During the two years they'd known each other Ted Vaughan had often brought Shepreth here, and for his part the Englishman had taken the Afro-American to visit some of the lesser-known archaeological gems within easy driving distance of the capital. Both had enjoyed the cross-cultural fertilization, and these days Vaughan could tell his Aztecs from his Toltecs, Shepreth his Mingus from his Monk.

As the pianist went into a solo, Shepreth wended his way through the tables to where his friend was sitting.

Vaughan opened his eyes. 'You're back,' he said, and closed them again.

'I got in last night,' Shepreth told him once the piece was over.

'How was Merry Old England?'

'In mourning. We lost a football match to the Germans,' he explained, seeing the look of incomprehension on Vaughan's face. 'I need something to eat,' he added, looking round for a waiter. The Luz de la Luna might not have had the world's greatest jazz, but the food was excellent. 'And then I need to talk to you,' he told Vaughan.

'Business?'

'Yeah. Off-the-record business, if there is such a thing.'

Vaughan smiled at that. 'After the set?'

'Sure.'

An hour or so later the two men emerged from the club and into the cool air. It was only just past ten o'clock, and the suburb of San Angel was far from sleeping. One group of teenage boys were honing their skateboarding skills in the parking lot next door, a mixed group of youngsters were talking and laughing outside the cinema just up the road, and in the distance they could hear the strains of the funfair wafting down from the Plaza San Jacinto.

'Have you got your car?' Shepreth asked.

'Yeah, it's over there.'

'Why don't we drive up to the plaza?'

'OK.'

They drove up the hill to find that many of the craft and artwork stalls in the square itself, and most of the fairground rides and freak shows in the adjoining streets, were still open for business. Vaughan found a spot to park the car, paid the local urchins a king's ransom to guard it, and the two of them walked slowly round the square, finally settling on a just-vacated bench close to the fountain. On the seat opposite a young couple were holding hands and staring into each other's eyes.

'Nice,' Vaughan said, lighting a cigarette. No matter how big an Hispanic population the US ended up with, Mexico would still feel a long way from home. He took a drag on the cigarette. 'So how can I help Her Majesty's Secret Service?' he asked playfully.

Shepreth had no desire to beat about the bush. 'You can tell us why your people are so reluctant to go after Angel Bazua.'

Vaughan grimaced. 'Ah, shit,' he murmured. 'Ask me something I know the answer to.'

Shepreth was silent for a moment. 'OK,' he said at last. 'We've got a pretty good idea of how big Bazua's European operation is. What's his volume of trade with the US like?'

'Big and getting bigger. Top twenty with a bullet. And we think he's recently done a distribution deal with Ignacio Payán in Ciudad Juárez, which would give him a seat at the big boys' table.'

'Which just seems to beg the question,' Shepreth said. 'Why the kid gloves?'

'Like I said, I don't know.' Vaughan hesitated for a moment. 'Off the record, right? I've asked my people in Washington, and they tell me he's in prison, the prison's in Colombia, there are easier fish to fry. All of which may be true, but it still doesn't feel right to me. Most of his organization's here and in Panama, and I can't see any harm in keeping tabs – if we don't, the bastard could have Mexico sewn up without even having to leave his goddam cell.'

Shepreth smiled. 'Do I detect some creative reading of your instructions from Washington? Are you keeping tabs anyway?'

'We're keeping a watch on Payán's people here, and of course that means investigating the people they're in regular contact with.'

'Like Bazua's people?'

Vaughan smiled. 'And I have a question of my own,' he said. 'Does the name James Docherty mean anything to you?'

'No,' Shepreth said without hesitation. 'Should it?'

'He's a fellow-countryman of yours. Ex-SAS, retired to Chile a couple of years ago. Two days ago he met with Bazua's top man here . . .'

'Lazaro Toscono?'

'The same. Docherty paid him a visit. We don't know why, but we do know that later that day some of Toscono's buddies in the police arrested Docherty, accused him of threatening Toscono and warned him to be a good boy in future.'

Shepreth pondered this information. Why would an ex-SAS man be threatening a drug baron?

'So he's not one of yours?' Vaughan asked.

'Not as far as I know,' Shepreth told him. 'Is he still in Mexico City?'

'He was this morning. He checked out of his hotel, took a cab to the post office and never came out again. At least, our guy didn't see him come out. It might have been just carelessness, but he hasn't left the country by plane and he hasn't checked into a new hotel under his own name.'

'You're still looking?' Shepreth asked, amazed as usual by how good the American coverage of the city was. One or other of their agencies must have someone on the payroll in just about every political, legal and military office in the capital, not to mention the various transport and communication agencies.

'Yeah,' Vaughan admitted. 'I'm curious,' he added by way of explanation.

So was Shepreth. It was almost midnight by the time Vaughan dropped him off at the Embassy-owned apartment, and in another couple of hours head office in London would be open for business. His body still seemed to be on English time in any case, and he felt more awake than he had earlier that evening. He made himself some coffee and liberally dosed it with brandy, then turned on the TV. A dubbed version of an old Paul Newman Western was showing – the one in which he played a white man who'd grown up with the Apaches. When it ended soon after one Shepreth flicked through the channels. One of them was showing a rerun of the England-Germany game.

He switched off the TV, took a shower, then encoded and faxed off his request for information on one James Docherty, ex-SAS. With any luck there would be an answer waiting for him when he woke up.

After ditching the BMW outside a Metro station in the Zona Rosa, Docherty had taken a taxi back to the Old City, collected his bag from the café owner who'd agreed to look after it, and checked into a far from salubrious hotel a couple of streets north of the Zócalo. He registered under the name Kenneth Dalglish, telling the receptionist his passport had been stolen that day. The man looked wounded by this news, but soon cheered up when offered compensation in the form of a ten-dollar bill.

The room looked like it was used for cockroach derbies, but the door seemed sturdy enough, and it would only be for the one night. In any case, Toscono had probably believed him when he said he had a plane to catch – it would have been too wounding for the Argentian's ego to suspect otherwise.

It was almost nine o'clock and Docherty hadn't yet eaten. The market streets north of Tacuba were still full of people, and a stall provided an excellent brace of *enchiladas suizas*, tortillas stuffed with chicken and smothered in sour cream. He could go back to watching the cholesterol later.

After washing the food down with a bottle of Negra Modelo – Mexico's best dark beer – he walked back down towards the Zócalo, keeping his eye out for a public phone. He eventually found one a stone's throw from the cathedral, on the edge of the still-busy square. Arranging a reversed-charges call to Chile was easier than he'd expected, and before a minute was up he could hear the phone ringing in their Santiago flat.

'Yes?' his wife asked briskly.

'It's me.'

The voice had softened. 'Jamie.'

'How's it going?' he asked. 'How are the kids?'

'Fine. Everything's fine. Marie won her race at school.'

'That's great.' He knew how pleased his daughter would be. 'Tell her well done from me.'

'How are you doing?' she asked. 'Have you seen Toscono again?'

'Aye, I have. I had to lean on him a bit, but he was a little more talkative second time around. He told me Guillermo Macías was one of several kids arrested for being in possession of gummed labels with left-wing slogans on them.' There was silence at the other end of the line. 'Are you still there, love?'

'I'm still here. After all this time, the stupidity of it all still takes my breath away.'

'I know what you mean. Anyway, Toscono claims he doesn't know what happened to Guillermo after he was "processed", but he seemed pretty certain the boy ended up in either a mass grave or the River Plate.'

'And?' she asked.

She knew him too well. 'He also told me that his boss, Bazua, has the Army's Dirty War files with him on Providencia.'

'What? All of them?'

'All the Army's. Not the Navy's,' he said gently. His wife and her friends had been tortured at the Navy Mechanical School outside Buenos Aires.

'My God,' she said softly. 'But he's not going to show them to anyone, is he?' she added a moment later. 'And especially not a retired British soldier.'

'He might give me the whole story on Guillermo,' Docherty said hopefully.

'Why would he do that?' his wife wanted to know.

'I don't know. Some of these bastards like to gloat. And if he just admitted to having the files . . . well, the Argentinian press would love the story. They might even get Menem to put some pressure on the Colombian government.'

'Knowing the files were still out there would certainly frighten a lot of people,' she agreed. 'I don't know, Jamie . . . what makes you think he'd agree to see you, or that the Colombians would allow it?'

'They probably wouldn't but . . . it just goes against the grain, leaving the job half done.'

'You've got something for Gustavo, and anything else will probably just hurt him more. Why don't you just come home?'

Docherty sighed. By morning his welcome in Mexico would be overdue, if it wasn't already. 'Aye,' he agreed. 'I'll get a plane to Buenos Aires tomorrow, and go and see Gustavo. I'll call you from there, or from Rosa's.'

'I'll be waiting,' she said, sounding relieved. 'I love you,' she added.

'And I you,' Docherty said. He hung up, wishing he was back in Santiago.

* * *

It was probably the birds rather than the whirr of the machine which woke Shepreth. His watch told him it was only just after six, but despite sleeping for only three hours he felt wide awake. In the main room the customized fax had disgorged three sheets of already decoded material; he took both them and a carton of juice out on to the small balcony, where the sun was making the most of the pre-smog hours.

James Docherty's life and career made interesting reading. He had grown up in Glasgow, the only son of well-known Clydeside shop steward Campbell Docherty ('reference MI5 file 4519/DX', the sender added helpfully). At school he had apparently been clever, serious and unruly – not necessarily in that order – and at the age of sixteen he had joined the Merchant Navy without consulting his family. Two years later, in 1969, he had signed up with the Army. He had passed through SAS selection training at the young age of twenty-two, and had promptly seen service in Arabia. Two years later he had married Christine Jess, but she had been killed in a road accident later the same year.

Docherty had obviously gone off the rails at this point. Reading between the lines, Shepreth guessed that his behaviour had been about to earn him a discharge when someone had shown the sense to grant him extended compassionate leave. The Scot had then spent five months travelling in Mexico.

Could his interest in Toscono date back that far? Shepreth wondered. It didn't seem very likely – the Argentinian had not taken up residence in Mexico until almost a decade later, after the military's fall from power in Buenos Aires. Or could the two men's paths have somehow crossed during the Falklands conflict?

He was letting his imagination race ahead of the facts.

After his wife's death and the long leave of absence Docherty had seen service in Northern Ireland, Yemen and Oman. By

1980 he had risen to the rank of sergeant – the highest an enlisted man could reach – and in that year he had successfully brokered a hostage crisis in Guatemala. Two years later, with the Task Force poised to begin the reconquest of the Falklands, he had led one of two four-man teams inserted into Argentina. Their mission was to keep enemy airfields under observation, and so warn the Task Force of air attacks.

Shepreth took a slug of orange juice. There had always been rumours of SAS activity on the mainland, but this was the first time he'd seen them confirmed in print.

And there'd also been someone working for MI6, he discovered to his surprise. A woman, moreover, an Argentinian exile who had endured torture at the hands of the junta who now ruled her country.

And Docherty had married her.

It was beginning to make sense, Shepreth thought. The SAS man hadn't come to see Toscono about drugs – he'd brought the Argentinian some unfinished business from the Dirty War.

He read on. Through the rest of the 80s Docherty had seen little in the way of active service. He had been an instructor in the SAS Training Wing, and as such had spent several periods on loan to foreign governments which wanted to set up their own élite units. Mostly though, he and his Argentinian wife had lived in Hereford. She had given birth to two children – a daughter in 1987 and a son in 1989.

Docherty's first retirement in 1993, at the age of forty-two, had been short-lived, for only a few months later he had been recalled to lead a four-man team into Bosnia. One of his SAS colleagues, who also happened to be an old friend, had apparently set himself up as a virtual warlord in the small town where his Bosnian wife had grown up. Docherty and his team had been told to bring him out, but instead of doing so they had reappeared a week later, minus one of their number, with a lorryload of wounded children. Neither the Foreign Office nor the Ministry of Defence had been pleased, but Docherty had claimed all the responsibility for himself and then announced that he was resuming his retirement.

Even that hadn't been the end of his active career – later that same year he and his wife had been members of a tour party taken hostage by Islamic fundamentalists in Central Asia, and both had played a big part in securing their own and the other hostages' survival. Since then they had lived in Chile. She was a travel writer and he was supposed to be writing his memoirs.

Shepreth drained the last of the carton and leant back dangerously in the rickety chair. Whatever it was that Docherty had wanted to ask Toscono, he might also want to ask Bazua. And if he did, then the SAS man might provide another way in, another key to the lock. He wouldn't even need a cover story, because he already had one that was true.

He wanted to talk to Docherty. After reading the MI6 version of his life and career he would have wanted to meet him anyway. Now he just needed Ted Vaughan to find the man.

Only seconds later the phone rang. 'He's staying at the Hotel León on Brasil, under the name Kenneth Dalglish.'

Shepreth laughed. 'I'll go and talk to him,' he said.

7

Having set his travel alarm for six-thirty, Docherty had completed his ablutions and packed by seven. Downstairs the receptionists were changing shift, but neither young man gave him more than a cursory glance – if Toscono had traced his whereabouts they hadn't been told.

He left the hotel and started zigzagging his way southwest through the grid of streets towards a travel agency he had noticed the previous day, hoping it would be open by eight. It was, and he emerged a few minutes later with a booking on the evening flight to Buenos Aires via Lima. The bad news was that it didn't leave until seven, leaving him most of the day to kill.

Breakfast took care of the first half-hour, and a poster on the café wall offered what seemed an excellent suggestion for the time remaining. Docherty had visited the archaeological site of Teotihuacán in 1977, but only two days off the plane from England he had been in no state to appreciate it. It was only an hour away by bus, which would give plenty of time to make his plane. And it would also get him out of the city for the day, making it harder for Toscono to find him.

His mind made up, he walked briskly back to the hotel, where he collected his bag and paid his bill. The receptionist had a shifty look on his face, but there was no one else in the lobby, and no one hanging around too obviously in the street. He set off in the direction of the nearest Metro station.

Shepreth's taxi was just drawing up on the other side of the road when Docherty came through the hotel doorway, bag in hand. The MI6 man passed a five-thousand-peso note to the driver, thinking he would have no difficulty catching Docherty up, but the man took an age rummaging for change. As he glanced up to make sure Docherty was still in view a young Mexican emerged from the hotel and started walking in the same direction. Shepreth wasn't sure why, but he knew the youth was tailing the ex-SAS man.

He joined the procession, keeping about twenty metres behind the Mexican, whose bright-red T-shirt made him easy to follow down the busy pavement. He had read about tails being tailed in thrillers, but never actually witnessed such an arrangement in real life. It felt vaguely farcical somehow, and would be even more so if someone was following him. He glanced around despite himself, and almost tripped over a loose paving stone.

Both Docherty and the youth turned right into República de Chile, confirming Shepreth's suspicions. The Scot, some forty metres ahead, kept disappearing from view in the bustle, but the red T-shirt was an efficient beacon. He followed it down into the Allende Metro station and the three of them stood there on the platform, still some twenty metres apart, waiting for a westbound train. Docherty obviously wasn't heading for the airport.

The three of them changed trains at Hidalgo and again at La Raza, before alighting at the Northern Bus Terminal. Looking like he knew where he was going, Docherty first put his bag into the left luggage and then walked through to the second-class section of the bus station, where he bought a ticket at the Autobuses Teotihuacán booth. The man was going sightseeing, Shepreth thought. The thought of a few hours at the ruins was appealing enough in itself, but, given the circumstances, felt rather anticlimactic.

The bus was not due to leave for another ten minutes but Docherty had already boarded. Shepreth looked round for the tail – he was involved in an animated conversation on one of the public phones. The MI6 man wondered if he should tell his fellow-countryman that he was being followed and decided against it – he was more likely to learn what was going on by just watching.

The youth was now buying a ticket at the booth. Shepreth joined in the queue behind him and waited his turn. The bus was almost full when he got on, and as he walked towards the back he gave Docherty the traditional half smile of gringo solidarity.

The bus took them out through the rings of the capital's growth, through overcrowded boulevards, industrial wastelands, shanty-covered hills and countryside living on borrowed time. Docherty found it profoundly depressing – the capital seemed like an unstoppable cancer, slowly consuming the country which supported it.

The sight of the great pyramids looming in the distance banished the gloom from his mind. He could remember how on his first visit the sense of excitement had kept bubbling up through the layers of grief, making him feel almost guilty. Now, walking from the parking lot towards the sunken square of the Ciudadela and the small pyramid which covered the Temple of Quetzalcoatl, he felt the same sense of wonder swelling in his chest and wished Isabel was there with him to share it.

He paused at the entrance to the Ciudadela, looking north up the two-thousand-metre causeway which formed the central axis of the ancient city. Teotihuacán was not built high on a mountain, nor deep in some dramatic valley, but there were few more breathtaking sights than this Street of the Dead, arrowing away across the plain to its end beneath the graceful Pyramid of the Moon. To the right of this giant's causeway, more than a kilometre distant, early-bird tourists were crawling insect-like up the massive stairway of the larger Pyramid of the Sun.

Once this had been a city of 200,000 souls, Docherty reflected. It had risen and fallen in the same epoch as the Roman Empire. It had been a ruin when the Aztecs found it.

The Ciudadela seemed overrun by visitors, so he decided to bypass it and head straight up the stone causeway towards those areas of the site the crowds had not yet reached. He ambled slowly northwards, conscious of the sun's heat beating on his head, but exhilarated by the brilliance of the colours all around him. Now that he was out from under the lid of smog which hung over the capital everything seemed brighter, more clearly defined, as if the sharpness of his senses had been turned up a notch.

The Pyramid of the Sun slowly loomed in front of him. He reached the bottom of the steps and started to climb, grateful that he – unlike countless sacrificial victims in the past – would be coming back down. The last time he'd been here archaeologists had just stumbled over a cave deep inside the pyramid which a later Aztec ruler had used to store the flayed skins of his victims.

The climb left him feeling glad he was still in shape, for all around him people were wheezing, massaging thigh muscles, or both. He did a slow circle, taking in the ring of grey hills which surrounded the flat, yellow-green valley, the sparse puffs of white cloud in the wide blue sky, and took a deep breath of satisfaction.

There was a sudden movement behind him, but it was only a couple of children chasing each other along the edge of the platform. As their mother yelled at them – she'd obviously had a real fright – Docherty scolded himself for not being watchful enough.

He walked back down and continued up the causeway towards the Pyramid of the Moon. Not many people had yet percolated to this end of the site, and the high platform's only occupants were a couple of Mexican girls, both of whom seemed more interested in slagging off their boyfriends than enjoying the famous view down the causeway. Docherty supposed it would only be a few years before his daughter Marie started tormenting boys – she already had both the looks and the brains to be a real heartbreaker.

The two girls started down, leaving him alone with his thoughts. The chat he'd had with Toscono was still very much on his mind, and he had to admit he'd enjoyed scaring the bastard. That probably wasn't something to be proud of, but fuck it, the man was a mass murderer and a drug trafficker – he deserved a few clouds in his fucking sky. And as for his boss . . .

The fact that Bazua had escaped payment for his crimes in Argentina didn't sit well with Docherty. The fact that he was still breaking laws with impunity and adding to the sum total of human misery sat even worse. And it wasn't just that people like Bazua had tortured his wife and her friends, though that would have been enough in itself. Docherty had been hooked on the drug of justice from an early age – it was 'the right of the weakest', his father had always said – and at the age of forty-five he still felt the need for an occasional fix.

But not this time, he told himself, as he watched a hawk riding the air currents above the site. This time he was going home.

He looked at his watch – he still had a couple of hours before he needed to take a bus back. Beneath his perch, on the far-right corner of the Plaza de la Luna, sat the restored Palacio del Quetzalpapaloti, possibly the only ruin with a roof in central Mexico. If memory served Docherty well, it offered both shade and beautiful frescos.

He made his way down and ambled around the interior of the palace, marvelling at the decorations. A sign pointed down a flight of stone steps to the remains of an earlier, half-buried building, the Palacio de los Jaguares. He descended the rough stairway into the relative darkness, where a German couple were examining a mural depicting jaguars in feathered head-dresses making music with enormous conchs. After a few moments they left him alone, but his privacy was short-lived, for as he stared at the murals there were more footsteps on the stairway behind him. Four feet appeared, then stopped; a few brief words were exchanged and two of the feet continued on down into the half-buried chamber.

They belonged to a tall, handsome Latino wearing blue trousers and a cream shirt. He walked forward, as if he too wanted to examine the mural. There was a friendly smile on his face, but his right hand was concealed in his pocket. 'It's beautiful,' he said in Spanish, looking past Docherty at the wall.

'Isn't it?' the Scot murmured. He turned his head back in the direction of the mural, but every muscle in his body was suddenly taut with expectation. This man might be a simple armed robber, but he doubted it. Toscono's set-up was obviously better organized than he'd expected.

The fact that the man hadn't yet produced a weapon suggested he had a knife rather than a gun, so Docherty wasn't surprised when the hand emerged from the pocket and swung viciously towards him, a long blade glinting in the half-light. He stepped aside in one motion, his right hand clamping down on the plunging wrist as his left delivered a karate chop to the side of his assailant's neck. The timing wasn't perfect but the man stumbled on to one knee, giving Docherty the chance to kick him hard in the small of the back. There was a loud grunt, and as the knife span away across the stone floor, the man's partner suddenly appeared on the stairway.

He had apparently given up knives in favour of a silenced automatic. Docherty was still bracing himself for the bullet when the man was suddenly catapulted forward. His head hit the roof above the stairway with a crack that seemed to echo round the chamber, his body slumped to the ground like a sack of cement and his gun did a lazy double somersault in mid-air before dropping on to his crotch.

The first man was raising himself to his knees, apparently oblivious to either his own or his partner's fate. Docherty hit him across the back of the neck this time, hard enough to knock him out. He looked up to find his saviour clambering over the body at the bottom of the stairs. It was the tall young man with the distinctly English look from the bus. 'We'd better get out of here,' Docherty said, and the new arrival nodded.

Upstairs in the Palacio del Quetzalpapaloti they found several tourists wandering round the courtyard, and it would only be a matter of minutes before someone decided to take a look at the jaguars. The two men walked swiftly back outside and headed across the grass towards the northern parking lot some two hundred metres away.

'There's usually some taxis waiting for people who can't be bothered to walk back,' the MI6 man said. 'My name's David Shepreth,' he added.

'I don't suppose I need to introduce myself,' Docherty said drily.

'No,' Shepreth admitted.

'On Her Majesty's Secret Service by any chance?' Docherty asked.

'Something like that.'

They was indeed a line of waiting taxis. 'And how did you manage to appear so conveniently?' Docherty asked as they walked towards the front.

'I followed you from your hotel. Actually I followed your follower.' He stopped ten metres short of the taxi. 'I need to talk to you,' he said, 'but not in a taxi. Any ideas?'

Docherty looked at his watch. 'I need to be at the airport in three hours,' he said. 'And first I have to pick up my stuff at the bus terminal.'

'How about Guadalupe?' Shepreth suggested. 'We can take the taxi there and walk up the hill.'

'Why not,' Docherty agreed, pleasantly surprised. He hadn't often met anyone from Intelligence who'd taken the trouble to find out anything about the culture of the country he or she was working in.

The taxi driver was pleased with their destination too, even after his first outrageous estimate for the fare was pegged back to something less than a minor fortune. As his two passengers settled back into their seats for the forty-five-minute journey he started off down the road which paralleled the ancient causeway.

Now that the immediate crisis was over, Docherty found himself feeling angry with Shepreth for leaving his intervention so late. But after a few minutes of staring out at the passing fields he reluctantly admitted to himself that the anger should be self-directed. He had put himself at risk, and for no other reason than overconfidence. His kids might not have any divine right to a living father, but they should be able to expect something better than this sort of carelessness.

Shepreth, on the other hand, was feeling pleased with himself. He had taken a chance following the youth rather than his fellow-Brit, but it had paid off. The youth had led him to the two *sicarios* and they had led him back to Docherty, who should now be feeling more than a little in his debt.

The taxi picked up speed once it reached the main highway, and soon they were passing through the landscape of denuded hills, rubbish mountains and rusting hulks which character-ized the capital's outskirts. The highway arced round the foot of the Virgin's hill and the giant Basilica came into view. The taxi dropped them outside, but the two men had no interest in entering the already crowded church. Instead they threaded their way through the traffic and started climbing in the footsteps of Juan Diego, the Christianized Indian who had started the whole ball rolling in 1531.

He had been happily crossing these slopes when the Virgin appeared to him with a message for the local bishop – a church was needed on this particular hill. Not surprisingly, the bishop proved sceptical, but a few days later the Virgin popped up again in front of Diego, ordering him to gather roses from the crown of the hill. He found the flowers, wrapped them in his cape and took them to the bishop, only to find that the image of the Virgin had become imprinted on the cloth. More than four and a half centuries later the cape still hung in the church below, attracting thousands of pilgrims every day.

Docherty and Shepreth had just reached the first of the small chapels built to commemorate the Virgin's visitations when the Scot broke the silence. 'So what do you want to talk about?' he asked.

Shepreth glanced around. There were pilgrims and tourists both above and below them, but they were about as alone as any two men could hope to be in the world's most populous city. 'We're both interested in Bazua, though presumably for different reasons,' he said.

'Drugs,' Docherty murmured. 'I don't know anything about the bastard's current activities. It's his past I'm interested in.' He hesitated for a moment, but could think of no reason for keeping the truth from Shepreth. 'Friends of friends in Argentina are still trying to find out what happened to their son in the Dirty War,' he explained. 'Bazua was in charge of the local Nazis, and Toscono was in charge of one of the arrest squads.'

'And he refused to talk to you.'

'The first time he did. I saw him again yesterday.'

'Ah,' Shepreth said. He'd been wondering why Toscono had sent his goons after someone whom he'd already ejected from his office. 'And what did he tell you?' he asked.

'He admitted he arrested my friend's son, but denied all knowledge of what happened to him after that. He told me that Bazua could fill in the details. The bastard apparently has a complete set of the Army's records for the period in question, with thousands of names and fates, and probably even a complete list of who got what in the torture chambers.' He smiled grimly. 'There was a lot of German and Italian immigration into Argentina, and someone once said the military inherited the German flair for keeping meticulous records and the Italian flair for battle. For a hundred years every cock-up has been brilliantly documented.'

116

They walked a few paces in silence.

'So you're on your way home?' Shepreth asked at last.

'Aye,' Docherty said. 'I have a feeling it wouldn't be so easy to arrange a private tête-à-tête with Bazua,' he added wryly.

'A pity,' Shepreth said noncommittally.

'Tell me about the drug angle,' Docherty said.

Shepreth waited until they were past the small crowd which had gathered around another of the chapels, then gave the Scot a brief outline of Bazua's trafficking business on both sides of the Atlantic and the Americans' flat refusal to sanction direct action against him. 'And it's not just the trafficking,' he concluded. 'The bastard's ploughing at least some of his profits into outfitting another invasion of the Falklands.'

'What?' Docherty asked disbelievingly.

'He already has a couple of boats, and his friends in Argentina are enrolling volunteers. The idea's just to establish a presence on the island, dare the British to chuck them off and dare the Argentinian government to abandon them.'

'I thought we still had a fucking great garrison on the island,' Docherty observed.

'It's not as big as people think, and it won't be there indefinitely. Bazua's probably willing to wait a few years.'

'Christ,' Docherty said disgustedly. It wasn't so much the Falkland Islanders he was worried about – though they deserved to be left alone – as the long-suffering people of Argentina. The thought of psychopaths like Bazua riding to power on the backs of a successful invasion brought a taste of bile to his mouth.

And then he remembered a conversation he'd had several years ago with Isabel and a couple of her fellow-exiles. 'The CIA had people in Argentina during the Dirty War,' he said slowly.

117

Shepreth didn't make the connection.

'Suppose Bazua's records contain evidence of American corruption,' Docherty said.

'It's twenty years ago,' Shepreth said instinctively, but his face was thoughtful.

'Which would give whoever it was plenty of time to climb the career ladder. They might well be in a position to block action against Bazua.'

Shepreth nodded. 'And they probably wouldn't even have to come up with a reason. Just a hint that Bazua was on the company payroll would be enough.'

They had reached the top of the hill, where the Capilla de las Rosas marked the spot where the miraculous flowers had sprung up. Docherty looked out at the vast city beyond – away to the south-west a plane was gathering height after take-off from the airport. He looked at his watch and turned to Shepreth. 'Time to go,' he told the younger man.

Shepreth didn't seem to hear him. 'What if I could get you in to see Bazua?' he asked.

Carmen stared out of the aeroplane's window at the egg-shaped island below. The sea was a patchwork of blues and greens, with the outline of the surrounding reef clearly visible. Most of the coastline seemed to be rocky, but there were a few sand beaches, and behind these the settlements had grown up. A road circled the island, linking these and leaving the mountainous centre to the flora and fauna. According to her guidebook, Providencia was famous for the variety of its lizards.

She had left Cartagena at ten o'clock that morning, and a good proportion of the intervening five hours had been spent waiting for her connection on the neighbouring island of San Andrés. Most of the other passengers seemed to be foreigners, and once the plane was down she expected a stampede for the tourist office, but in the event only one Japanese couple also needed official help. Listening to the choice of accommodation on offer, Carmen found herself wondering for the umpteenth time what she was doing.

The Cabanas El Paradiso – 'they are pretty wooden cabins by the sea' – sounded nice, especially for only ten thousand pesos, until she started thinking about how vulnerable she would feel alone in a cabin. The Hotel Princesa sounded nice too, and was even cheaper, but she wondered how good the locks would be on the doors of a cheap hotel. In the end she settled for the thrice-as-expensive Dutch Inn, on the dubious grounds that no one ever suspected rich people of criminal intent. Her choice was only about three kilometres to the south, in the hamlet of Aguamansa, and it seemed as if the taxi had hardly had time to get up speed before it was slowing to a halt outside the gabled wooden building.

The receptionist checked her in and showed her up to a large and lovely room, full of old wooden furniture and with windows overlooking the sea. He seemed to give her a strange look as he left her, causing her to wonder how many single young women came to the island. On the plane it had been all couples and groups as far as she could tell.

Well, she wouldn't be spending much time in the discos, always assuming there were any. She looked out of the window at the line of coconut palms waving in the breeze and realized that it was late in the afternoon. There was no point in wasting the last hour or so of light.

She changed into shorts, halter top and sandals, and went back downstairs. As she'd hoped, the hotel had bicycles for the use of its guests, and after checking the tyres and brakes on several machines she picked one out. A minute later she was setting off, somewhat unsteadily, along the coast road towards the next settlement. By the time she reached it her childhood cycling skills had kicked back in, and she was beginning to enjoy the ride.

The road turned inland now, cutting off the south-western corner of the island. It didn't look a likely spot for a prison, but there was no real way of knowing, short of exploring the area on foot. She would do that tomorrow, she told herself, cycling on. There was no shortage of buildings, many of them brightly painted smaller versions of her hotel, more Anglo-Caribbean than Hispanic, but none of them looked in any way official. Behind the ones to the right forested slopes rose up towards the distant peak in the centre, but there were no roads winding up through the trees.

The sea came back into view and she free-wheeled down the slope to where the road took a tight turn along the rim of some cliffs before running into the small but busy settlement of Aguadulce. Here there were many cheap-looking hotels and restaurants, shops advertising motorbikes and snorkelling gear for hire, and a busy dock at one end of the sandy beach. This might have been a better place to stay, she thought. Or not. Was it easier to escape notice in hordes of people or far away from them? There didn't seem to be an obvious answer.

It was getting dark now, but she cycled another kilometre or so beyond the last houses before turning back. By her reckoning she had traversed more than half the circular road since leaving the airport, but had seen nothing which looked anything like a prison. In fact the whole idea was beginning to seem unreal, and as she cycled back towards Aguadulce, intent on dinner, Carmen found herself wondering how many egg-shaped islands there could be in the Caribbean. Had she just jumped to the wrong conclusion? Or had Victoria's mind short-circuited in some strange way? Maybe the girl had spent a childhood holiday here, and memories from that time had become confused with those of the last year.

It was too soon to tell, Carmen told herself sternly. She still had the other half of the road to travel, and there was still the forested centre. There might not be any access by road, but prisons could always be supplied by helicopter, so she would have to keep an eye on the skies. This might be what her American tourists called a wild-goose chase, but if it wasn't, then she was closer to her sister than she had been for over a year.

The Prime Minister looked even more harassed than usual, as well he might. The nation was bored with him, the anti-European crusade in the name of British beef had proved a predictably damp squib, and his own back-benchers were queuing up to stab him in the back. Even England's football team had let him down, evoking memories of 1970 and Harold Wilson's kamikaze election. 'But what exactly are you advocating?' he asked Hanson.

It was late on Sunday evening, and the two men were sitting in shirtsleeves in the PM's private office, discussing the problem of Angel Bazua. Hanson had just finished his summary of the Argentinian's criminal and political activities with a recommendation for action of some sort. 'It's hard to be specific,' he said evasively, 'but I would have thought that at the very least we should aim for the destruction of the two boats. If we could also take out their owner I would be a lot happier.'

The PM grimaced. 'The British government doesn't usually employ assassination as an instrument of foreign policy,' he said mildly.

'Not lately,' Hanson agreed. 'But this is an unusual situation. It sounds ludicrous, but as long as he stays in prison this man is effectively beyond the law. And in the meantime,' he added, looking the PM straight in the eye, 'he poses a clear threat to the security of the realm.'

The PM sighed and examined the bottom of his empty glass. 'Who would you use?' he asked.

'The SAS, probably,' Hanson said, wondering whether he was going to be offered another drink.

But the PM had other things on his mind. 'The Colombians will probably break off relations,' he said gloomily, 'and I'll have the Foreign Office and Trade screaming blue murder at me for halving our market share in Latin America. And as for the Americans . . .' He trailed off. 'I don't think . . .'

'They'll all be angry,' Hanson agreed, 'but not necessarily at us.' He bit the bullet and helped himself from the bottle, then started to tell the PM about Docherty's involvement. 'He has a completely different reason for wanting to see Bazua, but if he does get inside the prison, he should be able to bring some useful information out. He has trained eyes, he's an SAS veteran, and whatever he sees should prove invaluable to an assault force. With good inside information the SAS might be able to do the whole thing incognito. They could even leave a few clues to the real culprits – another drug cartel probably.' Hanson paused, gathering his thoughts. 'If by some chance they are identified, then Docherty would also serve as a pretty good scapegoat. He lives in Chile, he married an ex-communist, and his SAS record offers ample proof that he's a born renegade. With that sort of ammunition we might be able to pass the whole thing off as a private affair, a mercenary operation paid for by nobody-knows-who.'

'We'll hang him out to dry,' the PM murmured.

'The man's a survivor,' Hanson said. He had read Docherty's file that morning, and felt more than a touch of guilt at what he was proposing, but a lot more lives would be ruined if Bazua wasn't stopped. 'He wants to get in to see Bazua, and his chances of coming out again are a lot better if the Colombian government has sanctioned the visit.'

'All right,' the PM said thoughtfully, 'we might fool the Colombians, but surely the Americans have the southern Caribbean under more or less continual surveillance. How are an SAS team going to get in and out without them knowing?'

'They aren't,' Hanson admitted. 'But if we bring them a present they won't be able to go off the deep end.' He explained about the Dirty War records which Bazua allegedly kept on Providencia, and Shepreth's suspicion that they were being used to blackmail high-ranking American Intelligence officials. 'If we can show them how one of their own people has been protecting Bazua then they'll hardly be in a position to complain,' he concluded.

It was a bit thin, but the PM didn't seem to notice. 'So all you want for now is an official request that this man Docherty be allowed access to their prisoner?'

'That's right.'

The PM sighed again. He had the distinct feeling he hadn't heard the last of this business. 'Very well,' he said with a thin smile.

Docherty ordered another glass of mescal and looked out across Oaxaca's sun-dappled main square. He had been in the south Mexican city for two days now, having taken the overnight train from the capital late in the day of his eventful trip to Teotihuacán. He had been sufficiently intrigued by Shepreth's plan to delay his return home, but it had not seemed a good idea to stay on in Mexico City, where Toscono's goons and probably half the police force would be looking for him.

Oaxaca had been his favourite Mexican town in 1977, and it hadn't changed as much as he'd feared. The town itself was a joy to walk round, the wonderful ruins of Monte Alban were only a hill climb away, and the main square, with its luscious foliage, beautiful cathedral and outdoor restaurants was the perfect place to sit and think. It was at one of these tables, nineteen years before, that Docherty had felt some balance shift inside his soul, as the dominance of his grief felt the first guilt-ridden challenges of a new joy in life.

Ah, Chrissie, he thought now. How different his life would have been if one stupid bastard had known how to drive. He would never have come to Mexico, never acquired the fluency in Spanish which marked him out for the Argentina mission, never met Isabel or adopted this continent so far from his beloved Scotland. It was sobering to think that a split-second decision by a complete stranger could turn your life upside down.

He had phoned Isabel to tell her his change of plan before boarding the train. She had taken the news calmly enough, but he could tell she was worried for him. If Docherty hadn't known that deep in the recesses of his wife's soul there lurked an unassuaged thirst for revenge against Bazua and his cronies, he would have felt a lot guiltier about putting her through the anxiety. As it was, maybe this whole business would complete the process of exorcizing her twenty-year-old demons. Or maybe he was kidding himself and Shepreth's offer had just piqued his curiosity.

He rather liked the young MI6 agent. Shepreth was obviously bright, and unlike most of his colleagues – or at least the ones Docherty had come into contact with – he hadn't immersed himself in self-serving cynicism.

The Scot looked at his watch – punctuality clearly wasn't one of Shepreth's strong suits – then signalled the waiter for a refill, thinking that he should have bought the whole bottle, worm and all. At the table next to his a bunch of English travellers, most of them in their thirties, were telling tales of the six-hour bus ride down to the coast, and he listened in, remembering his own descent of the hair-raising mountain roads in 1977.

The waiter arrived at the same time as Shepreth, who looked like the proverbial cat who'd got the cream. Another glass was requested, and they moved to a more secluded table.

'The government is asking the Colombians to let you in for a chat with Angel,' Shepreth told him.

'Good,' Docherty said. 'And what does it want in return?'

'Your eyes. If you can help us build up a picture of the inside, we'll be better able to judge the feasibility of an assault from outside by your old regiment.'

Docherty's eyes widened slightly. 'That's really on the cards?'

'Looks like it.'

'Any time-scale in mind?'

'The request for the visit was delivered today.' He shrugged. 'The Colombians may sit on it, of course.'

Docherty thought for a moment. 'I think I'd like a good look from the outside before I go in,' he said. 'Do we know where this prison is?'

Shepreth pulled a napkin towards him and drew a rough map of the island. 'It's here,' he said, indicating the location with a cross. 'When I get back to Mexico City I'm going to ask Ted Vaughan if he can sneak out some satellite photos. Don't worry,' he added, seeing the look on Docherty's face, 'I shall tell him to borrow a lot more than the Providencia shots.'

'They would be useful,' Docherty admitted, thinking more of a future SAS operation than his own reconnaissance. He couldn't quite shake the suspicion that there was more to all this than met the eye, although for the moment he couldn't see what it could be. But at least there was no doubting that the joint sponsorship of the British and Colombian governments would make his visit to Bazua's home from home a lot safer than it otherwise might have been.

And safety, he reminded himself, was what family men were supposed to place first on their list of priorities.

8

Carmen woke to her third day on the island feeling decidedly flat. She had ridden round Providencia twice on the previous day, once in each direction, and had seen nothing that might be a prison. She had wandered, with no little trepidation, down each of the two tracks that led into the south-western corner of the island, but found nothing. She had walked up the long path to the three-hundred-metre peak at the island's heart and seen only trees and colourful birds. And as the days had gone by those twin emotions of fear and hope, which had been her constant companions since setting foot on the island, had slowly dissipated.

Sitting outside the Dutch Inn with her breakfast coffee she asked herself how long she should keep looking. Another couple of days at least, but there would soon come a time when one more circuit of the island, staring at the same houses and beaches, would seem utterly pointless. But what else could she do?

Think, she told herself.

Maybe some sort of bluff . . . She had seen the military post outside Aguadulce, and for a few seconds had even thought it could have served as a prison, but it was obviously too small for the sort of set-up Victoria had described. The soldiers, though, would obviously know if there was a prison on the island, and if there was, where it was. If she came up with some story about a friend who had been arrested . . .

It wouldn't help. No one was going to say, oh yes, the prison's down the road – just knock on the gate and they'll let you in.

It suddenly occurred to Carmen that there was no reason why this prison would look like a normal prison. Victoria had always talked about 'him', as if he was the only one that mattered – maybe this was just a house which had been commandeered to hold one man.

But if it was just a house, how could she hope to find it? It would have to be well guarded, of course, probably with a wall or electric fence, but she had seen a dozen sprawling villas which answered to that description.

There had to be more, and a few moments later she realized what. In Miami Detective Peña had been quite certain that this man Bazua was still running his trafficking operations from the prison, and surely that meant he would need sophisticated communications equipment – a tall radio aerial, for example. She remembered seeing one of those, but where had it been?

It took her only a few seconds to remember. The house – a rather lovely one in Spanish colonial style – was on the seaward side of the road about a kilometre north of San Felipe on the island's west coast. In her mind's eye she could see the aerial rising up behind the house.

She gulped down the rest of her coffee, collected her camera and her father's binoculars from her room, and set off once more on the hotel's bike. Less than half an hour later she was passing the gates of the house, taking in the palm-lined drive, the house itself, surrounded by woodland, the silver sheen of the high aerial. There was no guardhouse by the gates, nor any sign of human presence – only a high stucco wall topped with three lines of barbed wire.

About twenty metres beyond the gate – out of sight, she prayed, of any surveillance cameras – she stopped, dismounted and made a pantomime of inspecting her back tyre. She took the hand-pump and started inflating the tyre, making sure to keep her face turned in that direction as her eyes behind the dark glasses examined the hill on the opposite side of the road. It was heavily forested and quite steep, and with any luck she would be able to find a vantage-point which overlooked the house behind her.

Apparently satisfied with her efforts, she climbed back on the bike and resumed her journey. About half a kilometre further on a stream passed under the road in a culvert, and beside it a rough path led up into the trees. That was her way in, she decided. On her way back to the hotel for more jungle-friendly clothes she felt the old knot of hope and fear rising once more in her throat.

Guadencio Santis López was playing eight-ball with one of his bodyguards when Miguel Domínguez tracked him down. As the President of Colombia was currently engaged in lining up a shot his Foreign Minister waited in silence, casting his eye around the newly converted pool room. The last president had used this room of the palace as a TV room and private cinema, watching endless soap operas on an enormous screen far into each night. It had been rumoured that the price of one drug baron's pardon had been the whole of *Dynasty* on video, and that the president himself had given up on his re-election campaign after watching the episode in which Fallon was abducted by aliens.

Pool had to be an improvement, Domínguez thought to himself.

'What is it, Miguel?' the President asked. He had apparently missed his shot.

'I've just had a visit from the British Ambassador,' Domínguez began.

Santis López looked at him in disbelief, as if such an event could justify interrupting his game. 'What did he want?' he asked, his eyes on the table.

'He wanted a personal favour. One of their soldiers – one of their heroes, I gather – is married to an Argentinian woman and he's trying to trace what happened to one of her relations during the Junta years. He wants to talk to Angel Bazua, and the British are asking us to arrange it for him.'

'Bazua's in prison on Providencia, right?'

'If you can call it that. I wish my home was half as comfortable.'

Santis López made a face as the bodyguard sank another ball. 'That was part of the deal.' He glanced across at Domínguez. 'Why are you bothering me with this?' he asked.

Domínguez chose to take the question literally. 'Because it doesn't feel quite right,' he replied. 'The British Ambassador even told me he thought the Americans had been stupid to accuse us of not cooperating with their anti-drug campaign.'

'They were.'

'I know, but . . .'

The bodyguard missed. 'Is there any reason why Bazua should object to seeing this man?' Santis López asked, measuring his next shot.

'My sources say he'll probably consider it entertainment,' Domínguez replied.

'Then give the British what they want,' the President said with a shrug. 'What can we lose?'

Docherty's plane from Oaxaca arrived in Mexico City soon after ten in the morning, and he spent most of the three-hour wait between connections reading an historical novel he'd picked up in a secondhand bookshop. Set in twelfth-century England and featuring monks, sociopathic nobles and obsessive cathedral-builders, it was thoroughly enjoyable.

As there was no direct flight to San Andrés from Mexico, he'd have another, albeit shorter, stopover at the airport outside the Costa Rican capital of San Juan. He'd never been there himself, but unfortunately he remembered Isabel's account of landing there. Apparently, the approach to the airport in question was down a deep valley where the crosswinds were fierce enough to turn even a large airliner into a flying see-saw.

It wasn't a very exciting prospect, and as the plane began to board he almost found himself hoping that Shepreth had finally graduated from mere unpunctuality to complete non-appearance.

The MI6 man arrived a few moments later, brandishing a large envelope. 'Copies of the photos,' he told Docherty. 'You should probably destroy them before you get to San Andrés.'

'I'll eat them on the plane,' Docherty said with a straight face.

Shepreth didn't seem to hear him. 'The Colombians have agreed to your visit,' he said. 'You're to present yourself to the military post on the island – it's just outside Aguadulce – at ten a.m. on Friday morning.' He looked at the Scot. 'I think that's it.'

'When are you coming over?' Docherty asked him.

'Tomorrow. Providencia's a small place and I didn't think it would be such a good idea for us both to arrive on the same day. I'll meet you on or near the dock at eight tomorrow evening, OK?'

'Aye,' Docherty said. He was pleased the Colombians had agreed to the visit and given him the chance to see a devil in the flesh.

Carmen reached back to scratch her right calf, wondering what had bitten her this time. As far as she knew, there were no poisonous reptiles on the island, but there were certainly plenty of biting insects. She had now spent most of two days lying face down on the ground, peering over a rotting fallen tree at the compound below.

She had no cast-iron evidence to show for it, but she was certain that this was the prison in which Victoria had been held captive. For one thing, the house had twice received visits from the military – on the first occasion it had been a lone officer in a jeep, on the second two other officers in a car. For another, there was the layout, which was more than twice as extensive as it appeared from the road. Behind the two-storey main house, facing each other across an open space, there were two barrack-shaped single-storey buildings, each about thirty metres long. In the space between them there seemed to be a swimming pool. Carmen couldn't actually see it, but the shimmering reflections on one of the gutters certainly suggested the presence of water.

In front of the house there was a short, palm-lined drive, which ended in a turning circle beside a double garage. The high stucco wall which fronted the road did not extend around the entire circumference – from the corner of the property which Carmen could see a high wire fence ran off through the trees in the direction of the sea. Unusually for a prison, the overhanging coils of razor wire had been arranged to keep people out rather than in.

Beyond the buildings and the probable swimming pool she thought she could see the beginning of a path, which would presumably lead down through the trees to the nearby shore.

But nobody had used it since she started watching, and nobody had conveniently appeared in a window. The previous afternoon, soon after the arrival of the two officers, she had heard shouts and what sounded like a bouncing ball, and for a few seconds a figure had come into view close to the beginning of the distant path. He had probably been collecting a stray basketball, but she hadn't actually seen a ball.

A couple of hours later, with darkness beginning to fall, she had had a fleeting glimpse of someone's head above the roofline, and though she couldn't put her finger on exactly why, she had been convinced that it was a woman. But there had been no time to take a picture – she would have needed a continually rolling camcorder to catch either of the human sightings.

A higher position might provide a view of the space between the buildings, but above her the slope of the hill flattened out for quite a way before resuming its climb. She had tried shinning up a couple of the trees, but in both cases it had proved a difficult, noisy and overly visible activity, and had offered nothing more than a better view of the surrounding foliage.

She needed better binoculars, she decided, or maybe just some old-fashioned luck. As another member of the insect kingdom drilled her ankle for blood she told herself not to get discouraged. If she stuck at it long enough she was bound to see something.

* * *

Docherty walked past the entrance to Bazua's place of detention, noting the electronically operated gates and the lens of the surveillance camera peeping out through the palm fronds. A few minutes later he reached the spot from which the path led up through the trees and, after a few moments' hesitation, started up it. He had decided that morning that there was really no need for the recce he had mentioned to Shepreth, but the path was there for the taking, so why not satisfy his own curiosity?

The going was easy enough for the first hundred metres or so, but then the path abruptly petered out, as if it had realized there was nowhere to go. This didn't surprise Docherty, but the discovery a few minutes later of a reasonably new bicycle did. The cyclist had dragged his machine a good thirty metres through the undergrowth before leaving it under some trailing fronds, which suggested an unusually determined attempt at concealment.

There was a metal tag attached to the handlebars claiming ownership on behalf of the Dutch Inn, Providencia.

Docherty squatted down, then rubbed some of the damp soil between his hands and applied a few streaks to his face. It wasn't an SAS make-up kit, but it would have to do.

The trail of the cyclist wasn't hard to follow through the heavy undergrowth. The footprints themselves suggested a small man, and the direction in which they headed implied an interest similar to Docherty's own. He moved forward as silently as the terrain allowed, remembering his days at the SAS Jungle Training School in Brunei almost a quarter of a century ago. 'I can hear you, Docherty!' the instructor had screamed, 'you sound like fucking Pan's People!'

What happened to them? Docherty wondered. He supposed most of them were grandmothers by now, which was a depressing thought.

He could catch glimpses of the road now, way below and to his right. And then he saw her.

She was about forty metres further down the shallow slope, just behind what looked like the rim of a ridge. Docherty steadied himself and trained the collapsible telescope on her. She was lying on her front, studying the view ahead with her own binoculars over a fallen tree. He couldn't see her face, but she had shiny black hair beyond shoulder length, a trim waist, nicely rounded behind and long legs. She was wearing a black, long-sleeved shirt, blue jeans and black boots. There was a camera on the ground beside her, but it didn't seem to be fitted with a telephoto lens.

'What the hell?' he murmured to himself. Why would a young woman be watching Bazua's prison?

He took his eyes away from the woman before her sixth sense had time to register his presence, and wondered what to do. She seemed to have the best spot, but he could hardly amble up and ask her to give him a turn. And there was no real need for him to examine the compound below – not yet at any rate. He obviously needed to talk to her, but this was neither the time nor the place, as she might well panic if he suddenly appeared out of nowhere, and for all he knew she was cradling a gun to her breast. He might not hear the shot but someone down the compound would.

He looked at her again. She was scratching her leg, and Docherty wondered if she knew how much insects loved rotting tree-trunks. In fact she seemed generally fidgety – like most people she was probably not used to holding her body in one position for any length of time.

It would also soon be getting dark, and he could see no sign of any night-vision equipment. She would probably be leaving soon.

He made his way back through the forest, descended the path and started walking south along the road. As he passed the gates of the prison compound he wondered whether she was watching him through her binoculars and hoped that she'd had the sense to use some sort of veil across the glass to eliminate tell-tale reflections.

In San Felipe he asked a friendly local about the Dutch Inn and discovered that it was an expensive hotel on the island's southern shore. Assuming that she'd choose the shortest route back, he walked on to Aguadulce, where an open-air bar offered both a drink and an ideal observation point.

She cycled through about forty-five minutes later, shocking him with a first sight of her face. In profile she looked stunningly like a young Isabel. It wasn't just the features, though the arrangement of the cheek-bones, the generous lips and dark eyes were all reminiscent of his wife – it was the intense look on her face, the seriousness of purpose, which reminded him of his first hours with Isabel, caught up in the throes of war at the other end of the continent.

He watched her cycle past the hotels and shops until she and the bicycle were just a spot in the distance. It was almost six o'clock, which gave him a couple of hours before his meeting with Shepreth.

The shop which rented out motorbikes was only a stone's throw away, and still open for business. A few minutes later he was cruising along the seaside road on a 250cc Yamaha, not quite Steve McQueen in *The Great Escape*, but close enough.

The Dutch Inn was a beautiful old building, standing between the road and a palm-lined beach. He hadn't yet worked out how he was going to ask for a woman whose name he didn't know without getting shown the door, but in the end there was no need, for as he propped up the Yamaha in the rear parking lot she emerged from a back entrance with a tall drink in hand and walked across to one of the empty tables which overlooked the beach. She had changed into shorts and a red halter top.

He walked inside, discovered to his amazement that the bar served draught Guinness, and carried a pint out to her table.

'May I join you?' he asked in Spanish.

She gave him the surprised look of someone deep in thought, and before she could say no Docherty sat down. Up close the resemblance was still striking, though perhaps not in a purely physical way. Now it was the sorrow-filled eyes which reminded him of Isabel, gazing out through the grimly held mask of determination. This woman had seen tragedy, and logic suggested that Angel Bazua had been the man responsible.

'I saw you watching Bazua's house,' he said softly.

She stiffened, not knowing what to do. Should she get up and walk away? Or run?

'I think we are on the same side,' he added, and allowed himself a smile.

She felt instinctively that he was telling the truth, but what did her instincts know? 'Who are you?' she asked. It was the first question that came into her head.

'My name's Jamie Docherty,' he said without hesitation. 'I'm British, but I'm married to an Argentinian, and we live in Chile. Do you know about the Dirty War in Argentina?'

'Yes, of course.' Was he going to give her a history lesson?

'My wife was one of the victims. One of the luckier ones – she was tortured, but instead of killing her they sent her into exile. She still has friends from those days, and one old man who's dying has become obsessed with the need to find out what happened to his son. He hired me to talk to the arresting officer, who now lives in Mexico City. I did that,

137

and he claimed that only his boss would know the details of what happened to a particular prisoner. His boss is Colonel Bazua. I'm going in to talk to him tomorrow morning.'

Carmen was getting over the shock, but was still having trouble grasping hold of what had been said. He had confirmed that it was Bazua's house – that was the first thing. And he had said he was on the same side, which might mean nothing but could mean everything – ever since her first talk with Victoria she had felt the weight of having to do it all alone. And he was going into the prison tomorrow. There had to be some way he could find out about Marysa.

Docherty waited and watched, knowing that it had been a shock to her, hoping that she would trust him. When she did speak it was his turn to be shocked.

'I think my sister is a prisoner in that house,' she said slowly. 'And two other women. They all disappeared more than a year ago, five of them, and until three weeks ago everyone thought they were dead.' She told him about the newspaper on the bus and her trip to Miami, the talks with Victoria and what she'd learned of Bazua's drug operation from Detective Peña, the realization that she could not risk asking for help from the Colombian authorities.

Docherty listened in silence, his sense of rage stirring deep within.

'Maybe when you are in the house,' she said, 'you will see my sister or one of the others – I have photographs in my room – and then I will have proof to take to someone.' She looked at him imploringly.

'If they are there,' Docherty said gently, 'I doubt if I will be allowed to see them. If the British government hadn't asked the Colombians to allow my visit I doubt whether I'd have got my nose in the door, and I don't think they'll be giving me a guided tour of the establishment. Of course I'll keep my eyes open,' he added, seeing her look of despair. 'I can even ask the bastard what he does for female company. But . . .' He hesitated for a moment, as the implications of her story sunk in. The presence of innocent women inside the compound would be a complicating factor if it came to direct action. And the woman she'd brought back from Miami would have precious knowledge of the layout.

Of course he couldn't tell the woman any of this – such a clear breach of security would give Shepreth and his people kittens.

But if tomorrow came and went and he had nothing to tell her, then what would she do? She didn't seem the type to just give up, but she was an amateur, so she'd either get caught watching the house and end up sharing Bazua's bed with her sister, or she'd manage to kick up an enormous stink and focus every mother's son's attention on Bazua's home from home. Even if the suits in Whitehall weren't scared off, the bastards in the prison would be on maximum alert.

No, he decided, they'd be better off bringing her on board.

His watch said twenty to eight. 'I'd like you to meet someone,' he told her, draining the last of the Guinness.

'Who?' she asked, suspicious again.

'His name's David Shepreth, which reminds me – I still don't know yours.'

'I am Carmen Salcedo,' she said.

'Pleased to meet you. Shepreth works for the British government, and they don't like Bazua because he's flooding London with heroin and spending his profits on outfitting a fleet to retake the Malvinas . . .'

She couldn't help the smile which crossed her face. 'I'm sorry,' she said.

'It is kind of ironic,' Docherty admitted. 'But a friend in need . . . If London's willing to shake the tree we may get the chance to catch our apples.'

She understood what he meant immediately. 'The enemy of my enemy is my friend,' she murmured.

'Unless he's a Rangers supporter,' Docherty added. 'Ah, never mind . . . My friend's waiting for me in Aguadulce, and that splendid machine over there is waiting to transport us.'

She looked at it doubtfully, but didn't really need persuading. The feel of her strong young body pressing into his back was somewhat disconcerting to Docherty, yet reminding himself that he was old enough to be her father didn't seem to make much difference. His mother had always said that men never really got past their teens – it was just that their bodies led women to believe they had.

The look on Shepreth's face as they walked towards his perch on the dock probably had nothing to do with her age. 'Just tell him what you told me,' Docherty said to her, and she did, walking along the dark beach between the two men. The stars were bright above, the ocean stretched away to the distant horizon and Aguadulce's single thoroughfare was alive with light, noise and the smell of cooking food. Every now and then they would hear the whisper of couples elsewhere on the beach, and on one occasion the less ambivalent sound of lovemaking.

As Carmen told her story, Docherty occasionally glanced across at Shepreth and was gratified to see what looked like genuine sympathy in the younger man's eyes. Not that the shorts and halter top didn't help.

There was also a hint of uncertainty in the MI6 man's expression, and Docherty guessed that Shepreth was having trouble deciding how much he should now tell the woman.

On impulse the Scot decided to force the other man's hand. 'If the government OK's direct action,' he said bluntly, 'then I think Carmen should talk to her friend Victoria again.'

'Direct action?' she asked, looking from one man to the other.

'It's a real possibility,' Shepreth admitted, giving Docherty a glance that was half reproach and half gratitude. 'But first our friend here has to beard the lion in his den.'

The following morning Docherty slowly walked the two hundred metres which separated his hotel from the island's military post, still wondering how he was going to present himself to Bazua. He was not expecting the Argentinian to offer him any details of Guillermo Macías's fate, and he doubted if he'd get far beyond the front door of the prison, but with any luck this would not be the end of the business, and there was always something to learn from any confrontation.

Anger seemed a likely tool. The official nature of the visit surely offered Docherty some protection, and if he could provoke Bazua into losing his temper the consequences might be more illuminating than dangerous. It was a theory, at any rate.

He reached the military post, which amounted to no more than a couple of one-storey pre-fabricated buildings in a walled compound situated between the road and the sea, and was shown into the OC's office. Captain Sonoma was outwardly polite, but there was also an air of genuine curiosity in the man's eyes, as if he already knew more about his guest than he was supposed to. He fitted the description of one of the officers whom Carmen had seen visiting the prison, and had probably learnt about the business with Toscono from Bazua himself.

Outside an empty jeep was now waiting, and as he climbed in Docherty took one last look round. Judging from what he'd seen so far, he put the post's strength at no more than twenty men. There was one UH-1H Iroquois helicopter standing on the pad, apparently ready for use, and another standing off to the side, minus its engine and tail rotor. Beyond them he could see a sleek-looking patrol boat tied up at the jetty.

Sonoma himself drove the jeep, greeting many of the locals with a smile or a gesture and keeping to a reasonable speed on the mostly empty road. He opened and closed the electronic gates with a remote control and finally came to a halt right outside the front door, where two young soldiers who hadn't been there the previous day were standing guard. At least they were trying to make it look a little more like a prison, Docherty thought.

He followed Sonoma in through the wide wooden doors and gained a glimpse of a courtyard beyond as he was ushered in through another doorway to the right. If he hadn't already known of the other buildings and recreation area from the American satellite photographs, he would have remained in ignorance of their existence.

The room he entered had the feel of a stage set. The wall coverings and curtains suggested an old-fashioned reception room, the table with its opposing chairs a setting for interrogations. They had tried to make it look like a prison visitor's room, he realized.

Sonoma indicated that Docherty should take the seat on the far side of the table, then sat down on an elegant-looking Spanish chair beside the door. They waited in silence for five minutes, then another five. The captain was clearly getting irritated but he made no move to find out what was causing the hold-up.

And then the scream sounded. It was muffled by walls and distance, and there was only the one, but Docherty was pretty sure it had come from a woman.

'One of the prisoners,' Sonoma explained. 'We have mental cases here.'

'Women?' Docherty asked in a neutral tone.

Sonoma hesitated for only a second. 'No, there are no women here,' he said.

Docherty was still deciding whether or not to let this go when Bazua walked in through the door, closely followed by two soldiers bearing automatic rifles. The fiction did not extend to the prisoner's clothes, which looked like the usual Club Mediterranean casual wear. The Argentinian didn't seem any older than he had in Shepreth's photograph. There seemed to be hardly an ounce of excess fat on the bronzed limbs, his muscle tone seemed excellent for a man in his early fifties and the light brown hair, though greying at the edges, was showing no obvious sign of thinning. Prison life obviously suited him.

He sat down and looked at Docherty, vague amusement in his eyes.

Docherty returned the stare. It would have been nice to see some of the corruption on the surface – a hint of dissipation in the mouth, a touch of evil in the eyes – but the man just looked like a happy thug. And he was going to tell Docherty sweet fuck all.

He owed it to Gustavo to ask.

'Señor Bazua,' he began, with at least a trace of civility. 'I am working for a fellow-countryman of yours named Gustavo Macías,' he went on, in a tone which suggested that as far as he was concerned this was no more than a job. 'His son disappeared after being arrested in Rosario in November

1976, when you were the Officer Commanding the local Army base. I have spoken to the arresting officer, whose name you probably remember' – Docherty allowed himself a slight smile – 'and he informed me that you are in possession of the relevant records.'

Bazua's smile was an ad for expensive American dentistry. 'I have never heard of any such records,' he said. 'And if I had, what possible reason would I have for sharing some information with an enemy of my country?'

Docherty looked at him. 'Common humanity?' he asked ironically. The eyes were a give-away, he thought. They weren't empty – they were cruel. This was not a man for whom killing meant nothing – this was a man who actually got off on it. Power was an opportunity for sadism.

'You will pay for what you did to Toscono,' the Argentinian was saying.

Docherty grunted. 'He was easy. A weak link in your organization, I'd say. Maybe you should employ more Colombians – they don't seem to scare quite so easily.' He gave Captain Sonoma a smile.

'You were in the Falklands,' Bazua said. There was a definite chill in his voice now.

Docherty thought about saying he'd been at Goose Green, but the news that the man on the other side of the desk might have killed his son could really trip Bazua over the edge, and the Scot didn't want to end up as the victim of a hard-to-credit accident. 'I've got nothing against Argentinian soldiers,' he said. 'The Argentinian Army's really brave when it comes to fastening electrodes or making people eat their own shit, but none of the real soldiers ever join the Army. As a matter of fact,' he went on conversationally, 'one of the twentieth century's greatest soldiers was an Argie.'

144

Bazua just stared at him.

'Che Guevara,' Docherty explained with a smile. 'Heard of him? Of course, he actually did some fighting, put himself at risk.'

'Why did you come here?' Bazua asked in a poisonous monotone.

'To ask you about Guillermo Macías. You refused to tell me anything.'

Bazua was on his feet. 'Get me out of here,' he said coldly.

'I think it's up to Captain Sonoma to decide when the interview is over,' Docherty suggested.

'It is over,' Sonoma said, as Bazua disappeared through the doorway, minus his escort.

'This must be one of those prisons where the accent is all on rehabilitation,' Docherty murmured to himself.

Captain Sonoma didn't say a word on the drive back to Aguadulce, and when they reached Docherty's hotel – which he hadn't mentioned – he just sat there, staring resolutely ahead, waiting for the Scot to jump out.

'Thanks for your help, Captain,' Docherty said cheerfully. 'I will make sure my government lets your government know how much your efforts are appreciated.'

'Thank you, Señor,' Sonoma said through gritted teeth, and let in the clutch.

Docherty smiled to himself and went in search of a drink. At least he hadn't been thrown off the island.

Two hours later he was halfway up the path to El Pico, where he had arranged to meet Shepreth and Carmen. The forest had grown more patchy as he ascended, and there had already been several spectacular views of the eastern coastline below.

He paused at the next one, as much to enjoy the view as to check that no one was following him. There had been no sign of anyone on the road, and this was the third time he'd broken his journey up the mountain, but it always paid to make sure. The three of them had chosen El Pico as a meeting place precisely because they didn't want to be seen together.

A young American couple in hippie-ish attire went down the path, but no one else seemed to be coming up. Docherty resumed the climb, and half an hour later he was at the summit. A German couple he had seen at breakfast that morning were standing together on one side of the flat peak, Shepreth and Carmen on the other. Docherty nodded at both couples and sat down on a convenient rock to enjoy the view.

When the Germans obligingly departed a few minutes later, Carmen almost ran across to Docherty. 'Did you see anything?' she asked excitedly, and Docherty hated being the one to dim the light of hope in her eyes.

'No,' he said. 'But I heard a woman's voice. It was raised, so it was hard to tell at first . . .'

'She was shouting?'

'Aye,' Docherty lied. 'The Army captain who took me in said it was a man, one of the prisoners, but he was lying. I'm sure it was a woman.'

'What did you see?' Shepreth asked.

'Hardly anything. They'd rigged up the first room inside the front doors as an interview room, and Bazua was brought to see me there.' He gave them the gist of the conversation. 'I got him angry, but it didn't help. All in all, I think I got more out of visiting the military post. There's no more than twenty men based there, and they seem to have only one working helicopter at the moment.'

'Yeah, but how many more men are there inside the prison?' Shepreth wanted to know.

Docherty shrugged. 'I doubt if there's any soldiers stationed there permanently – they'd probably ruin the social ambience. No, I reckon it's just him and his *sicarios* – probably no more than a dozen in all. I mean, it's obvious he's not expecting to be attacked, or at least not from the land or the sea. I'd guess his main fear is a bombing run by one of the other cartels, so he's probably got an air-raid shelter in there somewhere.' Docherty smiled. 'If it wasn't for the women and the records I'd be recommending that our boys try dropping a few.'

'But . . .' Carmen began, thoroughly alarmed.

'As it is,' Docherty went on, 'we'll have to go in on the ground, which means knowing the layout inside out. We've got the aerial photographs, which should . . .'

'I had a talk with a few of the locals this morning,' Shepreth interrupted him, 'and it seems that nearly all the building work on this island is done by a firm in Cartagena – Sánchez Construcción.'

'They are the biggest firm in the city,' Carmen said.

'So they should have the architect's plans of Bazua's prison,' Shepreth concluded.

'It's worth a shot,' Docherty agreed. 'And while you're there Carmen could try talking to her friend again.'

'I can try,' she said, without much enthusiasm.

'You should get off the island yourself,' Shepreth told him.

Docherty shook his head. 'It'll look kind of suspicious if I leave and then come back. And anyway, I don't think Bazua will risk having a go at me on Providencia – it'd look a bit obvious.'

147

9

Carmen and Shepreth managed to get seats on that evening's flight from San Andrés to Cartagena. They neither sat together nor acknowledged each other on either the short hop across to San Andrés or the hour-long trip south to the mainland, which they shared with a strange mixture of Colombians on business and gringo travellers leap-frogging past Panama on their way from Central to South America. At Cartagena airport they went through a pantomime of running into each other, then took a taxi together to her flat.

As Carmen had hoped, this was one of the weekends which Pinar spent in Bogotá with a tour group. It wasn't the possible lack of room which had worried her – Shepreth could easily sleep on the sofa in their living room – but the avalanche of questions which his presence would have precipitated. It had been a long time since she'd invited a man back to her home.

He hadn't wanted to come, of course, and had argued that it would be safer for her if he stayed in a hotel. She had talked him out of it, fearing that having got her away from Providencia he might just leave her high and dry.

The fridge was low on supplies, but there were enough vegetables for a stir-fry, which they ate in front of the TV. Both were conscious of the fact that they'd been thrown together by circumstance rather than choice, and felt somewhat awkward because of it. It was not much past ten when Carmen announced that she was tired enough for bed, and wished him goodnight. She lay down, intending to get her thoughts in order, but the next thing she knew it was morning and there was no sign of him in the flat.

A few angry moments later she noticed that his bag was still there. She'd just finished showering and dressing when he returned with a bag full of pastries for breakfast. 'It's a lovely day,' he said.

They sat out on the small balcony, eating the pastries and drinking coffee, enjoying the sunshine and the slight breeze blowing up from the sea. A month ago Carmen would have taken such simple pleasures for granted, but now she found herself treasuring each minute.

'You're going to call Victoria's aunt?' Shepreth asked, breaking the spell.

'Yes, I'll do it now,' Carmen said, getting up.

The aunt, whose name was Elena Marín, answered the phone almost immediately, as if she'd been sitting with a hand poised over the receiver. Carmen asked how Victoria was, and after a short pause Elena replied that she was no worse. 'Are you coming to see her?' she asked hopefully.

'This morning, if that's all right?'

'Oh yes. That would be wonderful.'

Carmen went back out on to the balcony and told Shepreth, who said, 'While you're seeing Victoria I'll take a look at Sánchez Construcción.'

Ten minutes later the taxi arrived to take Carmen out to Elena's house on the outskirts of the city. She hadn't earned any wages for several weeks now, and she'd intended taking the bus, but Shepreth had insisted on giving her the fare. Later that day she would have to see her parents, but she hadn't yet worked out what she was going to tell them. Her father wouldn't keep financing trips to Providencia without a good explanation – he'd be too worried that she would do something stupid.

Elena's house, though quite small, stood in almost a hectare of land. After greeting Carmen at the door, Elena led her through to the kitchen, from whose window they could both see Victoria. She was sitting with her back to one of several large trees just behind the house, staring into space.

'She spends hours like that,' Elena explained. 'She cries a lot, which I suppose is understandable, though it almost breaks my heart.'

'What did the specialist say?' Carmen asked.

'Not much. He recommended psychotherapy and gave me the name of a man here in Cartagena, but Victoria refused to talk to him.'

'I'd have thought a woman therapist would have been better,' Carmen said, surprised.

'I know. I talked to this man, and I don't think he believed the story we agreed on.'

'Hell,' Carmen murmured. They'd tried to re-create the circumstances of Victoria's ordeal in a different setting, because anything connecting her to Providencia and Bazua might get her killed.

'You know,' Elena said after a few moments, 'the terrible thing is, when she's not crying she actually seems quite happy.'

Maybe, Carmen thought, but it seemed like an amnesiac's kind of happiness. Shepreth had offered her a photo of Bazua to show Victoria, and she had brought it with her just in case, but the young woman in the garden didn't seem in any state to take a shock like that. As she stepped out through the kitchen door Carmen came to the sudden realization that before Victoria's healing could begin Marysa and the others would need to return.

'Hello,' she said from a distance, not wanting to give the woman a shock.

Victoria looked startled anyway.

'Remember me?' Carmen asked.

'Of course,' Victoria said, wrapping both arms around her knees and pulling them towards her chin. 'You're the one who brought me home.'

Shepreth strolled round the old part of the city for the best part of an hour before heading towards the head office of Sánchez Construcción. Carmen had already known where it was, because the firm's move into one of the oldest and most beautiful houses in the walled city had been big news a couple of years earlier. They had apparently had two reasons for doing a no-expenses-spared restoration job on the sixteenth-century house – the eldest of the Sánchez brothers was a history buff in his spare time and his two younger siblings were eager for the lucrative government contracts which similar jobs would provide.

The classic two-storey Castilian villa was in the heart of the old city, right next door to the San Ignacio church. It had an interior courtyard, and through the intricate wrought-iron gates Shepreth could see a riot of vegetation and hear what sounded like a fountain. There were no obvious signs of an alarm system, though, which was somewhat surprising.

Or maybe not, Shepreth thought, walking on before his loitering became noticeable. If the building was used only for office work and impressing clients then there was unlikely to be anything worth stealing on the premises.

The same could not be said of the next house in the row, which housed the City Museum. There was likely to be all-night surveillance in one form or another.

He walked on to the end of the street, spent a few minutes staring at the sea, then started back. There was no way he could go in over the iron fence facing the street, for even if the latter was, by some miracle, empty, there were too many overlooking windows. Entry via the museum would just double the risk of tripping an alarm. It had to be either the rear wall or the church.

The rear wall, he discovered, stood above a six-metre drop. Below it was a busy road, and beyond that the sea.

It had to be the church. The building itself stood about thirty metres back from the road, at the centre of a large paved area. Several large trees kept most of this in shade, and a dozen or more adults were chatting on the scattered iron benches while their children chased each other around the two circular fountains. Shepreth slowly circumnavigated the church, enjoying the age-old simplicity of its design and surreptitiously studying the wall which separated its grounds from the offices of Sánchez Construcción. It was only about two metres high, and in one place a bench had been placed right underneath it. Getting over would be no problem, but getting over unseen might be. Latin Americans loved spending evenings sitting out in places like this, and since it was Saturday there'd be a Midnight Mass.

He walked back to the flat, thinking about Carmen. It was a long time since he'd felt so attracted to someone, but he didn't really know anything about her. She'd told him she was a tour guide, and that she worked here in Cartagena, mostly for several foreign tour companies. She lived with a female friend and didn't apparently have a boyfriend, which would have been more surprising if he hadn't known about the abduction of her sister. Something like that might well have forced her in on herself.

She was obviously brave, stubborn and loyal. But was she clever, kind, naturally curious? Did she have a sense of humour? He couldn't remember ever hearing her laugh, but considering the circumstances that wasn't very surprising.

He let himself into the flat with the spare key she'd given him, set up and turned on the coffee machine, then stepped out on to the balcony just in time to see her paying the taxi driver. She looked up, saw him and smiled.

He had known this woman less than forty-eight hours, but it was hard to think of anyone he had felt so connected to.

'How was it?' he asked as she came into the kitchen.

'Sad,' she said. 'And not very useful. There was just one thing which might help – she went through the usual list of things like the water-bed and the fan and the birds singing and this time she added something – she kept talking about the moon filling the window. Which suggests an east-facing window. If she was in Bazua's bedroom . . .' She looked at Shepreth. 'I know it's really thin.'

'You never know,' he said.

'So how did you get on?'

'You remember the house?'

'Yes.'

'Well, the only way in seems to be over the wall by the church. If I can get over that without being seen . . .'

'You'll need a diversion,' she said.

It was a little after ten and the grounds surrounding the church were far more densely populated than they had been during the day. The two fountains were the preserve of the younger teenagers, the benches reserved for their paired-off elder brothers and sisters. On the pathway from the street to the open doors of the church several beggars were waiting for alms from the midnight congregation. Every so often a military patrol would ride past in a jeep. According to Carmen they followed a regular route around the walled city through the night, mostly to protect tourists who couldn't resist the spell of the narrow streets by moonlight.

The two of them had been sitting on the bench by the wall for about an hour now, since bribing the previous occupants to leave. 'Any minute now,' Shepreth said looking at his watch, and at that moment they could hear the jeep coming up the street. It drove slowly by, the driver waving at a group of girls while his companions smiled, their cradled sub-machine-guns pointing at the sky.

As the jeep disappeared from view Carmen got to her feet and started across the rough paving stones towards the opposite corner of the grounds. Shepreth had enjoyed the last hour, sitting close together and sharing family histories, and as he watched her walk gracefully away a pang of desire shot through his loins.

He watched her light a cigarette, stop by the litter bin as if she was searching for something in the plastic bag, then drop the bag in. He looked at his watch. About two minutes, she had said. When she was a kid she and her friends had done this all the time. And since the home-made fuses had never let them down they'd never been caught.

She disappeared behind the church on her way back round. Half a minute went by. A minute. She was only about ten metres away when the firecrackers went off in the litter bin, jerking every head towards them. Shepreth had been expecting it, and even he felt a momentary pull.

No one was looking their way. He put one foot on the top of the bench and rolled himself over the wall, almost in the same motion. Leaping over a wall without knowing what was on the other side was rather unnerving, but he landed in nothing more dangerous than a bush. He squatted there for a moment, letting his eyes get used to the darkness and listening out for any sign that his arrival had been noticed. On the other side of the wall the string of firecrackers exhausted itself, and he found he could hear the waves crashing against the rocks a hundred metres away.

Satisfied, he headed towards the back of the darkened house. The sudden sound of a distant police siren caused his stride to falter for an instant, before his brain reassured his nerves that it couldn't have anything to do with him.

It crossed his mind that the last time he'd broken into an office he'd nearly ended up in the Panama Canal. Which wasn't a pleasant thought.

Breaking into this one was easier than expected. He had no difficulty springing open the shutters on one of the rear windows, and the sash windows themselves weren't even properly fastened. A few seconds later he was examining a typical board room with his pencil torch.

The door was locked, but no match for his steel 'credit card'. He edged out into the courtyard, which was mostly in darkness – the setting half moon was casting its silver spell on only the uppermost leaves of the various ornamental palms and the apex of the fountain. There was no sign of any human occupancy.

He started working his way round the ground floor, unlocking and where possible relocking each door in turn. In one of the rooms facing the street he found what he was looking for – a mountainous map cabinet with some forty drawers.

After checking that the shutters were as lightproof as possible, he checked under P for Providencia. Nothing. Rather less hopefully, he tried B for Bazua. Nothing there either. He was just about to start going through the whole cabinet from top to bottom when another idea occurred to him.

He looked under 'M' for Ministry of the Interior, but eventually found it under 'I'. The Sánchez brothers had obviously done a lot of work for the government, most of it in Cartagena, from schools to military barracks, police posts to waste-disposal depots. And they had also built both a military post and a correction centre on Providencia. Shepreth spread the two sheets out on the floor. The correction centre plan not only included interior diagrams for the two buildings familiar from the satellite photographs, but also placed the two new constructions within the context of the site.

He was still rolling up the two sheets when he saw the photocopier. It would certainly be much better to leave the originals here, because if their absence was noticed and Bazua informed, he wouldn't need a brain transplant to figure out why they'd been stolen. But could he risk the light?

Who dares wins, he thought, remembering the SAS motto. His watch told him he had another ten minutes before the patrol went by.

He switched on the machine and when it had warmed up he folded the plan in two, put it in place and lowered the lid. If he'd been wearing a jacket he could have used it to cover the machine, but he wasn't. So he draped himself across it instead, rather like someone trying to X-ray their own stomach.

A faint light flared twice in the dark room. He stood up and went through the process again for the other half of the diagram. And then twice more for the military post. There were no cries from the street, no police sirens. He pulled out his shirt, stuffed the copies into his waistband and tucked the shirt back in.

He put the diagrams back, switched off the copier and made his way back round the ghostly courtyard to the room through which he'd entered. He relocked the door from the inside and went out through the window, pulling the sash down and then, with some difficulty, refastening the shutters from the outside. As he approached the wall he heard voices on the other side.

Shepreth had been gone only a couple of minutes when they appeared in front of her. She couldn't remember either of their names, but the faces were familiar from her school days.

'Remember us?' the older-looking one asked. He seemed more than a little the worse for drink.

'No,' she said coldly.

'I'm Ramón,' he said, sitting down beside her and stretching both arms along the back of the seat. 'And this is my brother Paolo.'

The younger man sat down on her other side, pulled out a packet of American cigarettes and offered her one.'

'I don't smoke,' she said. 'And if you don't mind, I'd like to be alone.'

Paolo actually started to get up, but thought better of the idea when he saw that his brother had no such intentions.

'A beautiful woman should not be alone on a night like this,' Ramón said sarcastically. 'Why are you so unfriendly?'

'I'm waiting for my boyfriend,' she told him.

'He is late?'

'I was early.'

'I don't think he's coming. Why don't you come for a walk with us?'

She gave him a scornful look. 'Why would I want to do that?'

'Because we can show you a good time. Go to a club maybe, or a party. Wherever we go it'll be better than hanging out in a churchyard.' He let his hand rest lightly on her shoulder. 'How about it?'

She brushed the hand away, and turned round to face him. 'No,' she said. 'Understand that? It's really simple. N-o. No. I do not want to go anywhere with you. I do want you to leave me alone.'

Ramón sighed. 'This boyfriend must be a real superman. I think we have to stay and see someone like that, just so that we know how to improve ourselves. Don't you think so, Paolo?'

Having arrived on the other side of the wall in the middle of this conversation, Shepreth's initial irritation soon turned to anger. The prospect of climbing back over and banging the two young men's heads together was an appealing one, but he was quite sure Carmen could take care of herself, and there had to be more prudent courses of action open to him.

He walked across to the wall which bordered the museum's grounds. There had been no sign of armed guards on the street in front of it, and it was possible that the building's alarm system was considered defence enough. In which case, he could use the grounds as an escape route.

He was raising himself up to take a look across the wall when there was a rushing sound from the other side, and a slavering mouth full of very sharp teeth materialized not much more than a metre from his face. He dropped back to the ground, his heart suddenly thumping at about five times its usual rate, just as the dog began barking up a storm on the other side of the wall.

In the distance a human voice was asking the dog what the trouble was.

'Shit!' Shepreth murmured to himself. The street had become his best chance.

He hurried down the side of the Sánchez Construcción villa and stopped at the corner for a look. The dog was still barking next door, but there didn't seem to be anyone out in front of the museum. Most of the street was out of sight from where he stood, and the chances of it being empty seemed somewhat remote. His watch told him the patrol would be passing in less than two minutes. The odds didn't look too good, but they were only going to get worse.

He ran for the wrought-iron gates, which seemed to offer the easiest climb, and concentrated on getting over them, not even looking up and down the street until he dropped to the pavement outside. About a hundred metres away a couple were walking towards him, but they seemed engrossed in each other. In the opposite direction a taxi had just pulled up outside the gates to the church grounds, but it was facing away. He was just congratulating himself on getting away with it when a shout came from behind him. Two armed guards had emerged from the museum and were walking towards him, sub-machine-guns at the ready.

Hearing the dog bark, Carmen put two and two together. Shepreth must have realized he couldn't rejoin her in the way he planned and sought another way out. She hoped he'd seen or heard the dog before crossing the other wall.

If he had, what would he do? There was no back way out, so it would have to be the front. She stood up abruptly and walked away from the bench, hoping that the bastards wouldn't follow her.

They did of course.

'If you don't leave me alone, I'll get a policeman,' she half shouted over her shoulder.

'We're doing nothing,' Ramón shouted back, but the foot-falls seemed to die away slightly.

She reached the gates and turned into the street just in time to see Shepreth halted by the guard's shout.

'David,' she yelled, turning his head once more, and ran towards him with outstretched arms. As they embraced like long-lost lovers, she saw over his shoulder that the guards were still coming forward. She freed herself from the embrace, glanced quickly back down the street and strode towards the approaching guards. 'See those two boys,' she shouted angrily, pointing back at the hovering Ramón and Paolo. 'They have been harassing me. I want them arrested.'

'That is not our business, Señorita,' the first man said.

'It should be the business of every man to protect innocent women,' she said haughtily. 'Come, my darling,' she said, taking Shepreth by the arm. 'We will be late.'

The following evening Docherty was lying on his hotel bed, Walkman on his chest, listening to soul singer O.V. Wright lament a wrong verdict by 'the jury of lurve'. He had spent a reasonably relaxing weekend, walking and swimming by day, reading and sleeping by night. He had really wanted to talk to Isabel, but there was every chance that the call would be monitored, and Bazua's reach certainly extended to Chile. Carmen had promised to ring his wife from Cartagena, so Isabel would know that he was all right, but he still missed the sound of her voice.

A police officer had joined him at his table during breakfast that morning. He said that he was from the local station in

Santa Isabel, and that he was obliged to ask Docherty some questions.

Actually there was only one – what the hell was Docherty still doing on Providencia?

'Taking a holiday,' the Scot had told him. 'I was hired to come here and talk to Angel Bazua, as I'm sure you know. And now that I've talked to him, I'm spending some of the money. You have a beautiful island here.'

The man had departed happily enough, though whether Bazua would be satisfied was something else again.

Lying there listening to O.V. Wright, he found it hard to believe in happy endings, but then who wanted to listen to the Osmonds?

There was a tap on the door. Docherty swung himself off the bed and walked silently across to the door. 'Who is it?' he asked, taking care to keep behind the jamb.

'It's me,' Shepreth said.

Docherty opened the door.

'I moved in down the corridor,' the MI6 man told him. 'Carmen's there now.'

Docherty followed the younger man to his room, which looked practically identical to his own. Carmen was standing with her back to the curtained window, looking happier than she had three days before.

'Did you talk to Isabel?' he asked.

'Yes. She's fine, the children are fine. She sends her love. I told her more or less everything and . . .' She hesitated.

'And she sounded worried,' Docherty suggested.

'Yes, she did. But she didn't say anything, just that you should be careful.'

'Aye,' said Docherty. There was no way round that one. 'So what have you got?' he asked the two of them.

Shepreth produced the architect's drawings with a flourish, and laid them out on the bed.

'You didn't have any trouble, then?' Docherty asked as he examined the plans.

Shepreth told him the story of the break-in, stressing the role Carmen's quick thinking had played in their getting away with it, and Docherty saw the look that passed between them. If they weren't lovers already, they soon would be.

'These were worth the risk,' he said shortly.

'And Carmen may have got something from Victoria Marín,' Shepreth said.

She explained about the moon-filled window, half expecting to see an incredulous expression on Docherty's face.

'This room or that one,' he said, finger jabbing at the plan. 'There's two obvious ways this could be done,' he went on. 'Assuming the SAS get the job, we could bring in a troop – that's sixteen men. The Royal Navy could bring them within range, but there's nowhere to put a helicopter down inside the compound, so if we want to catch Bazua by surprise – and for the sake of the women and the records I think we do – then they'd have to come in by boat. I don't know how sophisticated Colombia's defences are – not very, I expect – but I don't think there's much chance a Royal Navy boat would get past American surveillance. And since they can't be told what we're doing there's a good chance they'll alert the Colombians. And we don't want their air force turning up.'

'Maybe the Navy could come up with a cover story for the Americans,' Shepreth suggested.

'Maybe,' Docherty said, without much conviction.

'What's the alternative?' Carmen asked him.

'More stealth, less men,' Docherty said. 'Assemble a four-man patrol here on the island and bring them in one by one.

With surprise more or less guaranteed, I don't think the five of us would have too much trouble.'

'I have a feeling someone might point out you're no longer on active service,' Shepreth said, remembering Docherty's record.

'So I'm an on-site consultant,' the Scot said.

'And anyway there'll be six of us,' Shepreth said with a smile.

'Seven,' Carmen reminded him.

Later that night Docherty lay awake in bed, trying to remember how many of *The Magnificent Seven* had survived. Had Horst Buchholz been one of the three who rode away, or had they already left him behind in the village? He had been one of the three, Docherty decided, which meant four had died. He could remember them all – Coburn's knife dropping from his fingers, Robert Vaughn's fingers scraping down the wall, the gold-happy one whose name no one ever remembered. But most of all he remembered the children putting flowers on Charles Bronson's grave.

He didn't want Maria and Ricardo doing that, not until they were well into middle age.

10

The sun was barely over the horizon, the fields sparkling with dew in the early-morning light, as Lieutenant Colonel Timothy Greaves drove south from Hereford towards the Severn Bridge and the M4. There were shorter routes to London, but he had always loved this road through the Forest of Dean, and the meeting in Whitehall didn't start until eleven.

Of course, he could have saved himself the drive by arranging a flight to RAF Northolt, but in these days of military economy it was considered somewhat extravagant to use the RAF as a personal taxi service. And in any case who could think in a helicopter?

Greaves was not exactly looking forward to the meeting, but there were butterflies of excitement in his stomach nevertheless. It was nearly a year now since he had succeeded Barney Davies as the Officer Commanding 22 SAS, and he had spent quite a lot of that time waiting for the chance to play his part in one of those special operations which punctuated the history – the legend, almost – of the Regiment. They didn't happen very often, and when they did they were as likely to take place outside the public eye as in it.

The subject of that day's meeting would not be offered as grist for headlines, and that fact gave rise to a certain ambivalence in Greaves's mind. He would have to ask his men to risk their lives in the awareness that they would be unacknowledged in success and quite possibly disowned in failure. Several such missions had been carried out in Barney Davies's time, and Greaves knew that his predecessor's pride in their success had been more than a little tinged with bitterness. Too many men had died unrecognized.

Sergeant Jamie Docherty had been involved in several of those operations, including one of the most dramatic, the insertion of a four-man patrol into Bosnia. He was newly retired when the need arose, but had been reinstated for the duration of the mission.

Greaves had read through Docherty's file the previous evening and wondered. No other regiment in the British Army – probably no other regiment in the world – would have persevered with someone like Docherty when he went so comprehensively off the rails after his wife's death. And just about any other regiment would have court-martialled him for wilful disregard of orders at some point in his career. Yet there seemed no doubt that he'd been a brilliant soldier, at least insofar as the SAS defined the breed. His record in action showed that he'd frequently been better than his orders.

Greaves himself had seen precious little action since the capture of South Georgia and the reconquest of West Falkland. Then there had been training stints in a couple of African countries and a couple of mind-numbing tours in Northern Ireland. He shook his head, as if to dislodge the thought that soon he'd be sending more men into that murderously futile mess.

But first the joys of Colombia, he told himself, as he passed the midpoint on the swaying Severn Bridge. The river below seemed choppier than usual, despite the clear blue sky overhead.

His thoughts returned to the morning's meeting, the exact purpose of which seemed far from clear. During their telephone conversation the previous day Sir Christopher Hanson had implied that it was both a rubber-stamping exercise and a ritual sharing of responsibility, but Greaves had learnt to take anything Intelligence said with about a ton of salt. He feared a concerted attempt to impose political restraints on his military freedom of manoeuvre, and knew that he would have to resist any such pre-emptive tying of his men's hands.

In his written submission to the Prime Minister he had offered two possible courses of action, both loosely based on the suggestions emanating from Providencia. Hanson's man Shepreth was supposedly the source of these, but Greaves thought he could see Docherty's fingerprints all over them. He was also pretty certain that the politicians would refuse to sanction the larger-scale plan – no matter how it was dressed up, the dispatch of a full SAS troop sounded too much like an invasion.

But four men out of uniform could be inserted in secrecy, and once the job was done they could be passed off as mercenaries in the employ of a rival cartel. Admittedly there wasn't much chance of weapon supply or bodily extraction without the Americans taking notice – it was surprising any sunlight still reached the ground with all the surveillance planes and satellites that littered the skies above the Caribbean – but risk-free options seemed remarkably thin on the ground.

If the politicians asked for certainty he'd tell them there wasn't any, but that he certainly wouldn't bet against his men getting the job done as discreetly as was humanly possible.

* * *

The Prime Minister was already seated at the head of the rectangular walnut table when Greaves entered the room. This was not the first meeting he had attended in Whitehall, but it was his first view of the famous Conference Room B, which turned out to be stunningly ordinary.

There were six seats around the table. A man with thin, greying hair and piercing blue eyes sat facing the PM. Seeing Greaves, he got up and offered his hand, introducing himself as Christopher Hanson. There were two men on the other side of the table, one of whom Greaves knew, one he had frequently seen on *Newsnight* and *Question Time*. The former was Douglas Minchey, a junior minister at the Ministry of Defence, the latter Martin Clarke, who held an equivalent rank at the Foreign Office and was also rumoured to be a possible challenger for the Party leadership. They both nodded greetings, Minchey with a smile, Clarke with a frown that would have curdled milk.

The Foreign Office would hate this, Greaves thought as he sat down. The chair next to him was apparently spare.

The PM cleared his throat – nervously, it seemed to Greaves. 'Sir Christopher, if you could bring us all up to speed . . .'

Hanson obliged. Without once consulting his notes he told the story of MI6's increasing interest in Angel Bazua's twin career as drug smuggler and bankroller of Argentinian irredentism. He described the various and vain British attempts to interest the Americans in action against Bazua, and went through the events of the past few weeks – the accidental involvement of an ex-SAS man, his discovery of the Argentinian's possession of certain Dirty War records and the possible explanation of American behaviour which that suggested, the decision to ask the SAS proper to consider operational options.

The PM asked Greaves to outline what those were.

He was about to do so when the Foreign Office minister intervened.

'With respect, Prime Minister,' Clarke began, 'wouldn't it make more sense to discuss the potential consequences of any such action before we get down to specifics?'

'I think we're all aware that our relations with both Colombia and Washington could be seriously affected,' the PM said. 'And once we've heard what is possible we should have a better idea of how to minimize the potential damage,' he added dismissively, turning his attention back to the SAS CO.

Greaves outlined the two options he had submitted, on impulse stressing the purely military advantages of the larger-scale assault. He was conscious that when it came to playing politics he was an amateur among seasoned pros, but he was hoping that giving the Foreign Office something to shoot down would make them more inclined to let the smaller insertion go through. Out of the corner of his eye he could see a smile on Hanson's face, as if the MI6 man knew exactly what was going on.

'Which do you recommend?' the PM asked when he had finished. He still seemed nervous to Greaves.

'If we send in the larger force we can be pretty certain of achieving our immediate objectives – the destruction of Bazua and his boats. But the element of surprise won't be so great, there'll be more casualties and it will be impossible to conceal the operation from the Americans. The second option relies more on the skills of a few men, but as long as we solve the weapons supply problem the operation will be effectively over before anyone else knows about it. And if by then we have the means to mollify the Americans, then the Colombians will find it hard to prove our involvement.'

Clarke was not having any of it. 'The first option is clearly out of the question,' he said. 'A cynic might think that it had been conjured up just to make the second option look more reasonable. Either way, we'll be sending British soldiers on to the soil of a sovereign nation to blow up boats and kill people.' He locked eyes with the Prime Minister. 'Are we really going to sanction the use of the SAS to assassinate a drug baron?'

'Well, they can hardly bring him home,' the PM said coldly.

'If you really have moral qualms about this operation,' Hanson told the FO minister, 'I think you should save them for a more suitable occasion. Bazua is a mass murderer, drug dealer and worse.'

'And since when has MI6 set itself up as the moral guardian of the New World Order?' Clarke asked sarcastically.

'Gentlemen!' the PM admonished them. Greaves was expecting him to side with his minister, but he didn't. 'I would obviously prefer to work with our allies in this matter, but that seems to be the one option which is definitely denied us. And with all due respect to the Foreign Office's real concerns, I don't believe we can let the fear of American disapproval deter us from the pursuit of crucial British interests. I want those boats destroyed and I want this man brought to book.'

There was a glitter in his eyes as he enunciated the last sentence, and Greaves suddenly thought he understood why the man had seemed nervous before – it was because he had decided on a course of action which seemed completely out of character. But why? Greaves wondered. Was it the drugs that enraged him, the thought of another war or just Bazua's character? Was there anything there to undermine life-long habits of caution? No, he decided, and then he understood. The man was on his last legs politically and he knew it – there was no need to hedge any more. Like those beyond the age of responsibility he could do whatever he felt like doing. Taking on Bazua was like a last hurrah for seventeen years of Tory rule.

'So are we all agreed on the smaller-scale option?' the PM was saying.

There were nods from around the table, an almost infinitesimal twitch of the neck in Clarke's case.

Now Greaves knew why the meeting had been called. The PM had needed Clarke's metaphorical signature next to his own, just in case everything went wrong.

The SAS CO took the quicker route home, and despite stopping off for a late lunch in Witney was back in his office at the Stirling Lines Regimental HQ of 22 SAS by a quarter past four. He felt physically tired after seven hours of driving in one day, but mentally refreshed by the distance he had put between himself and Whitehall. The meeting in Conference Room B had left him feeling manipulated and none too respectfully inclined towards his political masters.

It had also left the Regiment with a job to do.

Once he was behind his desk, Greaves's first action was to order two cups of tea, his second to summon Major Jimmy Bourne, the long-time head of the Regiment's Counter Revolutionary Warfare Wing. The planned action against Bazua didn't come within the CRW Wing's purview, but before his retirement Barney Davies had recommended Bourne to Greaves as the best available source of personnel information and general advice, and on more than one occasion during the past year the new CO had been grateful for the tip.

'So we've been given the green light?' Bourne asked before he was even through the door.

'Plan B,' Greaves told him, indicating the waiting cup of tea.

'Good,' Bourne said, shovelling sugars into the dark-brown brew.

Greaves stopped counting after three. 'So who shall we send?'

'I've been thinking about that,' Bourne said, testing his tea for sweetness. 'It'll have to be one of our best, or Jamie Docherty will walk all over him.'

Greaves smiled despite himself. 'Does the bastard really expect a consultant's fee?'

Bourne grinned. 'That was a joke,' he said. 'But he'll bloody well expect to be consulted. I think we should give the job to my senior sergeant.'

'Wynwood, right?'

'Yep.'

'He just got married, didn't he?' There had been a photograph in the local paper which Greaves had found amusing – the bulky Welshman with the big grin and mass of dark, curly hair, the diminutive bride looking demure and serious enough for life in a convent.

'That was a couple of months ago,' Bourne said. 'A great bash,' he added wistfully. 'Anyway, he knows Colombia.'

'I know.' Wynwood had been one of two advisers sent by Her Majesty's Government to help train the Colombian Special Forces Anti-Narcotics Unit in the early 90s. After his partner and a prominent local politician had been kidnapped by the drug-dealing Amarales family, Wynwood had taken charge of the four-man patrol sent in to execute a rescue. The team had proved successful but not in the way intended, and had ended up having to walk across a mountain range to escape pursuit. Even then, two of their number had died at the hands of the Amaraleses' *sicarios*. 'The Colombians might remember him,' Greaves thought out loud.

'The name maybe, but we can change that. He's brilliant in the field, he speaks fluent Spanish and he'll get on with Docherty.'

'OK, I'm sold, he's the PC. What about the others?'

'Why not get Wynwood in here?' Bourne asked.

Greaves hesitated – even after a year back he was still not fully attuned to the Regiment's uniquely democratic ways – but only for a moment. 'Why not?' he agreed.

Joss Wynwood was just getting into his car, having decided to trim the odd half-hour off his working day. He and Sarah were going out for a meal with her elder sister and brother-in-law that evening and he wanted some time with his wife before they went. They could do a jigsaw together, or take a shower together, or . . .

It was his sister-in-law's thirty-eighth birthday, and he'd be thirty-nine himself in a couple of weeks. Next year he'd be forty. He had used to worry about getting older, but not since meeting Sarah.

He was just moving towards the gates, midway through fastening his seat-belt, when the trooper appeared in the side window, running along beside him and tapping on the glass. He rolled the window down and slowed the car to a crawl, letting the trooper slow to a walk as he delivered his message. The news that the CO wanted to see him made him feel like a schoolboy caught skiving off school early.

'Any idea what it's about?' he asked optimistically.

'Not a clue, Sarge,' the trooper told him with a grin.

Wynwood parked the car and walked thoughtfully across the parade ground towards the CO's office. The sky in the west was beginning to fill with clouds, which usually meant overnight rain. With any luck he wouldn't have to water the garden.

He knocked on the door and heard the CO's 'come in'. Wynwood hadn't had that much to do with Greaves since his appointment the previous year, but like most of the Regiment he'd been pleasantly surprised by the ease of the transition. Barney Davies had been a much-loved and respected figure, and so far Greaves didn't seem that much of a comedown.

It wasn't just the CO waiting for him inside – Jimmy Bourne was there as well. Maybe the CRW Wing was being abolished. He took the seat next to his immediate superior and prepared to be enlightened.

'There's another cup of tea on the way,' Greaves said by way of preamble. 'We've been given a job to do,' he continued, and proceeded to outline what it was.

Wynwood listened, feeling initially torn between wanting to go and not wanting to leave his current happiness behind. But as the CO, with occasional help from Bourne, sketched out the prospective operation, the Welshman's two decades of professional commitment reasserted themselves. The job itself seemed straightforward enough; the only obvious problem was weapons supply. The actual assault should present no real difficulties, as long as it was properly planned and executed. And as for the getaway, Bourne had apparently spent most of the morning confirming that a chopper from the Caymans could be customized to collect the team from just outside the twelve-mile limit.

'We think you're the best man to lead the team,' Greaves told him.

'Thank you, boss,' Wynwood said automatically. He had just seen the new film of *Mission: Impossible* and half expected to be handed a self-destructing tape. 'Who else have you chosen?' he asked.

'No one yet,' Bourne said. 'You're here to help us pick the names out of a hat.'

Terry Stoneham left the car by the wooden gate, not really caring whether he was infringing on a farmer's right to move his livestock, and started up the public footpath, kicking stones as he went. Every time he saw the kid a great bundle of conflicting emotions seemed to knock him sideways, and as usual he found himself wondering why he was putting himself through it all. Mark was Jane and Don's child in every way that counted. It might have been his sperm which fertilized the egg, but Don had been the one at the birth, the one who had watched the first walk and heard the first word. He was the one the kid called Dada.

He kicked another stone, with slightly less vicious intent.

Jane had asked him to let go, stand back, give up the kid. All his friends in the Regiment thought he was just digging himself a hole to be miserable in. Even his parents had told him to think about what was best for the boy, and God only knew how much they wanted a grandchild.

But he couldn't bring himself to do it. He didn't know if it was a real attachment or pure stubbornness, just as he still didn't know whether he'd really loved Jane or only thought he did.

His early life had not prepared him for this. In a world of broken families and free-wheeling angst his parents had loved each other and him – just about the only thing he'd been deprived of was a sense of deprivation. He'd been a happy baby, a happy child, a happy youth and a happy grown-up, right up to that moment when his pregnant wife had told him about her lover.

But that was two years ago, he told himself as he reached the top of the hill. Just before the hostage crisis in Samarkand which he and Rob Brierley had sorted out with a little help from the locals. Well, quite a lot of help actually. He had really fancied Nurhan, the woman in charge – in vain, unfortunately – but at least the fancying had helped dull the pain of his ex-wife's betrayal. He had noticed today that he no longer found Jane in the slightest bit sexy. He had given up on her, so why couldn't he give up on a kid he only saw for a couple of hours each week, a kid moreover who didn't really seem to know who the occasional visitor was?

He thought he'd make a good father one day, but then Don already seemed to be one, and an art teacher was less likely to get killed than an SAS sergeant, even one who seemed permanently stationed in a classroom full of smart-arse trainees.

Stoneham smiled to himself and ran a hand through his straw-coloured hair. 'Ah, what the fuck,' he murmured to himself and gazed out at the fuzzy line of the distant Black Mountains. Maybe he could get a security job with Princess Di, entrance her with his ready wit and manly body, and get a cut of the millions Charlie had lobbed in her direction.

He laughed and looked at his watch – he had a class in half an hour.

There was no irate farmer waiting by the gate and the traffic was kind, so he made it with three minutes to spare. The trainees were full of enthusiasm and long on naïve questions, and by the end of the class he felt old for his thirty-four years. Still, he'd outlived Jesus, he thought, as he headed for the canteen and a possibly life-threatening meal. He was only ten metres from the doors, and could almost smell the spotted dick, when the adjutant collared him. The CO wanted to see him at eight the following morning, and he should cancel his classes for the coming fortnight.

* * *

At twenty to eight the next morning the 'Twins' were mopping up the last of their fried eggs with slices of white bread. Both accent and appearance offered proof positive that there was no blood relationship between Corporals Sam Blackman and Charles McCall. The Liverpudlian 'Blackie' had dark hair and an almost gangling frame, the Glaswegian 'Bonnie' ginger hair and a riot of freckles, but since their simultaneous badging in 1990 the pair had seemed virtually inseparable. They were now in the last stretch of their second three-year term in the SAS and had no intention of missing out on a third.

But shit happened, as the Americans said, and on this particular morning they were anxiously wondering why the CO had developed this sudden yearning to see their pretty faces.

'It can't be about that fight you got us into, can it?' Blackie asked plaintively.

'Which one?'

'In the Slug & Pellet.'

'It was you got us into that one, staring at that tart's tits.'

'It was you asked if they were real. That was what really set her boyfriend off.'

'Yeah, yeah,' Bonnie agreed, remembering the breasts in question.

'Anyway, that was two weeks ago,' Blackie said. 'He'd have had us in before now.'

'So what did we do last weekend?'

'We went to that party in Ludlow.'

'We crashed that party in Ludlow,' Bonnie corrected him. 'And you tried to go swimming in the punch-bowl.' He sighed. 'But let's look on the bright side. He doesn't want to tear us off a strip – he wants to tell us what a great job we've been doing. Or maybe there's a job waiting for us, and we can get out of fucking Hereford for a while. Give the women a chance to miss us. You know, build up expectations for when we return.'

'Yeah, right. An all-expenses-paid fortnight in sunny Belfast.'

'It could be another HAHO drop on to the mountain above the bad guy's lair,' Bonnie said reminiscently. He and Blackie had been part of the back-up troop parachuted into Colombia in 1990. They had been on the ground no more than a couple of hours, but just about every minute, not to mention the preceding hour-long drop, was etched in the memories of the two men.

'Christ, I hope so,' Blackie murmured.

'Or they could send us after that Bosnian Serb – what's his name? – the one they want for the war crimes.'

'Karadzic.'

'Yeah, that's him. Well, someone's got to arrest the bastard, haven't they?'

Blackie shrugged. 'It'd be a change.'

'Those Bosnian women won't know what hit 'em.'

'Your sledgehammer wit, you mean?'

Bonnie grinned. 'You're just jealous. That new barmaid at the Pig's Head thought I should go professional.'

'She was winding you up.'

'No chance. I think I'm in there this weekend.'

'If you're not in Bosnia,' Blackie said, looking at the canteen clock. 'I think it's time we got our orders from Jimmy.'

They gulped down the last of the sludge-like coffee and started across the parade ground in the direction of the CO's office. In the distance the unmistakable figure of Senior Staff Sergeant Wynwood was coming towards them. 'Christ, maybe we are going back to fucking Colombia,' Blackie muttered.

'Change of venue, lads,' said Wynwood. 'It's the Kremlin for us.'

'So what's it about, boss?' Bonnie asked innocently.

'All will be revealed shortly,' Wynwood told him. 'As the actress said to the bishop.'

'I bet that made his cassock bulge,' Blackie murmured.

In the briefing room they found the CO, Jimmy Bourne and Terry Stoneham already waiting. The mounted water-buffalo's head, a forty-year-old souvenir of the Regiment's time in Malaya, gazed moodily down at the assembly. As they took their seats, Bonnie and Blackie noticed the large-scale map of the Caribbean draped across the easel.

Bourne started the ball rolling with a brief biographical sketch of Bazua and his activities. Stoneham, Bonnie and Blackie, who were hearing of the man for the first time, looked suitably angered by his presence on the planet. The involvement of Jamie Docherty – a famous SAS old boy – was greeted with interest.

'Can we call him Grandad?' Bonnie wanted to know.

'If you want to end up feeding the sharks,' Wynwood told him.

'Right,' Bourne said, leaning towards the map. 'Now for the interesting bit. You four are off to the delightful Colombian island of Providencia.' He tapped a point in the Caribbean which seemed closer to Central America than Colombia, then folded the sheet back to reveal a smaller-scale map of the island itself. 'Wynwood and Stoneham will arrive tomorrow afternoon, Blackman and McCall will spend a day on the adjoining island of San Andrés – an uneventful day, I should stress – and then move over to Providencia the following day. That night – preferably that night – you will break into Bazua's home and sink his boats.' He did a round of the four faces. 'All clear so far?'

'Not really,' Blackie said. 'Why do we need to break into his house to sink his boats? They're not in the swimming pool, are they?'

Bourne grinned. 'We didn't want to make it too simple in case you got bored. For one thing your chances of escape will increase about a hundredfold if you destroy Bazua's communications with the outside world. For another, Bazua has something the Intelligence boys want to get their hands on – he has military records from the 70s Dirty War in Argentina.'

'Most 70s records are crap,' Bonnie murmured.

'Why do they want them?' Stoneham asked.

Bourne looked at Greaves, who nodded. 'They may find out that Bazua has an important friend in American Intelligence,' he told them.

'What about Bazua?' Stoneham asked. 'Do our masters want him dead or alive?'

Bourne looked at Greaves again.

'We don't want him brought out,' the CO said. 'The government couldn't put him on trial without admitting that British troops had snatched him from Colombian soil.' He paused, looking almost embarrassed, Wynwood thought. 'I've been put in a difficult position,' Greaves went on, 'which I'm afraid means that you're in one too. MI6 want this man dead, and they will also be involved in this operation – they already have a man on the island. I can't say that I'd shed too many tears if Bazua gets killed, but I have been given no orders for his assassination. So I'm afraid you're going to have to play it by ear.' He paused again. 'And there's another complication. There are several women on the premises – we don't know how many. Five were kidnapped on the mainland a year or so ago and taken to the island, and as far as we know three of them are still there. They're Bazua's prisoners – slaves virtually. And there may be more than three.'

'Christ,' Stoneham said, 'are we supposed to bring them out with us?'

Greaves sighed. 'If you can. I think that's another decision that can only be taken when the time comes. As far as Her Majesty's Government is concerned the important thing is to get in and out without leaving any British fingerprints, and as far as I'm concerned the number-one priority is getting you all back in one piece. Working within those parameters . . .' He shrugged. 'But to get back to where we were. Shepreth – that's the MI6 man – will have the primary responsibility for grabbing the records and taking care of Bazua; you will take out the boats and assist him in whatever other ways are necessary. Is that clear?' he asked, thinking it was anything but.

The objectives were diverse, the chain of command confused, and there'd be no chance of a rescue if things went badly wrong.

But if the men in front of him shared his doubts, there was no sign of it on their faces. All four of them had an expectant gleam in their eyes, like kids who'd been promised an adventure in the woods.

'We'll clarify as we go along,' Wynwood said.

On Providencia the days were passing slowly. Shepreth and Carmen were seeing a lot of each other – it seemed safer to pretend that they were strangers enjoying a holiday romance than unattached loners with no apparent agenda, and if Shepreth had had his wish they would have been doing more than pretending. In Cartagena he had begun to hope that she reciprocated some of his feelings, but since their return to the island she had retreated back inside herself. Shepreth hoped it was the proximity of her sister rather than second thoughts about him which had caused the change.

He had not tried to keep her in the dark about the imminent operation, telling himself that she would be needed to reassure the women once they were released. Which might well be true, but it wasn't the real reason he was wilfully ignoring every security regulation in the book. He was emotionally involved, and pleased about it. He had a personal stake, and he liked it that way. He couldn't see any reason why his professional obligations should come into conflict with his personal loyalties but if they did then he'd follow his conscience. And if that cost him his job, then the hell with it. He wanted Carmen, but that was only the half of it. He wanted to feel better about himself.

For her part, Carmen was only too aware of Shepreth's more basic urges, and at times the temptation to respond was almost irresistible. But she didn't let herself. It would have been more than a betrayal of her sister – it would have been wrong for her and Shepreth too. She liked him, and she could already imagine falling in love with him, but she couldn't shake the feeling that jumping into bed with him in the middle of all this would cause either or both of them to emotionally short-circuit.

When it was over . . . well, then she'd be more ready to trust her own feelings and to believe that his interest was more than an awkward blend of lust and sympathy. In the meantime she tried not to let herself think about what might be going on in the house on the other side of the island, and not to let impatience rule her days.

She was not the only one eager for action. Docherty was once good at waiting, but age had made him more impatient, and he missed his wife. He liked both Shepreth and Carmen, but apart from hurried meetings in the hotel room, he had no contact with them. He liked Providencia, but he'd finished his book and the three tapes he'd bought for the Walkman were wearing out. He'd walked just about every path on the island by the Tuesday, and he'd never been one for just lying on a beach.

When Shepreth delivered the news of the SAS team's imminent arrival he breathed a deep sigh of relief, but later that evening he noticed that the age-old mix of fear and excitement had acquired a new ingredient – guilt. He had always thought that there had to be things worth risking his life for, but the older he got the fewer they seemed to be, and he wasn't completely sure that Angel Bazua was one of them.

Or that Isabel would think he was.

11

Providencia was a small island, making secret meetings hard to arrange. If the four of them were seen gathering in one of the more secluded spots then suspicions were likely to be aroused, and on balance Docherty reckoned that a meeting in one of the small settlements, in full view of the locals, carried the lesser risk. So he and Shepreth first 'bumped into each other' in the bar of an Aguadulce hotel, then 'just happened to wind up in conversation' with two fellow-countrymen who had just arrived from San José.

Joss Wynwood and Terry Stoneham both looked fit, Docherty thought. In fact, almost too fit for the travellers they were supposed to be. He had met them both before, but they were from a later SAS generation, and he didn't know either of them that well. He had spent more time with Stoneham, particularly in the days following the Samarkand hijack business, but he was also well aware of Wynwood's reputation and pleased to see that the Welshman had been chosen to lead the SAS team.

After about ten minutes of innocent male chatter about football, women and the local beer, Wynwood quietly wondered whether this might not be the best place to talk.

Docherty took one last look round the room. There didn't seem to be anyone in earshot, and in any case the people they most needed to worry about would have a hard job understanding English, particularly the Welsh and Scottish versions spoken by Wynwood and himself. And talking here would certainly look potentially less suspicious than hiding in a hotel room or wandering down to the beach together in the dark. 'Aye,' he decided. 'Why not?'

'The other two will be here tomorrow,' Wynwood told Docherty and Shepreth. 'Blackman and McCall – do you know them?'

Docherty shook his head.

'They're full of bullshit, but I'm told they're reliable when it counts,' Wynwood said. 'Terry and I will hire a boat in the morning and go for a ride. After dark we'll be picking up the you-know-what, which we'll need to stash somehow – I don't fancy leaving the stuff in the boat for twenty-four hours.'

Docherty thought for a moment. 'On the hill above the target,' he suggested. 'We can dig a scrape in the trees.'

'Sounds good. Have you taken a look at the seaward side yet?'

'I have,' Shepreth said. 'We took one of the tour boats which circle the island. It kept much further out from the shore in that sector, but I got a reasonably good look through the glasses. There were a couple of men on the dock with SMGs – Uzis, I think – but they didn't look like they were expecting trouble. The wire fence follows the shoreline by the way, just inside the trees, and there's a gate by the dock.'

'Electrified, I presume,' Wynwood said.

'Nope,' Docherty told him.

'Christ, they're making it easy for us.'

Docherty shrugged. 'Not many people break into prisons,' he said.

'I suppose not,' Wynwood muttered. 'What's our best estimate of enemy strength?'

'We don't really have one,' Docherty admitted. 'There's no way of seeing right into the compound, and however many people there are in there, they never seem to leave. Carmen watched the place for two days. She saw four officers visit, but nobody else went in or out.'

'Sounds like a social club,' Wynwood commented.

'It is one.'

'Sounds like a brothel,' Stoneham observed.

'It's that too,' Docherty said, 'only I don't think the women are getting paid. One of them's Carmen's sister, by the way.'

'Ah,' Wynwood said. That hadn't been in the briefing.

'That's why she's here,' Docherty explained. 'What are your orders about the women? What are the rules of engagement, come to that?'

Wynwood smiled. 'I don't think there are any.' He looked at Shepreth. 'But MI6 is supposed to be taking out Comrade Bazua.'

'Are they indeed?' Docherty asked.

'If possible,' Shepreth said curtly. 'The records are more important. Without them, Bazua's days will be numbered in any case.'

'And the women?' Docherty asked again.

'We'll take 'em with us if we can,' Wynwood said. 'If there's twenty of them, they won't all fit in the boat.'

'Carmen will have to come in with us,' Shepreth said. 'She'll be able to reassure the other women, and we may need help from them.'

Wynwood grimaced. 'Makes sense,' he agreed.

187

'You were complaining that it sounded too easy,' Docherty reminded him.

Next morning Wynwood and Stoneham walked down to the dock in Aguadulce and took their time picking out a boat for hire. Since it was the low season the choice wasn't great, but there was one sturdy-looking eight-metre boat which looked more than adequate. It was fitted out for deep-sea fishing and reminded Wynwood of Humphrey Bogart's boat in *To Have and Have Not*. Now all he had to do was train Stoneham to walk like Walter Brennan and find himself a Lauren Bacall.

Not that he needed one. For a few seconds he let Sarah swim round his mind, and could hardly believe how much he missed her.

Stoneham, meanwhile, was negotiating with the boat's owner, an English-speaking West Indian sporting a Boston Red Sox baseball cap. He was initially reluctant to let them have the boat without a chaperone, but once Wynwood had demonstrated that he could handle the boat, knew what a reef was and was prepared to pay twice what the boat was worth for a week's hire, the objections seemed to melt away. 'But no drugs!' was his parting shot. 'Just girls,' Wynwood agreed. 'And a small arsenal,' Stoneham added under his breath.

They spent the morning circling the island at a leisurely pace, getting used to the boat and stopping on two occasions to make use of the snorkelling equipment they had also hired. It was the second time in a year that Wynwood had enjoyed the beauties of the reef – in the previous autumn he had honeymooned on the similarly named island of Providenciales in the Turks and Caicos Islands, where his old SAS comrade Worrell Franklin ran a clinic with his Gambian wife.

Soon after two they passed the target's dock for the second time, and as on the previous occasion there were two men on guard. This time they were both smoking, and Wynwood was sure he could detect the smell of marijuana across the water. The dope was probably a first line of defence against the Latino pop which was pouring from their boom box, but if things got really bad they could always shoot themselves with the Uzis that were leaning against one of the concrete capstans.

Half an hour later the two SAS men docked the boat at Santa Isabel and washed down a delicious lunch of fresh lobsters with tolerable local beer. Stoneham leaned back in his chair, belched and announced that a soldier's life was sometimes hard to bear.

Wynwood was glad his companion had cheered up – on the flight from RAF Brize Norton he had seemed almost suicidal.

They got back to the boat with about three hours of daylight remaining, and Wynwood steered them away from the island on a north-north-west heading. An hour and a half later they reached the prearranged spot. Stoneham decided to try his hand with a fishing rod, something he had never tried before, and after a while he realized why. Wynwood collected a beer from their cooler and watched the sun going down over the empty sea, thinking about Sarah and how lucky he was.

'Nice place,' Bonnie McCall said, surveying the activity on Avenida Colombia. He and Blackie Blackman were sitting on the wall between the beach and the road, watching the ebb and flow of San Andrés Town's night-life. The other side of the Avenida was lined with busy hotels, and the smell of frying fish made Blackie feel almost nostalgic for Blackpool.

'Pity we can't make the most of it,' he said, as their eyes swivelled to follow two nubile locals. One of the girls said something in Spanish, the other glanced over her shoulder, and both giggled.

'We promised the boss we'd be good,' Bonnie said in a tone of mock anguish.

Neither man said anything for a couple of minutes; they just sat there listening to the swish of the waves behind them and the confused rhythms of competing discos further up the road.

'It's all a bit unreal, isn't it?' Blackie said after a while.

'Yeah. I was just thinking that I should have told my folks we were off on a jaunt. I didn't want them to worry, but if I don't beat the clock they're going to get a hell of a shock.'

'Nah,' Bonnie said. 'What's the point of worrying them and *then* giving them a shock?'

'Yeah, maybe.'

'Yeah, well. So should we have another pint, do you think?'

Blackie shook his head. 'No, let's be really good. I've got a feeling we may be needing all our brain cells tomorrow.'

It was two minutes to eight when Wynwood heard the plane in the distance, and soon he could see it – a growing black speck in the star-filled sky to the north. It was a Cessna of the type most frequently used by drug smugglers, and had been chosen for that very reason. Why should the American operatives in their AWACS and satellite-tracking rooms take more than a passing interest in a smuggler's plane heading south *towards* Colombia?

The Cessna was almost overhead now, and first one, then a second, parachute appeared, pale white in the moonlight, drifting slowly down. The first of the crates hit the water with a mute splash some two hundred metres away, the second moments later not half that distance from the boat. Stoneham engaged the engine and began chugging towards it.

A few minutes later both crates had been manhandled on to the deck. The two men disengaged the parachute lines, knotted the material around rocks Wynwood had collected for that purpose on the beach at Santa Isabel, and threw them overboard. They then turned their attention to the crates' contents. Inside the first, tightly wrapped in waterproof oilskin sacks, were six Heckler & Koch MP5SD silenced sub-machine-guns and a supply of C3 plastic explosive with detonators, fuses and electronic timing devices. Inside the other, similarly wrapped, were six Browning High Power 9mm pistols, two PRC 319 satellite radios, six Davies CT100 microphone/receiver sets, six lightweight Bristol Type 18 armoured jackets, six pairs of Passive Night Goggles (PNGs), one nightscope, a dozen stun grenades and a flotation bladder with a small bottle of carbon dioxide.

'Where's the Chieftain tank?' Stoneham asked.

'They always forget something,' Wynwood muttered. 'You start sorting this lot out while I get us headed in the right direction.'

Stoneham unwrapped everything and started sorting it into two piles. In one he placed two of the MP5s, handguns, CT100 sets, armoured jackets, half the explosives and one of the PRC 319s. This pile was then carefully rewrapped in the waterproof oilskins and attached to the flotation bladder. He then turned to the other pile, packing everything but the PRC 319 into the bergen backpacks which had previously held their clothes and personal effects. That done, he took over the helm, leaving Wynwood free to align the satellite radio's antennae and type the single word 'received' on the miniature keyboard. A little while later he received an equally terse reply from Grand Cayman, nearly six hundred kilometres to the north: 'acknowledged'.

191

For the next hour they sat mostly in silence, watching the hump-shaped island slowly loom larger. There were a few clouds in the western sky now, but the almost full moon hung suspended among the stars to the east. Passing the scattered lights of Santa Isabel and Pueblo Viejo to port, they moved in towards the island's western coastline a kilometre or so to the north of the target's dock. A torch blinked twice on the rocky shore, and for a moment Wynwood found himself wondering how many boats had surreptitiously edged their way in towards Caribbean shores over the past five hundred years.

Docherty and Shepreth, both knee deep in the gentle swell, took charge of the loaded bergens and vanished back into the darkness as Stoneham headed the boat back out towards the open sea. After drawing a wide semicircle around Bazua's dock he headed the boat in towards another cove that they had scouted earlier that day. This one was surrounded by mangroves, and after inflating the flotation bladder with carbon dioxide Wynwood clambered down into the water and attached it to a convenient root. The buoyancy had been calculated just right for the weight, holding the bundle a foot or so beneath the surface.

He climbed wearily back on board and Stoneham headed down the coast to Aguadulce, where, to his surprise, the boat's owner seemed to be waiting for them. As they pulled in to the dock he walked to and fro, apparently checking the boat for signs of major damage. Finding none, he seemed reassured. 'Catch anything?' he asked, as Wynwood leapt out to tie her up.

'Threw 'em back,' the Welshman replied.

By this time Docherty and Shepreth had reached the hiding-place on the hill. They had felt exposed walking down the road, but only two cars had passed them, both driven by local West Indians. The second had stopped to offer them a lift, exhaling ganja fumes through his wide smile.

Docherty had dug the scrape earlier that day, so now all they needed to do was drop in the bergens and cover everything with the already made roof of cut branches and large leaves. 'You go first,' he told Shepreth when they were done. The MI6 man nodded and slipped off through the trees. He had a knack of moving quietly, the Scot thought.

The slight sounds faded away, leaving only the breeze in the foliage above, the occasional chirp of a night bird, and the sound of his own heart. Way above him the upper branches of the trees were swathed in the light of the moon.

He squatted on his haunches, remembering the desert mountains of Oman, the bare hills of southern Argentina, the snow-filled valleys of central Bosnia. What a life, he thought. He wouldn't have swapped it for the world.

On the other side of the island Carmen was sitting at her favourite table outside the Dutch Inn, staring out at the darkened sea. She knew what was supposed to be happening that evening, and she had tried to picture the different scenes in her mind, but her subconscious kept pushing her forward twenty-four hours to the moment of truth.

She had resisted being left out, but now, in the privacy of her own thoughts, she could admit how terrified she was. In Cartagena it had all seemed like a game, but now it all seemed real again, and she was worried that she might let Shepreth and Docherty down.

She should do something to take her mind off it, she thought. But what? She was hardly in the mood for dancing, and going for a walk at night seemed like asking for trouble.

She could always go to bed, but she knew that her chances of getting to sleep were slim. Tomorrow was probably going to be the most exciting day of her life – she would either rescue her sister or end up sharing her prison.

The idea made her shiver.

She thought about the Englishmen. They seemed confident enough, but for all she knew they were hopelessly outmatched. Bazua would hardly have lasted as long as he had if he'd been a pushover.

12

Blackie and Bonnie came over on the early-afternoon shuttle from San Andrés, took a pick-up around the island to Aguadulce and spent an idle half-hour lounging in the bar of the Hotel Princesa. At three o'clock Wynwood passed through the bar, but made no attempt to talk to them – the sign that everything was still going according to plan. A few minutes later the two young men walked back outside, where they shook hands and parted like recent acquaintances. Blackie walked down the beach towards the dock, leaving Bonnie waiting by the side of the road for a pick-up going north.

The Glaswegian had to wait only ten minutes, and the journey up to Puerto Viejo took less than that. He walked down the dirt track to what the guidebook claimed was the island's cheapest hotel, paid for a room, dumped his bag and went out again, walking north around the rim of Santa Catalina Bay to Santa Isabel, where he ate an early lobster supper at the same restaurant Wynwood and Stoneham had used the day before.

After watching the sun sink into the bay over a couple of Cokes he started walking slowly back to his hotel, reaching it just before eight. He took a vigorous shower, laid himself out on the bed of his spartan room and stared at the patterns of peeling paint on the ceiling. At £2.50 a night the place was a steal.

At ten he turned the light off, waited a few minutes, then slipped out of the door. There was music spilling out of an open doorway across the yard, and a couple on a bench above the beach seemed to have their tongues in a knot, but no one looked his way as he turned the corner of the building and hurried up the dirt track to the main road. There was a light on in the two-storey shop at the intersection but it went out as he approached.

He took the road south, still walking briskly. The moon was rising in the east, and for a while he could see its light scattered across the sea to his right, but then the road cut inland, running almost like a tunnel through the tropical woodland. He walked on, trying to calculate the distance. The path was supposed to be slightly over a kilometre from the shop, and just as he began to think that he must have walked that far, there it was, winding up alongside the stream into the darkness of the forest. He took the prescribed fifty paces and gave a faint whistle.

There was an answering whistle, and a few moments later Wynwood emerged out of the darkness. The Welshman was already kitted up, his face beneath the PNGs artistically streaked with camouflage cream, a CT100 unit fastened to his collar, an MP5SD cradled in his arms. He gave Bonnie a pair of PNGs and gestured him to follow, and for the next few minutes they threaded their way along an invisible path through the dense foliage. Several times Bonnie felt the brush of unknown entities on his face and offered up several silent prayers to the effect that any poisonous spiders or snakes on the island had already been endangered out of existence.

There was another faint whistle from Wynwood, an echo up ahead, and in the green glow of the PNGs Bonnie could see three other figures sitting on the forest floor. One was a wiry-looking, short-haired man with a half-amused expression on his face, the second a taller man of not much more than Bonnie's own age, the third . . . was a woman. Like everyone else she had darkened her face with make-up, but unlike the others she wasn't wearing body armour.

'Get kitted up,' Wynwood told him.

'Yes, boss,' Bonnie said, and did as he was told, wondering who the woman was. By the time he had finished there were still nearly two hours of boredom to enjoy before they moved off down the hill.

Stoneham had casually picked up Blackie from his dockside vantage-point soon after four, introduced him to the boat's owner as a fellow-Brit that he'd just met, and offered him a few hours of fishing. Blackie had been suitably thrilled, and, pantomime over, they had taken the boat a couple of miles offshore, where they watched the sun go down and argued over whether Sheringham or Fowler should be partnering Shearer in England's attack in the '98 World Cup.

Once the sun had gone down they moved lazily north, heading in to shore to collect the weapons bag from among the mangrove roots. They then rode at anchor for a while, as Stoneham put together several explosive devices.

By ten-thirty they were off Aguadulce again, eating sandwiches and taking turns observing the small military post through the nightscope. As on the two preceding nights, there was virtually no visible activity – just a single uniformed sentry sitting in an upright chair at the landward end of the protruding dock and one window showing light in the command building.

There was no sign of anyone aboard the patrol boat which was tied up on one side of the jetty.

At eleven-forty the light went out, and at midnight the sentry was relieved. His replacement walked down to the end of the dock and back before settling into the already warmed seat.

Two minutes later Blackie lowered himself over the side of the boat and began swimming towards the shore, the waterproof pouches containing the two bombs strapped across his chest. The water was warm, he was a good swimmer and as far as he could tell there weren't any sharks closing in for the kill.

As he approached the jetty the patrol boat came between him and the sentry's line of sight. He worked his way round to the stern, where he fastened the first of the two explosive devices to the rudder-propeller assembly which lay just beneath the surface. He then carefully inched through the water to a position beneath the landward end of the dock and looked at his watch. There were two minutes to wait. He hung there in the water, one arm wrapped around a jetty support.

Stoneham started the engine right on cue, and there was an almost imperceptible rise in the decibel level as he brought it in towards the dock. The sentry heard the boat too, if he hadn't already noticed it with his eyes. There was a scraping sound as he got up from his chair, and then the creak of boots on wooden boards. He yelled something in Spanish – something along the lines of 'You can't dock here, you fucking idiot!' – and there was an obsequious reply from Stoneham, requesting further directions. Blackie pulled himself out of the water and on to the jetty. Twenty metres to his right the sentry was standing there gesticulating, his back turned toward the base. Blackie took the five steps necessary to get him through the gate and sank to his haunches. He could hardly believe that something so obvious could have worked, and he felt grateful that he hadn't had to cut the sentry's throat. Or at least not yet.

The compound seemed deserted. It was even less well lit than the dock, with three of the four floodlights either off or broken, and two bare light bulbs shining forlornly above the doors to the two main buildings. Behind him the conversation was still going on, the sentry sounding increasingly exasperated with this stupid gringo God had pushed in his direction.

Blackie moved towards the helicopter pad, checking the fence to his right for possible ways out. He found several. Over the years the sea had eaten away at the foundation and in several places the bottom of the fence simply lifted like a flap. It looked like the sentry was going to see another dawn.

After securing the second explosive to the underside of the helicopter's nose cone, Blackie scuttled back to the fence and slipped underneath it. The rocks below were slippery, but the sentry was still standing with his back to the shore, watching Stoneham turn the boat around. Blackie slid into the water and began swimming after it. Five minutes later he was clambering over the side.

They headed out to sea, not turning north until they were some three kilometres from land and the lights of Aguadulce were strung like a necklace beneath the silhouette of the hills beyond. Almost immediately they turned back towards the shore, and soon after twelve-thirty they were lying about two hundred metres off the coast and about twice that distance south of the target dock. The two boats earmarked for Bazua's Falklands invasion were drifting at anchor some fifty metres offshore.

They were now within CT100 range of the others.

'The charges are set,' Stoneham reported to Wynwood, and as he said the words his ears picked up the sound of a plane. 'What the fuck?' he murmured to himself – there were no night flights to or from the island.

'It's up there,' Blackie told him, pointing. 'It's a big plane, an airliner.'

'It's a Caravelle,' Stoneham said, half to himself and half to Wynwood. 'It's coming in to land at the airport.'

'That explains it,' Shepreth whispered to the others.

Fifteen minutes earlier four men had emerged from the house below, clambered into the Cadillac which one of them had collected from the garage and disappeared in the direction of Santa Isabel. None of the departees had been in uniform, which seemed to suggest they were Bazua's men.

'The Caravelle must be *en route* from Colombia to Mexico,' Shepreth went on. 'Probably with about five million dollars' worth of heroin on board. Bazua's boys will be making sure nothing leaves the plane while it's refuelling.'

'Sounds reasonable,' Wynwood murmured. He did some mental arithmetic. It would take them ten to fifteen minutes to reach the airport, the same to get back, and the jet would probably be on the ground for at least half an hour. Say an hour in total. The poor bastards were going to miss the party.

He took a quick glance at the others, all of whom looked as tense as he felt, and gave the signal for go.

They worked their way back to the path and descended it in single file. A car went by on the road below, its headlights flaring green through the PNGs and the noise of its engine slowly fading to the north, leaving them with only the sounds of the breeze and the burbling stream.

Reaching the moonlit strip of road, they broke into a steady trot, ears and eyes alert for the sound of traffic, ready to dive back into the shadows of the trees. A hundred metres later they turned off, clambering across the crumbling wall of the property next door to their target. The large house that loomed away to their right was in no better shape than the wall, but would doubtless make some developer a fortune in the future.

It was Docherty who had scouted this route and he was in the lead now, working his way through the overgrown garden and adjacent woodland to the fence which surrounded Bazua's luxury prison. As Bonnie went to work with the wire-cutters, the others squatted down to wait. By Wynwood's watch it was twelve forty-eight.

The seconds ticked by, punctuated by the click of the cutters. Shepreth shared a nervous smile with Carmen, and resisted the temptation to reopen the earlier argument about the body armour. She was right – provided she kept out of the way as she'd promised, he would be the one who needed it.

Carmen was grateful for the smile. She felt scared, and would have been more so if it hadn't all seemed so unreal. Here she was squatting by a wire fence in the middle of the night with a bunch of gringos, her face covered with gunk, a gun tucked under her belt. She had never fired one in her life.

The click of the wire-cutters had stopped. Bonnie lifted the flap and beckoned to the others.

Wynwood examined his watch again. 'We're going through the fence,' he said softly into the microphone.

'Acknowledged,' Stoneham murmured in all their earpieces.

'Remember,' Wynwood reminded the others. 'Don't speak any English if you can help it.'

They squirmed through the hole one by one and headed on through the forest, Wynwood in the lead, followed by Bonnie, Docherty, Shepreth and finally Carmen. In the distance a thin wash of green light seemed to be filtering through the trees, but it was impossible to tell whether it was man-made or a trick of the moon.

They had only about two hundred metres to travel, but it seemed a long time before the first rectangular shadow appeared in front of them. This was the northernmost of the two specially constructed buildings which extended in a westerly direction behind the main house, on either side of the swimming pool. There were only a few narrow windows visible, and none of these showed any illumination, but a faint green glow above the roof suggested a light source in the open courtyard beyond.

It was now twelve fifty-seven. The column split into two groups, with Wynwood and Bonnie moving to the left and the others to the right, heading for opposite ends of the building in front of them.

The threesome didn't have so far to go. Docherty took off his PNGs and inched an eye round the first corner. There was no one visible, and no light from the end window, which they were hoping was the one that Victoria Marín had seen filled by the moon. The only other east-facing window was in the building on the other side of the pool, and the satellite photos had shown a basketball hoop on that end wall.

It was twelve fifty-eight. Shepreth had ushered Carmen into the nearby trees, and was now employing the same hopeful gestures dog owners use when trying to persuade their animals to stay. Docherty advanced along the end wall and put an eye round the next corner.

To his left a faint yellow glow filled the distant doorway to the main house, but no lights showed in any of the windows.

202

During their various stints on watch over the past week Carmen and Docherty had never seen any signs of life in this part of the compound, and the current plan of attack was based on the assumption that it was unoccupied.

The two buildings on the other side of the swimming pool were definitely in use, and thin lines of brightness around the central windows and doors of one indicated that the communications room was still operational. Both the room to its right and the small building to its left – which they had guessed contained a back-up generator – were in darkness.

There were no outside lights burning, but the pool's underwater lights were on, casting a shimmering blue glow over the whole courtyard.

A dull thump sounded in the far distance, then another. If he hadn't known better Docherty would have assumed there was a fireworks party in Aguadulce. His watch told him it was exactly one o'clock.

As Shepreth appeared at his shoulder, Wynwood and Bonnie came into view away to the left, carefully skirting the back of the villa. The young Glaswegian took up a position from which he could cover both the gate through to the interior courtyard and the doors facing the communications room. Wynwood was about twenty metres away from the latter when its door suddenly swung open and a man strode out. He saw the SAS man coming towards him, took in the gun and camouflaged face, and opened his mouth, either as a prelude to shouting or simply to gape with surprise. Wynwood's MP5 spat fire, throwing the man back, and there was the sound of something breaking in the room behind him.

Docherty had already started forwards along the front of the other building, and as the first *sicario* went down he opened the first door and tossed in the stun grenade, then pulled it

203

shut once more. The thunderclap seemed to rattle the window, and a line of light flashed in the gap beneath the door. He stepped quickly in across the threshold and dropped to one knee, MP5 at the ready, but it took only a second for his senses to conclude that the room was empty.

'Shit,' he murmured. So much for moons in the window.

On the other side of the swimming pool Wynwood had reached the communications room door at a run, which was just as well, as another of Bazua's men was halfway to his feet, gun in hand. Wynwood put a triple tap through his upper trunk, spinning him back and round across the chair he'd been sitting in. Man and chair collapsed in a heap, taking the floor fan with them. This ended up on the dead man's face, whirring at the ceiling.

Wynwood's eyes scoured the room. There was a sophisticated array of radio equipment, plus the usual telephone and fax, but there was no sign of any records – no computer, no filing cabinets, no leather briefcase with the words 'Dirty War' embossed in gold.

Docherty and Shepreth were only a few metres from the next door when it burst open, disgorging two men, both dressed only in shorts. As one fired his Uzi from the hip in the general direction of the communications room the other took off at a run for the far end of the swimming pool. Bonnie ducked back inside the doorway, which gave Docherty a safe shot at the man with the Uzi, whose body was propelled forward into the pool, where its impact on the water made a resounding splash and caused shivers of blue light to dance wildly over all the walls.

The other man was past the end of the pool now, and had almost reached the shelter of the main villa, when Bonnie cut him down. The Colombian's gun seemed to keep firing as it cartwheeled out of his hand and glass cascaded down from broken windows in the main house.

Four down, Docherty thought, but where the fuck was Bazua?

The sound of running feet made him spin round, just as the two guards from the dock emerged out of the trees to his right. Shepreth opened up first, and one man went down, but the other turned tail and ran, spraying bullets behind him as SAS fire zipped through the foliage to either side.

It was like a shooting gallery, Docherty thought. But where were the fucking prizes?

There were more doors to open – the one leading into the room with the basketball hoop outside, which Wynwood was now moving towards, and the last two on this side of the pool. The first of these, the one from which the two *sicarios* had burst, opened into a dormitory of sorts, with several beds, posters of naked women with their legs invitingly spread, a large TV. There was even a pool table, but Bazua wasn't cowering underneath it.

For Carmen, the last couple of minutes had been endless. She had heard gunfire, explosions, a splash, breaking glass, and for all she knew her English allies had all been killed by Bazua's men. Her mind told her this was unlikely and that she should stay where she was, but apparently neither her heart nor her feet agreed, because a couple of seconds later she found herself tentatively extending her head round the corner of the building.

She gasped at the scene in front of her, the bodies littering the courtyard, another floating in the pool. But none of them, she realized with a leap of her heart, were dressed like the Englishmen. Two of these were walking along the far side of the pool, and as she turned her head Docherty and Shepreth emerged from a door further down the near side. They were alive . . .

And then she saw the door open in the far corner, the figure in silhouette, head looking this way and that, gun in hand.

'*Atención*,' she screamed.

Docherty spun round, saw her standing there and followed the direction of her outstretched arm. The door which they had assumed led only to the back-up generator was open, and there was a flicker of shadow on the inner wall as someone disappeared inside.

'I'll take it,' Docherty yelled in Spanish, forgetting he was wearing a microphone and almost deafening the others. 'You take the last room,' he yelled over his shoulder at Shepreth, and didn't bother to wait for the MI6 man's agreement. Skirting the end of the swimming pool at a run, he almost skidded to a halt by the side of the open doorway. A quick glance inside revealed both the expected generator and a flight of steps leading down into the bowels of the earth.

He started down the steps, forcing himself to take it slowly and carefully. At the bottom of the steps corridors ran off to both left and right, and he took the former, which led directly into a luxurious suite of rooms.

Docherty took them one by one, rerunning the old 'Killing House' training like a mental video, refusing to let impatience and his strong intuition that the rooms were empty lead him into a fatal mistake. The largest room boasted a huge round bed and not much else. Another good-sized room contained two tan leather sofas, a TV and a sound system; a third served as a small office. There was a swish-looking bathroom and toilet. At the corridor's end there was a room containing six bunk-beds.

They were all empty.

And then the sound of a distant shot echoed in the enclosed space.

Moments after hearing their bombs go off in the Aguadulce military post three kilometres to the south, Stoneham and Blackie had slipped into the shallow water and started towards the dock. On the way they heard the Uzi bursts, and were not surprised to find that the guards had abandoned their position. 'We're on the path,' Stoneham told Wynwood, just as another burst of automatic fire split the night.

'One headed your way, Terry,' Wynwood said in his ear.

The two SAS men headed carefully up the dark path, counting on the PNGs to give them the edge.

They had been walking only a few seconds when they heard the man coming towards them, and a few moments later they could see him. Both men stepped behind convenient trees, and Stoneham spent several valuable seconds trying but failing to remember the Spanish for 'stop'.

'Stop, you bastard,' he screamed in English, but the Colombian's only answer was to tighten his finger on the Uzi's trigger and keep running, presumably in the hope that the spray of bullets would act like a shield. It didn't. The two MP5s almost cut him in half at the chest, his mouth gushed blood, and he was dead before he hit the ground.

'One down,' Stoneham reported in.

'Come on in,' Wynwood told him. He and Bonnie had just checked the remaining room, which had turned out to be the prison armoury, containing, in Wynwood's rough estimation, well over a million pounds' worth of brand-new weapons and equipment.

* * *

In the basement Docherty regained the bottom of the steps in time to greet the descending Shepreth and Carmen.

'Look after her,' Docherty told the MI6 man curtly, without pausing in his stride. The corridor ran straight ahead of him into the distance, and he guessed with a sinking heart that it had been designed as an escape route. Forty metres later he reached another flight of steps, and realized that he'd been right. As he started ascending, a car's engine burst into life, and he knew that Bazua was gone.

The steps emerged into the garage, and as he ran out through the open door headlights swept past the gates and on to the road. He heard the others coming up the stairs and turned, and it was then that he saw the woman's body. She had on only a T-shirt, and her face had been all but destroyed by the bullet. She'd broken free of Bazua's grasp, Docherty guessed, and the bastard had just shot her in the back of the head. 'The fucker's escaped,' he said into the microphone, disgust in his voice.

He looked up to see Carmen falter in her stride, the guilty relief in her eyes as she realized it wasn't her sister.

'It's Irma,' she said, as if she was talking to herself.

Docherty looked at his watch. Six minutes had passed since the bombs had gone off in the Aguadulce military post, and they couldn't count on many more before the local authorities put in an appearance.

Carmen had other ideas. 'We can go after him,' she said, pointing to the other car standing there.

'No we can't,' Docherty told her, and she looked as though she'd been slapped.

'But . . .'

'He's heading for the airport,' Docherty said, remembering which way the car had turned outside the gate. 'Even if we could catch him there's no way we could get off the island, not now. The locals are probably on their way already.'

'He's right,' Shepreth agreed.

The look on Carmen's face clawed at Docherty's heart. 'We'll get the bastard,' he told her. 'It just won't be today.' He didn't add that Bazua might well dump the other two women the first chance he got.

'You promise you'll carry on?' she asked fiercely, gazing from one face to the other as if determined to catch them in a lie.

'Aye,' Docherty said, looking her straight in the eye. 'Now let's get going.'

They retraced their path down the tunnel and as Shepreth searched through the small office Carmen wandered round the room with the bunk-beds, staring at the various pieces of women's clothing, the magazines, the cosmetics by the mirror. She looked about fifteen, Docherty thought.

'Only two beds have been slept in,' she said suddenly.

She was right. He put an arm round her shoulder, meaning to pull her gently away, and at that moment his eyes caught sight of the painting on the wall in the main bedroom. A Spanish woman was sitting at an open stone window, and the space itself was filled by the moon.

'That means there were only two women here,' Carmen said, a hint of hysteria in her voice.

'Maybe,' Docherty agreed. 'Or maybe one was with Bazua,' he added gently.

She gave him a look that was half hope, half heartbreak.

'There's nothing here,' Shepreth said behind them. 'He must have taken the records with him.'

'Then let's go,' Docherty said, propelling Carmen towards the corridor and steps.

'Victoria told me he was like a worm that burrowed,' she said, 'but I just thought she was talking about sex. If I had . . .'

'Forget about ifs,' he told her. 'They're only there to keep us humble,' he murmured.

In the compound outside Bonnie was keeping watch while Wynwood placed the charges in the armoury. The body in the pool was floating happily on its back. Another day of the dead, Docherty thought.

Wynwood emerged a few moments later, having lit the five-minute fuses. 'There's enough weapons to mount another Falklands invasion in there,' he told Docherty. 'But no luck with the records,' he guessed, noticing that both Shepreth and the Scot were empty-handed. He shrugged. 'Well, let's get the fuck out of here. Terry and Blackie are planting the charges on the boats.'

It was twelve minutes past one.

They headed up the path in single file, with Docherty bringing up the rear. He was just thinking that the five minutes must be up when he heard a tooting horn from the direction of the villa – the local military had arrived at the gates and were demanding entry. There was another toot, longer this time, and then, as if in response, a yellow flash lit the sky. It was instantly followed by the sharp rip of the first explosion. That was the communications room, Docherty guessed, and the fuller-throated roar of the next detonation proved him right.

They reached the dock just as Stoneham and Blackie returned from fixing their charges, and with all seven of them on board Wynwood headed the boat north at its maximum speed of about fifteen knots. If the commandant of the military post in Aguadulce had instantly asked his superiors on San Andrés for help a helicopter could be arriving at any minute, but Wynwood wasn't expecting any such quickness of thought or independence of action. The commandant wouldn't have wanted to involve outsiders without clearing it with his real boss, but he would only now be discovering that Bazua had flown the coop, and it would take him a few minutes to realize that he had been left in an impossible position. At that point he might cut his losses and ring either San Andrés or the mainland.

If he did, Wynwood reckoned, they had about fifteen minutes in which to lose themselves on the open sea before a search got underway.

They had travelled about a kilometre when the first charge went off behind them. Wynwood looked back to see the second jagged flash erupt against the dark background of the coastline, and then a third, a fourth, a fifth, a sixth. Stoneham and Blackie had done a thorough job on Bazua's navy.

He looked round at the others. There were grins of relief on the two younger men's faces, but on Stoneham's and Docherty's he saw a reflection of his own sombre realization that their mission had been a partial failure. Then he told himself that meant it had also been a partial success. They had destroyed the bastard's boats and his weapons stash, they had driven him out of his safe haven, at least for the moment, and all without suffering a single casualty, which had to be worth something. Bazua would find it hard to replace what he'd lost. Acquiring new and sophisticated military equipment was never simple, even when money was no object, and governments willing to let drug barons run their organizations from prison were, mercifully, thin on the ground. No doubt the man had friends in Mexico, but they wouldn't be as powerful as the ones he'd made in Colombia. And next time he might not be so lucky.

But it wouldn't be the SAS who got the bastard. And Wynwood couldn't help finding that hugely disappointing.

A few metres behind him, sitting in the boat's stern, Docherty's thoughts had been moving in much the same direction. His script, though, had a different ending – even without the promise to Carmen he would probably still have considered Bazua unfinished business, and with it there was no room for doubt.

He looked round for her, and saw that her head was cradled in Shepreth's shoulder.

'Boss,' Blackie said suddenly, and everyone turned to follow the direction in which he was pointing, certain that the Colombian military was in hot pursuit.

They had forgotten the Caravelle, which was climbing into the sky above the diminishing hump of Providencia. It seemed to pass directly over their heads before veering away in the general direction of Mexico.

'Where's a terrorist bomb when you need one?' Bonnie asked no one in particular, as the Caravelle vanished among the stars.

Shepreth walked forward to talk to Wynwood. 'I need to let some people know about that plane,' he said.

'People where?' the Welshman asked him. 'We've only got Grand Cayman listening in.'

'They can pass the message.'

'OK. Terry, take the helm, will you.'

Stoneham obliged, and Wynwood set up the PRC 319 on the cabin roof, typing in the message as Shepreth dictated.

By the time he'd finished they were more than halfway out of Colombian waters, and as the remaining kilometres slipped by the eyes of the team were more or less permanently focused on the southern horizon. Even though an attack from the air seemed unlikely, a fast patrol boat could still try to take them into custody.

But neither aircraft nor boat loomed in the south, and Stoneham had no sooner announced that they were in international waters than a moving speck appeared in the northern sky. As this swiftly grew into the expected Mk 3 Sea King they made ready to leave the boat. The pilot hovered overhead as the rope ladder was lowered, and one by one they clambered up it, leaving the empty craft bobbing happily on the swell below. As the pilot turned the helicopter back towards the north another member of the crew poured mugs of tea from a giant Thermos.

13

The day had dawned a dull grey in London, and it had been raining on and off ever since. The perfect weather for his mood, Sir Christopher Hanson thought, as he threaded his way through the maze behind Whitehall in the direction of the Prime Minister's back door. He had been up all night anxiously waiting for news from the Caribbean, and still hadn't shaken the feeling of disappointment which had eventually accompanied it.

Of course the night hadn't been a dead loss – there had been achievements too, and it was these which he planned on stressing in his report to the PM. Hanson thought about opening with 'Well, there's good news and there's bad news – which would you like first?', but he knew that all he'd get from his audience would be a stony look. It was hard to believe these days, but the man had possessed a sense of humour when he came into office.

It was only seven a.m. but the PM was already at work in his private den. He gestured Hanson to a chair and pushed aside whatever he was working on with ill-concealed irritation. The MI6 chief found himself wondering whether a Labour government really would make his life more difficult, as all his subordinates expected.

'They're back on Grand Cayman,' he said, sitting down. 'No casualties.'

The PM looked confused for a moment, then comprehension dawned. 'Good,' he said. 'And the Argentinian?'

'He escaped,' Hanson said flatly. 'Probably to Mexico.'

The PM grimaced.

'But they destroyed his base, his ships and his armoury,' Hanson went on, exaggerating only slightly. 'It'll take him a long time to recover.'

The PM didn't look mollified. 'How did he get away?' he asked.

'I'm not sure. There'll be a full debriefing as soon as the men arrive back here. I thought it would be wise to get them away from the . . .'

'The scene of the crime,' the PM suggested drily. 'Yes, you're probably right.'

'I do know that an illegal flight landed on the island in the middle of their operation, which was something that no one could have foreseen.'

The PM scratched his forehead. 'I don't suppose they got their hands on the military records?' he asked.

'I'm afraid not. He must have taken them with him.'

'If they exist. So we've got nothing to show the Americans?'

'No,' Hanson admitted. 'But I'm told the team didn't leave any fingerprints behind them, so we could at least try feigning ignorance. Just play dumb, as the Americans would say.'

The PM made a scornful-sounding noise. 'They may not have left any fingerprints but I'll bet the sky was lit up for miles around. And what are the chances the Americans didn't track the helicopter back to the Caymans?'

'Smugglers use the Caymans. And we may have been lucky – the Yanks aren't omniscient. Maybe just this once

216

their operator didn't notice the blip on the screen.'

'You're grabbing at straws, Christopher,' the PM said. 'I think I'd rather go with your earlier suggestion than simply deny all knowledge. Washington won't believe a word of it, but they might buy the idea that the attack was mounted by a renegade ex-SAS man.'

'There's still the flight to Grand Cayman,' Hanson said. 'This man – I've forgotten his name . . .'

'Docherty.'

'He could have got hold of a helicopter on the black market, couldn't he?'

'Probably, but . . .' Hanson paused. He had spent the last couple of hours thinking about how to pursue Bazua, and had come to the conclusion that in Mexico the only real help he could offer Shepreth was Jamie Docherty. Neither the Americans nor the local authorities could be used for obvious reasons, and the chances of getting the PM to sanction another SAS operation on the North American mainland were non-existent. 'If the worst comes to the worst,' he said, 'then we can throw him to the Americans, but I'm sure you'll agree that the optimal outcome for everybody – remains the elimination of Bazua and the seizure of his records. And I think Docherty can still be useful in that regard. He knows Mexico.'

The PM shook his head, but there was a thin smile on his face. 'And what do we tell the Americans in the meantime?'

'Tell them you don't know what happened but that you're determined to get to the bottom of it. Imply that some of our people may have taken matters into their own hands. He should understand that – his own people are doing it all the time.'

The rap on the door woke Docherty, and there was a moment of disorientation before he remembered where he was. They had landed in a secluded corner of the empty airport soon after five, and a minibus had driven them not much more than a kilometre to the hotel, where he had just about managed to set Isabel's mind at rest, and bless the fact that he was no longer in command of anyone, before collapsing on to the soft bed. Wynwood and Shepreth had no doubt been up for hours, reporting back to their superiors in the UK.

It was Wynwood at the door, and by the look of his red-ringed eyes he hadn't had any sleep.

'What time is it?' Docherty asked between yawns.

'Nearly nine. Yes, I know,' he added in response to Docherty's look of reproach, 'but we're off in about half an hour. Fancy a cup of coffee before we go?'

'Sure,' Docherty said. He had not only come to admire the big Welsh lunk over the past few days – he had grown to like him too.

He reached for his only pair of trousers, thinking that some of his increasingly hard-earned fee from Gustavo Macías would have to be spent on another set of clothes. Downstairs the hotel restaurant was still serving breakfast, but the two men just ordered coffees and took them out to one of the gaily coloured metal tables which sat beneath the palms around the empty pool. As they lowered themselves gingerly into the metal chairs a couple of buses full of tourists swept past on their way to the airport.

'They're not wasting much time bringing you home,' Docherty observed.

'No,' Wynwood agreed. 'The other three are pretty pissed off – they were hoping for at least a couple of days on the beach.'

'But you weren't?'

'I've just got married,' Wynwood said, as if that explained it.

Remembering the first few weeks of his marriage to Isabel, Docherty guessed it did. 'Congratulations,' he said.

Wynwood smiled. 'So what'll you do now?' he asked.

Docherty shrugged. 'God knows. Or Shep does.'

'I wish we could have finished it,' Wynwood said.

'Aye,' Docherty agreed, thinking about Carmen. 'But then think how happy we'd have made the bastard's competitors.'

Wynwood grinned. 'So tell me – is there life after the SAS?'

It was phrased like a joke, but Docherty knew it was a serious question – one he'd asked himself often enough before his retirement. 'Aye, there is. And a family helps. But it's hard at first. I think if you've been doing something long enough, retirement usually is.'

'Yeah,' Wynwood agreed, thinking of his dad, who still got up wanting to go down the pit, even though the nearest working one was now a couple of hundred miles away.

'Any idea what you're going to do when the time comes?' Docherty asked.

'None,' Wynwood replied cheerfully. Over the Scot's shoulder he could see Blackie and Bonnie ogling one of the chambermaids in the foyer, and a few seconds later Stoneham appeared in the doorway. 'The car's here, boss,' he said, walking towards them. 'Good to work with you,' he told Docherty, extending a hand.

'Likewise,' Docherty said, taking it. 'Give my love to Hereford,' he told them both, and a couple of minutes later he watched as their car disappeared in the direction of the airport. They'd sleep all the way home, he thought, and when they got there everything would seem a bit unreal for the next few weeks. They were the SAS – they did things other people thought only happened in films. A picture of the Brecon Beacons filled his mind's eye, and then his old CO's face on that night in the Glasgow pub when he'd asked Docherty to go and look for John Reeve in Bosnia. He could see the Dame lying beside the lorry, the wonder of death in his eyes, and he could hear Razor mixing proverbs in the scrape above the airbase at Rio Gallegos. There was no fool like a friend in need.

He missed it all right. But he wouldn't have given up the life he had now to get it back, even if he could.

It was still only nine-thirty, but he felt wide awake now, and decidedly hungry. The hotel served up the sort of English breakfast which reminded him of his childhood – the holy trinity of bacon, eggs and toast, his dad had used to call it – and which Isabel was reluctant to sanction at home. He was on his second cup of coffee when Carmen appeared in the doorway, eyes blinking in the strong sunlight.

She was also wearing yesterday's fighting clothes, and they didn't look any better on her than his did on him. Her eyes looked more subdued than tired, and they sat in silence for several moments waiting for her coffee to arrive.

When it did she tore open two sachets of sugar and stirred them in. 'I want to say something,' she said without looking up. 'Yesterday . . . when you promised to keep looking – I know that you had to say that or . . .' She looked up. 'I can't hold you to that promise. You have a life of your own to live.'

He smiled. 'Thanks,' he said. 'But if it's at all possible I intend to keep looking. The problem is, I'm just a private citizen these days – I don't have the resources we'll probably need to trace Bazua's movements.'

'I know,' she said with a sigh. 'Neither do I.'

Assistant Secretary of State Calvin Stahoviak had come in to Foggy Bottom that morning expecting nothing more than a chance to catch up on his paperwork. Instead he was listening to a crisis call from John Holzman, the US Ambassador in Bogotá.

'You know people who start spraying you with saliva when they get really mad?' Holzman was asking him. 'Well, Domínguez is one of those. By the time he'd finished I felt like I'd been caught in the rain. But this is serious,' he went on, hearing Stahoviak's grunt of amusement, 'and they really are pissed with us. Their goddam honour has been insulted. At the moment they're just venting, but unless they get some real satisfaction we're in for trouble. Just lodging a protest isn't going to cut it this time.'

'What will?' Stahoviak asked. He was wondering which particular bunch of morons in either Intelligence or the military was responsible for sticking a hornet up Bogotá's backside.

'The sight of heads rolling,' Holzman said. 'And if you want really happy people then mount them on stakes and mail them to the Presidential Palace.'

'Shit,' Stahoviak murmured, more to himself than the ambassador. 'I'll get back to you, John,' he said, and resumed eating the chocolate croissant he had picked up *en route* from home. The accompanying frappuccino had seemed like a good idea on the sweltering street, but in the chronically over-air-conditioned State Department offices it almost made him shiver.

He sipped at it nevertheless, wondering how the Colombians might express their anger. There were the old diplomatic stand-bys of course, like rabble-rousing among the other Latin American countries at the OAS or the UN, but with Colombia there was also the added problem of never knowing quite who you were dealing with. Official government, cartels, guerrillas – they all seemed willing to help each other out when it came to sticking knives in poor old Uncle Sam.

He finished the croissant, reached for the phone, and spent the next hour tracking down the guilty party, only to find that it was the fucking Brits.

Stahoviak felt almost as intrigued as angered by this piece of information. What in God's name did they think they were doing shooting up islands in America's backyard? 'Are you one hundred per cent certain?' he asked his source at the Customs Service.

'Yep. Our AWACS tracked their chopper from the Caymans to a point just north of Providencia – consistent with a pick-up from a boat – and then back again.'

'So what did they want on Providencia?'

'Probably Angel Bazua.' The Customs man explained who Bazua was, and why the British in particular had a grudge against him.

'Did they get him?' Stahoviak asked.

'No idea. But the AWACS tracked another flight – a large jet this time – which left Providencia for northern Mexico at around the same time. Bazua could have been on that.'

'OK, thanks,' Stahoviak said, and hung up. The Brits might have a good reason for running amok on Providencia, but that was neither here nor there. This was American turf, and they didn't get to play on it without an invitation. Someone would have to do some tough talking, and it might as well be the President.

He asked his secretary to connect him to the White House.

Carmen and Docherty were still sitting in the chairs by the pool when Shepreth found them. From the look of suppressed excitement on the younger man's face, the Scot guessed it was good news. Maybe Bazua's plane had crashed.

'We're still on the case,' Shepreth said.

'We?' Docherty asked.

'Ah,' Shepreth said, smiling. 'I've been asked to put a proposition to you. Her Majesty's Government would like to offer you a twenty-grand consultancy fee. For assistance in the field.'

Docherty's surprise was short-lived. After all, who else did they have available? They needed people with military experience when it came to taking on the private armies of the drug barons, and while they might get away with using the regulars on an isolated island like Providencia, the Mexican interior would be a very different kettle of fish. And if things went wrong he would be the scapegoat on the spot.

He saw that Carmen was waiting anxiously for his reply, and fought back the temptation to refuse the bastards' money. If he did they'd probably spend it all on raising cabinet ministers' salaries. 'So when do we leave?' he asked.

Shepreth looked at his watch, 'I'm off in half an hour – the quick way, via Miami. But since Bazua has probably told our American Mr X about your visit it seemed wiser to book you and Carmen via Honduras. There's a plane to La Ceiba at four this afternoon, and from there you can pick up a connection to Tegucigalpa. It'll give you both time to pick up some clothes,' he added with a smile. 'The tickets will be waiting for you at the Islena Airlines desk. You OK for money?'

'Aye,' Docherty said – he still had a wad of Gustavo Macías's traveller's cheques burning a hole in his back pocket. 'I'll phone your flat first thing tomorrow morning.'

Shepreth got up, hovered for a moment as if uncertain whether to give Carmen a goodbye kiss, then just placed a hand lightly on her shoulder before turning and striding off.

'He's sweet on you,' Docherty observed.

'I know,' she said noncommittally, but there was pleasure in her eyes.

* * *

In London it was almost five in the evening, and the sun was making a last-ditch attempt to put in an appearance. The Prime Minister took a deep breath and picked up the receiver. 'Bill,' he said, as if the call was a pleasant surprise.

'John,' the voice on the other end began, the southern US twang adding a layer of amiability to his tone, 'I suppose you can guess the reason for this call.'

There didn't seem much point in simply feigning ignorance – that would just put the President's back up. 'I hear there's been some excitement in the Caribbean,' the Prime Minister said mildly.

'And is the British government claiming responsibility?' the President asked, both irritation and amusement in his voice.

'As of this moment,' the PM said carefully, 'the official position of the British government is to deny any involvement in the events which took place last night.'

The President sighed audibly. 'OK,' he said. 'But would you like to tell me – off the record – just what the hell is going on?'

'I'd be delighted. Angel Bazua has been using his so-called prison as a base for both drug trafficking and other activities hostile to the interests of the British Crown. We have made repeated requests for American cooperation in confronting the Colombian government and all have been refused.'

'The DEA tells me he falls just outside their top ten of major-league players, and our policy, as you know . . .'

'Our information differs,' the PM said, as gently as he could manage. It was time to bite the bullet, as his audience would no doubt say. 'And we think we know why it differs,' he went on. 'We believe that Bazua has an American protector – or even protectors – someone highly placed in one of your agencies responsible for combating the cartels. And once we had realized that this man or men existed . . .' He let the words hang for a second. 'Well, I'm sure you'll understand that we had no choice but to act unilaterally.'

There was silence on the other end.

'Mr President?'

'You don't know the identity of this man? Or men?'

'No, but I can send you everything we have which points to his existence.'

'Thank you. I'll look into it.'

'And I shall start an investigation into the possibility that British forces' equipment was illegally used in a raid against this Colombian island. And I shall tell the Colombians that if we indeed find that this has occurred, then we will build them a prison to replace the one that was destroyed. I'm sure prison design is much the same the world over.'

The President couldn't resist a guffaw. 'I'll be getting back to you, John,' he said, and hung up.

A few moments later he was on the phone to Langley, thinking that if there was one thing he didn't need right now it was a goddam Intelligence scandal. Not with the election less than four months away.

Shepreth spent most of his two flights, not to mention the one-hour stopover in Miami, thinking about Carmen. He had got used to her being there, a thought that rather frightened him, particularly since he was far from sure that she reciprocated his feelings. Sometimes he was convinced that her emotions were so overloaded by worry for her sister that she didn't really see him at all, or at least not as anything more than someone to help her find Marysa.

His plane touched down in the Mexican capital soon after six. He took a taxi to his flat, asked the driver to wait while he showered and changed, then directed him to San Angel and the Luz de la Luna. Arriving between sets, he found Ted Vaughan alone at his usual table, drinking in the Mingus record that was playing on the sound system.

Vaughan raised both eyebrows when he saw Shepreth. 'I'm not sure I should be seen with you,' he said, 'but since I can't wait to hear all the fucking details of your people's latest brainstorm, I suppose I'll have to be.'

'I'll tell you everything,' Shepreth promised, 'but not here. Fancy another drive up the hill?'

'Sure,' Vaughan said, getting up and draining his glass. 'I was just about to leave anyway – I've got an interdepartmental briefing in a couple of hours. I only came down here to get a fix of the real world before listening to those turkeys talk.' He glanced sideways at Shepreth. 'You ever think you're in the wrong job?'

'A little more with each passing day,' the Englishman said as they reached the street. The same group of youths as last time seemed to be practising with their skateboards. Maybe they never went home.

'I think I've reached the certainty stage,' Vaughan said.

As they got into his car Shepreth was thinking that he had never heard his friend sound quite so jaded. He knew that as a kid Vaughan had seen his family torn apart by the crack epidemic, and he guessed that if the American didn't feel he was making a difference in the war against drugs then the job would have little appeal. Vaughan wasn't someone who liked playing games. He was clever, but he worked from the heart.

They drove up to the Plaza San Jacinto, and Vaughan found a parking space on a nearby side-street. As they strolled round the noisy square Shepreth filled the American in on everything that had happened since their last meeting – from

Docherty's discovery that Bazua had the Argentinian Army's Dirty War files to the raid on Providencia early that morning.

Vaughan was not happy to hear that Bazua might have an American protector. 'You don't have a shred of proof,' he argued, but his tone lacked conviction.

'We don't,' Shepreth agreed, 'but it's the only thing that makes sense.'

'Shit,' Vaughan said, as much in sorrow as in anger. He shook his head. 'It sure would explain a lot,' he murmured.

'Do you know where Bazua is now?' Shepreth asked.

'We've got a pretty good idea. The Caravelle was seen coming in to land on a dry lake bed in south-western Chihuahua. We'd already tipped off the Mexican Feds after your message came through, but this place is in the middle of nowhere – it's still Indian country, for Chrissake – and they still had about twenty miles to go when they met the bad guys in a convoy coming the other way. A bunch of Ignacio Payán's men, complete with a local police escort. There was a stand-off, but the Feds had only about a third as many men, and they backed down.'

'Was Bazua with the bad guys?'

'If he got on the plane in Providencia he must have been. The Feds found it empty, and there were no other roads out of there.'

'Were there any women?'

'No one mentioned any.'

Shepreth hoped that was all it was. He didn't think it was possible to throw someone out of a pressurized jetliner, but then for all they knew Bazua had left the women behind on Providencia. 'So where does this Payán hang out?' he asked the American.

'Would you believe a monastery?' Vaughan said. 'Name of Ixmíala. It's one of the ones the Spanish built in the first

227

fifty years they were here. You know the kind: half monastery, half fortress.'

'I know,' Shepreth said. He'd visited a few during his off-duty explorations of the Mexican countryside. 'I'll need the precise location,' he told Vaughan.

'You're still after the bastard then?'

'Yep. And a satellite photo of the monastery wouldn't go amiss.'

'I'll do what I can,' Vaughan promised him. He flashed his even teeth in a smile. 'If you're right, and some bastard in Washington is keeping the rain off Bazua's head, then I want to be one of the first to know his name.'

Soon after ten the following morning Shepreth, Docherty and Carmen were gathered round the map which the MI6 man had spread across the Scot's hotel bed. 'The DEA think he's holed up here,' Shepreth said, pointing to a spot in the mountains some thirty kilometres west of the small Chihuahua town of Norogachic. 'He somehow persuaded the local state government to sell him one of the old fortress monasteries. It's in the mountains, and accessible only by dirt road or helicopter.'

'Tarahumara country,' Docherty murmured reminiscently. He had a vague memory of the name, but couldn't picture the town. What he remembered were mountains that glowed in the sunset, clear rivers running through canyons deeper than Arizona's most famous tourist attraction, and a people who had so far been spared the two-edged sword of progress. It had been like visiting the world when it was young.

'You've been there?' Carmen asked, surprised.

'Aye. I spent about six weeks there twenty years ago. Did a lot of hiking in the mountains. It's a beautiful place.'

'I don't suppose you've got any contacts in the area?' Shepreth asked hopefully.

Docherty shrugged. 'It was twenty years ago,' he said again, 'but who knows? Most of the time I was there I stayed with one Indian family, and I don't suppose they've moved very far. It's an enclosed world.'

'Not any longer,' Shepreth said drily. 'The drug people have moved into the area in a big way over the last five years. And not just to establish secluded stopovers for stuff heading north – they've got the Tarahumara into the poppy-growing business.'

'There's hardly any decent soil in those mountains,' Docherty said. 'They probably need the money to feed their children.'

'A few of them may be making money,' Shepreth said, 'but some are getting killed, and a lot more are getting beaten up. According to Vaughan it's like the Wild West revisited.'

'That's a shame,' Docherty said.

Shepreth was examining the map again. 'Where exactly did you stay?' he asked.

'I was based in a village near Batopilas,' Docherty said, pointing it out. 'That's where the family lived.'

'It's almost next door,' Shepreth said.

'It's about seventy-five miles away by dirt track,' Docherty corrected him. 'Or a two-day hike across the mountains.' The Tarahumara were famous for their walking, he remembered. Some of their young men could give the SAS a run for their money across the Brecon Beacons.

'Why would this drug lord want to live somewhere like this?' Carmen wanted to know.

'He's also got a big villa in Ciudad Juárez,' Shepreth told her. 'We don't know how much of the year he spends in the monastery.'

'He probably likes hunting,' Docherty murmured, and looked up from the map. 'It's not a small area, but the Tarahumara are – or were – a tight-knit community, and someone in Batopilas will know what's happening in Norogachic. I'll get up there and nose around – with any luck the Torreses will still be there.' Paco, the teenage son with whom he had spent a week hiking in the wilderness, would be over forty by now. 'I think you two should head for Divisadero,' he went on, pointing it out on the map. 'It's on the Copper Canyon Railway, just above the Copper Canyon itself. They were building a couple of swanky hotels when I was there, and you can enjoy the view for a couple of days while I do all the work. I'll get in touch when I have something.'

'Sounds reasonable,' Shepreth said, his dislike of the enforced inaction more than offset by the thought of the company he would be keeping.

'OK then,' Docherty said, 'seconds out, round two. And I expect I'll be needing a handgun,' he added as an afterthought.

14

As the small plane touched down on the runway at Hidalgo del Parral the mountains to the west were silhouetted against the deep-red sky. Docherty descended the rickety steps and headed across the tarmac towards the taxi rank, where several welcoming smiles were competing for the right to fleece the gringo. The lucky winner drove him straight to the town's best hotel, sorely disappointed by the Scot's ability to remark in fluent Spanish that he'd noticed the faulty meter.

After eating an excellent *comida corrida* at a nearby restaurant Docherty took a stroll round the town centre. Hidalgo del Parral was famous for being the site of Pancho Villa's assassination, and the habit of violence seemed to have lived on in the groups of surly-looking youths who watched him walk by, pursuing him with menacing murmurs of '*Gringo*!' But then he didn't suppose there was much else in the way of entertainment on offer.

Soon after dawn next morning he walked down to the bus station, where a red-eyed driver pointed him in the direction of the pick-up point for those heading west into the Sierra Tarahumara. Half an hour later he was sharing a wooden bench in the back of a four-wheel-drive Dodge pick-up with a mixed bag of Mexican farmers and forestry workers. They took on more passengers in the old mining town of San Francisco del Oro, and then, on a rapidly deteriorating road, began slowly climbing into the mountains. About eight dusty, bone-rattling hours later, Docherty stepped gingerly down on to the square at Batopilas, a small town surrounded by soaring canyon walls. His body might be aching, but he felt that familiar intoxication of the spirit which only the world's high places seemed to conjure up.

He bought and consumed a couple of *empanadas* on a bench in front of the old adobe church, then went in search of transport for the last few kilometres to Uruáchic. A forestry official answered his thumb, and an hour later he was being dropped off in another smaller square in another smaller canyon. The village had changed little in twenty years, though there were more shiny pick-ups in evidence, not to mention electricity pylons. Docherty walked down to the store which the Torres family had run, and ducked in through the low doorway. It took a few seconds for his eyes to get used to the dark, but there it all was – the worn leather saddles hanging from the wooden beams, the ubiquitous crates of Coca-Cola, the hessian sacks full of maize and beans.

He realized the man behind the counter was staring at him. A second later, they recognized each other.

'Jaime!'

'Paco!'

The two men hugged, and stared at each other some more. The lithe teenager with whom Docherty had gone hiking in the mountains had not put on much weight, but his face was gaunter, and his dark eyes seemed more hooded than before. 'Come,' Paco said in Spanish, 'we'll go to my house. It is time to close anyway.'

He insisted on carrying Docherty's bag as they walked the couple of hundred metres to the farmhouse on the outskirts of the village. Paco's mother, Juanita, was a Tarahumara, but his father, Fidel, was half-Mexican, and they had inherited the house from the Mexican side of his family. The outbuilding where Docherty had slept for several weeks was still standing, dwarfed by the canyon wall behind it.

Juanita and Fidel were sitting out on the porch, enjoying the last hour of sunshine before shadows filled the canyon. They looked old now, though they were probably only in their early sixties, and it took both of them a while to recognize Docherty. When they did, huge smiles creased their leathery faces.

Another woman was standing in the doorway. 'This is my wife Siniya,' Paco said, and the woman shook his hand, curiosity in her large, dark eyes. 'You will eat with us?' she said in halting Spanish, reminding Docherty that a lot of the Tarahumara spoke only their own language.

'I'd be honoured,' he said.

'And then the two of us will go walking in the mountains,' Paco insisted, before he saw the reproachful look in his wife's eyes. 'Or perhaps not,' he added, and everyone laughed.

Three children joined them at the huge table inside. His two eldest sons, Paco explained, were both married and living in Batopilas. He asked Docherty whether he was married, and was clearly pleased with the answer. No doubt he remembered that the Scot had been lugging around a broken heart the last time they met.

Between mouthfuls of bean stew and the local maize beer the adults swapped stories of the past twenty years, while the younger children stared at Docherty through saucer-like eyes. It was not until afterwards, when Paco and Docherty were alone on the porch with second bottles of Tesquina, that the question came up of what had brought Docherty back to Uruáchic. 'It is wonderful to see you again,' Paco said, 'but there is a seriousness in your eyes, my friend. I do not think you have come to the Sierra for a holiday.'

Docherty grunted. 'I wish I had,' he said. 'But first, tell me what is happening to the Tarahumara. I have a friend who tells me that there has been trouble here in the last few years.'

Paco shook his head, but not in denial. 'Much trouble,' he agreed. 'It is the drugs, of course, or the people who deal in them, and it has been going on for a long time now. The men first came with the packets of seeds, and they promised ten times more for a single crop than anyone could earn from corn or beans.' He shrugged. 'Some people planted the seeds,' he said, 'and at first they made a lot of money. Each year that the rains failed a few more would decide to grow the marijuana or the poppies, because otherwise they were afraid their families would starve. But they did not get rich – the buyers offered less and less for each crop, and if anyone refused then men with guns would visit them. They have frightened teachers away from several schools and they stopped the building of a clinic.' He stood up. 'Come, I want to show you something.'

They walked down the empty street towards the dimly lit centre of the village. Paco opened the wooden door of the small adobe church and went in, lighting a candle from the supply inside the door. He walked to one side and held it up to the wall, which Docherty could see was pock-marked by bullet holes, and then held it above the deeply stained wooden floorboards in the aisle. 'There was a meeting here six months ago, a meeting of farmers to discuss how they could fight back against the drug people. And in the middle

234

of it three men walked in with guns and opened fire. Four of the farmers were killed, and many more injured.'

'What did the police do?' Docherty asked.

'Nothing.'

'And the state government, the *Federales*?'

Paco shook his head. 'They make noise about stopping the drugs, but that is mostly for the *Nortamericanos*.' He smiled. 'They spray the crops, pretending they are killing them, but they are spraying water.'

'The drug people – do they have one leader?'

'In this area it is a man named Ignacio Payán. He has a fortress in the mountains near Norogachic.'

Docherty felt both satisfaction and a twinge of guilt. 'I have business with this man,' he began, and Paco's face dropped. 'He has kidnapped a woman, the sister of my friend. And he is protecting a man named Angel Bazua, who killed many of my wife's friends.'

Paco was smiling again. 'You are still a warrior, yes?' he said.

'Old habits die hard,' Docherty admitted. 'I need to get into this fortress and get the woman back. I will also kill Bazua and Payán if I can.'

'All by yourself?'

'Another man is waiting with my friend in Creel, but that is all.'

'These are vicious men,' Paco said, looking down at the bloodstained floor. 'I have a cousin in Norogachi,' he said. 'He has been trying to organize people against Payán for several years, and though they have run his truck off the road and given him several beatings he refuses to accept defeat.'

'I'd like to meet him,' Docherty said.

* * *

On the same day that the Scot had taken his flight to Hidalgo del Parral, Carmen and Shepreth had flown further north, to the larger city of Chihuahua, and early next morning they boarded the Vista Tren for their five-hour journey to Creel on the famous Copper Canyon Railway. The train was predictably full of tourists, most of whom were travelling all the way to Los Mochis on the Pacific coast, but the two of them made no attempt to socialize. Carmen just stared out of the window at the green ranching country and distant mountains, while Shepreth read a novel he had found in his hotel room the previous night.

At first sight Creel looked like a set for a Hollywood Western – streets of log cabins complete with ranchers and Indians, a trading store and a Jesuit mission. The bank, post office and hotels looked a little more modern, and the forest managers in their gleaming new pick-ups looked as if they'd strayed into the picture by accident. The Nuevo looked like the best hotel on offer, and after taking two rooms they wandered round the town, ate dinner and went to bed.

There was still no word from Docherty the following morning, and Shepreth managed to persuade Carmen that going on one of the organized minibus trips to an impressive waterfall would be better than sitting around waiting. Through the first hour of the four-hour journey she felt as listless as the day before, but gradually the brightness of the colours and the clarity of the mountain air revived her spirits, awakening a feeling in her chest and stomach which she eventually recognized as simple happiness. This realization brought guilt in its wake – how could she feel happy when she knew what Marysa was going through? – but deep down in her soul Carmen knew that at that moment there was nothing more she could be doing.

The Basaseachic Falls, which their guide proudly announced were the highest in North America, were certainly beautiful, but as Carmen stared at the tumbling shroud of water she felt something more than mere wonder. The Falls were like a reaffirmation. The water fell and fell, and life went on.

That same morning Paco took Docherty into Batopilas and found him a lift to Norogachi. The road up the canyon was in no better state than it had been the day before, and the bottoms of the passengers in the back of the pick-up rarely spent more than a few consecutive seconds on the wooden benches. Docherty found such physical preoccupations almost a relief – he had woken that morning with thoughts of an old Western on his mind and had instantly realized why. In the film, which he remembered from his schooldays, John Wayne had spent years looking for a niece who had been captured by Indians. And when he had finally found the grown-up girl his first inclination had been to kill her, because her years as an Apache squaw had turned her into one of them.

What had happened to Carmen's sister? Docherty wondered. Could anyone come all the way back from where she had been?

The pick-up reached Norogachi just before eleven. He recognized it now – the two barrack-like buildings sandwiching the adobe church with its corrugated-iron roof, the convent school and the small hospital. If he walked a little further down the road he would be able to see the Copper Canyon stretching and deepening into the distance.

He walked the other way, following the directions Paco had given him to a small adobe house near the river. As he walked towards the door two men emerged, one of them cradling an AK47 in his arms.

Docherty stopped. 'I would like to see Manolo Torres,' he said, reaching slowly into his pocket. 'I have a letter of introduction from his cousin.'

The one without the gun came forward to take it, then disappeared inside the house. A few moments later another man emerged, gesturing Docherty forward. 'I am Manolo,' he said. He had the same mouth as Paco, but his nose was sharper, the eyes even darker. And he looked more wary, which probably wasn't surprising.

He led Docherty through to the yard behind the house, stopping on the way to pour his guest a cup of coffee from the pot on the stove. A long bench stood up against the house and a few feet away an antique typewriter sat on a collapsible metal table. On the other side of the yard two women were sitting outside an outhouse, rolling ground corn into tortilla balls.

'I remember your first visit,' Manolo said conversationally. 'I was only about ten.'

He didn't have the full use of his left arm, Docherty noticed, and wondered if that was a consequence of the beatings he had received. 'Your family treated me very well,' he said, conscious of how inadequate the words sounded.

Manolo nodded. 'So what do you want from me?' he asked. 'Paco says you are an enemy of Payán, and that you need help, but help with what?'

Docherty began at the beginning.

The minibus got back to Creel just before dark, and after showering off the dust Carmen and Shepreth walked down the main street in search of somewhere nice to eat. Although it had been a gruelling day neither felt tired, and both were aware that they felt easier with the other, as if some invisible bridge had been crossed. In the restaurant they worked their way through a bottle of wine and talked about everything but the reason they were here in the mountains of northern Mexico, only realizing that the establishment was closing when the proprietor started stacking chairs on the other tables.

Not wanting the evening to end, they walked to the empty station, where the risen moon was reflecting in the rails. She took his arm as they walked down the dusty platform, and as they turned by the signal she stopped him and looked up into his eyes.

He leant down to kiss her, gently at first, and then, as their tongues entwined, with mounting passion.

He cradled her face in his hands and looked into her eyes. Like a little boy seeking reassurance, she thought, but there was kindness there too, and desire. She took one of his hands and placed it over her left breast, so he could feel the hardening of her nipple, and they kissed again. 'I don't want to sleep alone tonight,' she told him.

'That makes two of us.'

They walked back across the square, fighting and losing the temptation to run as they reached the main street. They rushed in through the hotel doors like a whirlwind, laughing their way up the stairs and clawing most of each other's clothes off before he realized they'd forgotten to shut the door.

That done, they stood there embracing each other's nakedness for a minute and more before lying down together, kissing and feeling each other's excitement mount. As he finally entered her, Carmen had a sudden vision of her sister's face, but when she opened her eyes to his all she saw was the mirror of her own desire.

* * *

239

Shortly after darkness filled the canyon two young Tarahumara arrived with the horses. Docherty, who had not ridden for more than a decade, mounted his with some trepidation, but the animal greeted him with nothing more fearsome than a stamping of the front foot. Manolo, who had abandoned his jeans for a more traditional-looking loincloth, looked as if he'd been born in the saddle.

They rode west down the canyon, keeping to the southern side of the swift-flowing river. The dirt track on the far bank would have allowed a faster pace, but Manolo was wary of meeting a four-wheel drive full of either Payán's men or the local police. If anything went wrong he didn't want anyone to know he'd been out.

After about an hour they left the canyon floor, turning up a long and gently sloping cleft which brought them out on to a moonlit rim about five hundred metres above the barely visible river. Another valley, steeper this time, led them up to a dry and broken plateau, and in a niche among the rocks Manolo made a fire and heated up maize coffee to wash down their tortillas. As they sat eating, the Tarahumara, his face thrown into stark relief by the firelight, recounted the story of his people's struggle with Payán and the authorities. He didn't glorify his own role; in fact he seemed genuinely amused by the fact that he had become a living symbol of the resistance. And he made no attempt to hide his feeling that they were fighting a losing battle.

Which feeling, Docherty thought, probably explained why the man was taking a chance on helping him. If the gringo proved to be a superman, then they would all benefit, and if he proved a damp squib, then the Tarahumara would be no worse off than they had been before he arrived.

It was just gone eleven when they put out the fire, checked that the horses were secure and started across the broken plateau on foot. The moon was high now, spreading its light across a vast panorama of mountains, and for the best part of an hour Docherty followed Manolo across the rocky landscape, clambering in and out of deep clefts in the rock, striding across stone slopes which time had worn as smooth as a marble floor.

They were heading down a dry stream bed towards a group of stunted trees when Manolo suddenly stopped, so that Docherty almost banged into him. Over the other man's shoulder he had a fleeting glimpse of something slithering away into the rocks. 'We are almost there,' Manolo said softly, as if that were the reason he had halted, and a couple of minutes later they were looking out across the head of a deep valley. Almost directly in front of them the crenellated walls of the Ixmíala fortress monastery glowed in the moonlight.

Their view of the walled compound was from the side. On the right, nestling against the head of the valley, were two buildings, the church rising up behind the two-storey living quarters. A wide flight of steps led down from the front of both buildings to a large open space, and an arched gateway in the wall to the left disgorged a dirt track which disappeared into the darkness of the valley beyond.

Two four-wheel drives and an R44 Astro helicopter were parked on the open ground which fronted the monastery buildings; this space, Docherty remembered, was called an atrium. The stub of stone in the middle would once have supported a cross, and the broken towers at each corner of the wall were what remained of the chapels. Atriums were intended for the use of overflow services, though how the local clergy ever expected to fill a church in a place like this was beyond him.

He indicated to Manolo that he wanted to move left, for a better view of the front of the buildings. The Indian nodded, and led the way.

241

Docherty's intentions were purely professional, but he couldn't help spending a few seconds admiring the front of the church. The details of the carved door and stone columns were hidden by distance and darkness, but the gabled belfry, with its seven bells still hanging in the seven arches high above the door, possessed the sort of simply beauty which he had always loved.

Almost reluctantly he trained the SAS nightscope on the building which stood to the right of the church. There was an open chapel at the front, and the glow of light was visible through an open door in its inner wall. As he watched, several figures suddenly walked into that glow, almost eclipsing it. There were four of them, all men, all in uniform.

'The local *Federales*,' Manolo sneered.

They climbed into one of the pick-ups, which reversed before speeding off down the valley road in a moonlit cloud of dust. Docherty directed the nightscope back towards the interior of the building and kept his eye on the inner glow for several minutes. No one extinguished it by shutting doors, and soon the lights were going out on the second floor.

Manolo put words to what the Scot was thinking. 'There would be no trouble getting in,' he said. 'We have sometimes thought about such an attack ourselves. But where would we run to afterwards? We have to live in this land.'

Docherty didn't, but then getting away from it didn't look much easier. As the two of them walked back across the plateau, reclaimed their horses and rode back down to the canyon, he went through their options. There didn't seem many to choose from.

Shepreth and Carmen emerged from the hotel room at about nine, both wondering what had hit them. They had spent more of the night making love than sleeping, but it wasn't just that – neither he nor she had ever been gripped by such a desperate passion. It might be wonderful – it was wonderful – but it also felt almost unreal, and that feeling was exacerbated by the receptionist's news that there was a message from a Señor Docherty.

'Arriving early afternoon,' was all it said.

They had breakfast, stared at each other for a while, then went back to bed.

They came back downstairs soon after noon, and Shepreth called up Vaughan from the booth in the lobby. 'I'm in the Nuevo Hotel in Creel,' he warned the American. Privacy was not guaranteed on calls originating anywhere in the Sierra Tarahumara.

'Your client also seems to be in Chihuahua,' Vaughan told him. 'According to my head office he's trying to do a deal with them, a cross-border deal. Know what I mean?'

Shepreth guessed that Bazua was trying to buy immunity with the Dirty War files. 'And are your people interested?' he asked.

'Hard to say,' Vaughan told him. 'But if you want to make a deal with him yourself I wouldn't waste any time.'

'Right. Thanks, Ted.' Shepreth hung up the phone, feeling worried. If Bazua dealt his way across the border then MI6's hopes of getting hold of the Dirty War records would disappear. And there was also a very good chance that he would consider any current female companions surplus to requirements.

'Bad news?' Carmen asked, appearing beside him.

He had just finished telling her what Vaughan had told him when Docherty came through the hotel doorway. The Scot looked rather dusty, having spent the last four hours bouncing north on the mail bus from Batopilas.

They went upstairs to Shepreth's room, which didn't look as if it had been slept in. And there was also a subtle change in the way his two partners were looking at each other, Docherty realized. As Shepreth told him the news from Mexico City he grinned at the two of them, feeling pleased for them both.

'We can go in tomorrow night,' he said when the MI6 man was finished, and went through what he'd discovered over the previous couple of days about the Tarahumara situation in general and Payán's fortress in particular. 'They won't take part in any assault,' he said, referring to the Indians, 'and with good reason – their people would bear the consequences. Unlike us, they haven't got another home to run to. But they'll help us with intelligence – Manolo is talking to some of the women who are driven up to do Payán's cleaning and laundry – and they'll lend us horses. Can you two ride?'

They both could. Shepreth had learned during a short and boring posting in the Middle East, Carmen during family visits to an uncle's ranch in the Magdalena Valley.

'Does that mean your sister can ride too?' Docherty asked her.

'Better than me.'

Shepreth was spreading out his map of the area. 'Where are we riding to?' he asked pointedly.

Docherty didn't answer right away. 'There's no problem getting in,' he began, 'but there's only one road out of the valley and not many more out of the area. Even if we got a good jump on them I don't reckon much of our chances of getting out of the state. And to get a good jump we'd have to either find and kill everyone in the place or find and destroy every means of communication they have – radio, mobile phones, whatever. Which doesn't seem very realistic.'

He looked from one face to the other. 'The alternative is an hour's walk across the mountains to where the horses will be waiting, and then an eighty-kilometre ride down the Copper Canyon to Divisadero here.' He pointed it out on the map.

'The train?' Shepreth said doubtfully. 'We'd be on board the damn thing for about seven hours, and even then we'd only have got as far as Chihuahua.'

'Aye,' Docherty admitted, 'but that's one of the things in its favour – no one'll be expecting us to just jump aboard a train that's headed for the state capital.'

'What's the other?' Carmen asked.

'The train will be full of tourists. If all they see tomorrow night is a couple of gringos, then they're going to have a much harder job picking us out from a train full of tourists than they would in a stolen pick-up. The Mexican police can't arrest a whole trainload of gringos.'

'That makes sense,' Shepreth admitted.

'Where do we go from Chihuahua?' Carmen asked.

'North, I suppose,' Docherty said. 'But let's get within striking distance before we worry about that one.'

15

Docherty landed on his toes and immediately sank to his haunches, his eyes scouring the fortress monastery's compound. The façade of the church rose above him, the gable belfry silhouetted against the stars, while away to his right the Astro helicopter and a Dodge pick-up stood almost side by side in the middle of the stone-paved atrium.

Shepreth dropped down beside him, and the two men slipped across the ten metres that separated them from the wooden doors of the church. As Docherty had feared, they were bolted from the inside. The sentry would have to be taken out.

Half an hour ago he had been sitting smoking a cigarette just inside the open chapel, not more than twenty metres from where they now stood. He was tempted by the thought of just walking round the corner, trusting that surprise would immobilize the man for the necessary few seconds, but only for a moment. Surprised people were hard to predict, and this one was carrying a noisy-looking Uzi.

Docherty and Shepreth were carrying silenced Browning High Powers and wearing borrowed AK47s slung across their backs. The Scot gestured what he wanted the MI6 man to do, and Shepreth obliged, first taking himself round the corner of the church façade furthest from the sentry and then starting to tap the stone with the butt of his Browning.

It was not a threatening noise, but it was food for the curious. Docherty heard the chair scrape back, the boots on stone, and waited in the doorway of the church.

Perhaps the man was careful not to walk too close to the façade, or perhaps he wasn't thinking about it one way or the other, but he was way beyond the reach of an outflung arm when he passed the doorway, and Docherty had no choice but to take him out with the gun. The Browning coughed twice, the silhouetted head jerked and the body concertinaed on to the flagstones, muffling the rattle of the Uzi which fell beneath it.

Docherty waited a few seconds but heard nothing, and went to drag the body into the church doorway, where it sat like a gruesome Guy Fawkes. He then inched his way along the façade for a view of the open chapel. The guard's seat was empty and a packet of cigarettes lay beside it on the floor.

Shepreth was back at his shoulder now. The two of them moved silently across the chapel and the adjoining empty room to the doorway which led into the inner courtyard or cloister. According to the intelligence Manolo had gathered from those who had visited or worked there, between four and six men habitually occupied the three rooms on the opposite side of the cloister from the church. Payán's room were almost directly above where they now stood, with windows facing out across the atrium and the valley below. His recent guest had also been given a room on the first floor, on the southern side of the cloister, above the rooms occupied by Payán's men. The woman – and there was only one – had the room next to Bazua's.

The cloister itself was dark, but there was a light on in one of the downstairs rooms, which hadn't been the case half an hour before.

Shit, Docherty thought. The light could mean anything from a change of sentries to an unexpected crap. There didn't seem much point in investigating, or at least not until they had finished their business on the second floor. Following his mental map, Docherty led Shepreth towards the nearest of the two flights of stairs.

As the two men emerged on to the upper veranda they could hear talking below them, which meant that at least two of Payán's men were awake.

The door to Bazua's room was slightly ajar, allowing a shaft of moonlight to illuminate the empty bed. Shepreth slipped inside, leaving Docherty to keep watch, and took out his pencil torch. There wasn't much to look at – only a bed, a washstand with a bowl of water, an open suitcase on the floor. He knelt down beside the latter and was wading through the clothes when he noticed the rectangular bulge in the lid pocket. He pulled the zip open, extracted the heavy ledger and shone the torch on a random page: '. . . *from 180 to 220 volts, two sessions with the submarine* . . .'

'I've got them,' he whispered to Docherty, undoing the buttons of his shirt so that he could carry the ledger inside it.

And after that things began to go rather quickly.

They were heading for the woman's room, and still about ten metres from the door, when it suddenly opened. A tall man stepped out, his nakedness exposed by the light shining out of the door, his half-erect penis sticking out in front of him like a miniature battering ram. He walked across to the edge of the veranda, where he stretched his arms above his head before dropping his hands on to the wooden rail.

Both Docherty and Shepreth recognized the man from Vaughan's photographs – it was Ignacio Payán.

The Mexican's face twitched in their direction, as if he had suddenly become aware that he was being watched, and his mouth was still opening when the two Brownings sent four bullets through his upper torso. He tottered for a moment, then collapsed on to the wooden floor with a loud thump, cutting off the conversation below.

Shepreth had already resumed his stride towards the woman's room, but he was still six metres away when Marysa Salcedo appeared in the doorway with Angel Bazua's forearm locked around her neck and what looked like a table fork pressed against her throat. They were both naked.

Shepreth stopped in his tracks about two metres ahead of Docherty.

'I'll kill her,' Bazua said, then shouted for help.

The odds could only get worse. Hoping Bazua wouldn't catch the movement in the shadows until it was too late, Docherty raised the Browning and fired, taking off the Argentinian's right ear in a spray of blood. The hand with the fork recoiled, jerking Marysa's head sideways and giving the Scot a clear second shot.

He sent it through Bazua's right eye, just as an answering shout came up from below.

Shepreth ran forward as Marysa was dragged down by the dead hand around her neck. She pulled herself violently away and then started pawing at his back in what looked like a paroxysm of grief.

Shepreth reached her side and pulled her gently away. Bazua's bare back was oozing blood from the cuts she had gouged with her nails.

'We've come to take you away,' he said in Spanish, half

conscious of running feet below. 'Your sister Carmen's outside waiting for you,' he added.

At the word 'Carmen' she turned her face towards his as if she couldn't believe it. 'Carmen is here?' she asked.

'Yes,' Shepreth told her. She was as beautiful as her sister, he thought, but there hardly seemed room for anything but fear in her eyes.

Docherty emerged from the room with a handful of clothes just as feet sounded on the front stairs. As he scooped the naked woman up in his arms and half ran with her towards the other end of the building, Shepreth brought his AK47 into position and fired off a burst in the direction of the charging shadows on the stairs.

In the other stairwell Docherty was helping Marysa into her clothes, but hardly noticing what a lovely body she had. 'I can manage,' she told him curtly, and he realized that he'd been stupid to assume that Victoria Marin's psychological escape route would also be hers. Whatever arrangements Carmen's sister had made with herself for the sake of sanity, they obviously hadn't included a flight into dreamland.

'I'm ready,' she said.

Docherty indicated that Shepreth and Marysa should go first, and as the MI6 man led the woman down the stairs the Scot fired a last burst down the length of the veranda with his own AK47.

At the bottom of the stairs Shepreth found there was only one way out, and that led into the open cloister. He hesitated a second, saw no one on the far side, then grabbed Marysa's hand and made a dash for the door which led into the church. Finding it shut but mercifully unlocked, he heaved open the heavy wooden door, bundled her through and stepped in after her, just as bullets ricocheted around the stone columns to his left.

Docherty was still in the other doorway. The flash from the guns told him Payán's men were in the far corner of the cloister, and that to reach the outside world they would have to cross his line of fire. 'I'll keep the bastards busy,' he yelled to Shepreth. 'Get her over the wall and come back in through the open chapel.'

'OK,' Shepreth shouted back, just as the Scot opened up with a murderous burst from the AK47. He grabbed Marysa's hand and hurried her through the empty church. There were no seats, no pulpit – only a wide stone floor dappled by the silver moonlight from the windows.

Reaching the front door, he removed the long wooden bolt and gingerly pulled open one door. Docherty was still firing repeated bursts across the cloister next door, and if any of Payán's men had made it through to the atrium Shepreth couldn't hear or see them. He ran for the wall, one hand ready with the Browning, the other pulling Marysa after him. 'Carmen!' he shouted.

'I'm here,' came a hopeful voice from beyond the wall.

'Your sister's coming over,' he told her, cupping his hands like a stirrup to help her up on to the top of the wall. The moment her foot had left his hand he was heading back towards the buildings at a run, only slowing slightly as he turned the corner towards the entrance to the open chapel.

They were only about five metres apart when they saw each other, and their fingers must have clenched on the triggers at exactly the same moment. For the longest split second of his life Shepreth stared down the barrel of the Mexican's gun, then a hammer seemed to hit him on the chest, knocking him his back on to the edge of the steps. I'm dead, he thought, but the stars were still shining above him.

And then he realized that Bazua's ledger had saved him.

252

He stumbled to his feet and started forward again, a little more cautiously this time, his hand shaking slightly from the shock. The man he had killed was face down on the flag-stones, arms by his side, as if waiting for a massage.

Shepreth walked carefully through the open chapel to the doorway which led on to the cloister, and inched an eye around the jamb. Three of Payán's men were sheltering behind the old stone columns, one firing, the other two reloading. He aimed at the former's legs and the man dropped with a squeal. The other two made a dive for the shelter of the nearest room. 'Clear,' he yelled to Docherty, and watched the distant figure of the Scot scurry along behind the far columns and disappear into the open door of the church. One more burst of fire into the relevant room and Shepreth abandoned the cloister, running back out through the open chapel.

Docherty was waiting in front of the church, slamming another magazine into his AK47. 'Go,' he told Shepreth, turning the gun on first the helicopter and then the pick-up.

The explosion of the helicopter's fuel tank almost knocked Shepreth off his feet as he ran for the wall; the boom from the pick-up was almost anticlimactic in comparison. He clambered over to find the two women waiting, Carmen's anxiety dissolving into a huge smile as he appeared. A moment later Docherty was jumping down beside him, urging everyone up the slope which the three of them had descended not half an hour before.

As they climbed the path the whole head of the valley seemed lit by the burning vehicles below, but no figures emerged into the atrium. Payán's men no longer had their leader to make their decisions for them, and his right-hand men in Chihuahua and Ciudad Juárez were a long way from the action. Docherty reckoned that their chances of reaching the border had improved considerably in the last half-hour.

Getting across it was another matter. If there was an American name inside the ledger Shepreth was carrying, then that American would soon be pulling out all the stops to recover it. One of his agents at the border crossing perhaps, obeying orders he didn't understand. 'Could you come this way, sir? I'm afraid we'll have to look after these records for you . . . A possible threat to national security . . .'

And that was an optimistic reading – Mr X would no doubt prefer that they were killed. Docherty kept walking, half of his mind celebrating their success, the other half searching for ways to make it stick.

A few metres behind him Carmen was also counting blessings and curses. Her whole being seemed to be almost quivering with relief that her sister was alive, that Shepreth hadn't been badly injured or killed, that they were on their way. But it had taken only a few seconds for her to realize that her sister was not the same person she had been a year ago. Of course she hadn't really expected that she would be, but she couldn't help hoping . . . Now only time would tell how serious the damage was, and the sense of heartbreak which that provoked seemed so at odds with the happiness which kept bubbling through her whenever she thought about Shep.

He was bringing up the rear, still a little in shock from that moment when he thought his life was over. The bullet had caught a corner of the ledger – another couple of inches down or to the right and he wouldn't have been walking anywhere.

They were ascending the dry stream bed now, and the fires in the valley below were no longer visible. The moon was riding high in the centre of a shimmering universe, the shadowy mountains stretching away, and the thought crossed

Shepreth's mind that it wasn't the sort of place from which you took a taxi home.

For the next hour Docherty navigated their way across the broken plateau towards the niche in the rocks where he and Manolo had waited two nights before. There they rejoined the Tarahumara, along with one of his young disciples, their backpacks and the six horses.

Docherty returned the AK47 to its rightful owner. 'Payán is dead,' he told Manolo.

The Indian's lips creased in a smile. 'And the man you were looking for?'

'He is dead too.'

Manolo nodded gravely, then gave a wan smile.

They mounted the horses. Despite Carmen's assurance Docherty was half expecting problems with Marysa, but the opposite seemed the case. Once in the saddle she seemed more animated than before and more at ease with her mount than Docherty was with his.

The six of them made the long descent in single file, reaching the canyon floor soon after two-thirty. Even with the benefit of the hidden moon the trail was almost invisible to the naked eye, and for the next few hours they were totally dependent on Manolo's knowledge of the canyon. They were still about eight kilometres from the station at Divisadero when the first rays of light began working their way down the eastern canyon wall, and Manolo led them out of the main canyon and up a narrow wooded cleft past a succession of small waterfalls.

'The walk to the station is all uphill and sometimes steep,' he told Docherty. 'It will take the women at least two hours.'

The Scot did a quick calculation. The train was due at ten past one, but it was unlikely to be less than half an hour late.

They didn't want to be hanging around the station for too long but then they could hardly afford to miss it. 'We'll be here for about five hours,' he told the others, adding that they should try to get some sleep if they could. Which of course was easier said than done. His own brain seemed determined to watch endless reruns of the night's events, so he just lay there with his eyes open, head on the backpack, staring up at the kaleidoscope of colours on the soaring canyon wall.

The next thing he knew, Manolo was shaking him awake with the news that it was almost eleven o'clock. He woke the others, and wished he'd been more careful with Marysa, whose eyes sprang open with an expression he wished he hadn't seen. Then they closed again and she pursed her lips, as if she was trying to squeeze something from her memory.

Ten minutes later they were ready to go. Docherty thanked Manolo and asked him to give his goodbyes to Paco. 'Tell him I will bring my family to meet his,' he said, hoping it would be possible.

The walk to Divisadero took less than the expected two hours but it was hard work just the same. They arrived at the station looking like one more group of exhausted gringo backpackers, and were duly set upon by the sellers of Indian trinkets and Mexican snacks. There was no sign of Payán's men, either uniformed or otherwise. If a search was underway – and it was hard to believe that it wouldn't be – then it hadn't yet reached here.

Docherty bought a couple of *burritos* and sat down to eat them, his eyes scanning the station area. He was pleased to see that there were several other gringos waiting for the train – a couple who looked and sounded like Germans, two obviously American young women and a lone male with the Australian flag plastered across his backpack.

The minutes ticked by, and eventually the train arrived – a line of dirty green coaches pulled by a blue diesel. Apparently it stopped for fifteen minutes at Divisadero, during which time the tourists were expected to gape at the canyon below, take photographs and buy souvenirs. The four of them watched out of the window, expecting at any moment to hear the whirr of an approaching helicopter above the idling hum of the diesel.

The train eventually clanked out of the station. Docherty bought their tickets to Chihuahua and surveyed the other occupants of the first-class carriage, at least half of whom were gringos. He caught one of the men smiling at him, and realized it was a smile of envy from another middle-aged man, one who hadn't got a woman as gorgeous as Marysa sitting next to him.

Creel was the train's next stop, and if any station in the mountains was being watched then that would be the one. It seemed to take an age to reach, but when they finally pulled in alongside the crowded platform there was no line of men waiting with guns. There were two uniformed policemen standing beside the doorway to the station building, but their wholehearted attention was almost immediately claimed by the two American women who had got on at Divisadero, and who were now asking for directions.

In the seat behind, Carmen and Shepreth were both remembering their first kiss on this very platform, three long nights ago.

The train resumed its journey, following a succession of winding valleys down from the mountains. Docherty's mind continued to race with unverifiable assumptions and unanswerable questions. No one had seen Carmen, so their pursuers were probably looking for two gringos and one woman. Did they have any photographs, either of Marysa or himself? He could just imagine Bazua taking humiliating shots of women, and it was hard to believe that someone hadn't taken his own picture on Providencia. But maybe he was just being pessimistic. Maybe there was no pursuit.

As they neared the small town of Cuauhtémoc he wondered whether it would be safer to leave the train rather than go on to Chihuahua. No, he decided. They would probably be the only gringos getting off there, and at Chihuahua their fellow-tourists would serve as camouflage. They would stay on board.

The sun went down behind the train, and the last hour of the journey was travelled in almost complete darkness. They stepped down on to Chihuahua's single platform fearing the worst, but another pair of uniformed policemen did nothing more threatening than ogle the gringo women, and during the taxi ride to the city centre they could all feel the tension beginning to drain from their bodies.

The main square was full of life, and there the taxi driver dropped them off at a car-hire firm that was just about to close for the day. They wanted an early start to visit the ruins at Casa Grande, Shepreth told the reluctant proprietor, and once a sizeable bonus had changed hands the man was able to appreciate their urgency. Five minutes later they were on the way out of the city in a dark-blue Nissan Cherry, with only three hundred and fifty kilometres of modern highway between them and the border town of Ciudad Juárez. For the next three hours Docherty and Shepreth took turns at the wheel, and as they sped along the straight and frequently empty two-lane road the Scot began to feel more optimistic.

That feeling took a bit of a dent when the lights of the state police car brightened in their rear-view mirror. As it passed them the officer in the passenger seat stared across, turned to say something to the driver, then gave Shepreth the signal to stop.

'Shit!' the two men murmured in stereo. Glancing in the back, Docherty saw that the two women were awake again. He took the Browning from the dashboard compartment and pushed it into his belt beneath the hanging shirt.

The two Mexican policemen climbed out of their car and walked carefully back towards the Nissan, each with one hand on the butt of his holstered gun.

'*Buenas noches*,' Shepreth said.

'*Buenas noches*,' one of the men replied curtly, as he did a round of the faces. 'Passports,' he demanded.

Docherty groaned inwardly – Marysa wouldn't have one. He handed the nearest man his own, reckoning that it would be better if the cops had their hands full when he pulled the Browning on them, but at that moment Carmen cheerfully produced two passports from the pouch she wore around her neck.

Docherty hardly had time to feel relieved before another problem reared its head – did the Mexicans know they were looking for Colombian women? Would Bazua have bothered to advertise the fact? Would Payán's men have known? As the Scot's fingers inched towards the butt of the Browning once more his mind wrestled with the various options. Should they take their own car or the police car? They could lock the two officers in the boot of one of them . . .

The Mexican was still studying Carmen's passport. Now, Docherty thought, but at that moment bright lights flashed in the rear-view mirror.

The car was going fast, and as it went by they had a brief glimpse of young American males, a brief sonic deluge from their car stereo. The Mexican stared after the vanishing tail-lights, a frown on his face, and almost absent-mindedly handed back the passport. A few moments later he and his partner were in pursuit.

The four of them just sat there for a moment.

'How come you had Marysa's passport?' Docherty asked, still staring through the windscreen at the disappearing police car.

'I've had it all the time,' she told him. 'I wanted a picture of her to show people on Providencia.'

They resumed their journey, and some fifteen minutes later they passed the policemen and the American youths, one of whom seemed to be counting out dollar bills. Forty-five minutes after that they were entering the outskirts of Ciudad Juárez, eyes peeled for a suitable-looking motel. The border was now only a few kilometres away but Docherty had no intention of attempting a crossing until he was certain that all the other options looked worse. As things stood at the moment there were people in authority on both sides of the Rio Grande who had a vested interest in stopping them.

They chose a mid-priced motel, and after they had been given the keys to two of its rooms by a sleepy-looking girl of about twelve, Shepreth phoned Vaughan at his apartment in Mexico City. 'Just get over the border,' the DEA man told him. 'My friends in Washington tell me the President already has a private investigation going – it's just a matter of time.'

Shepreth explained that they might run into problems if they just presented themselves at Mexican emigration.

'It seems like about ten million people have managed to get across without presenting themselves to anybody,' Vaughan murmured. 'OK, just sit tight,' he added, rather more sympathetically. 'I'll see what I can arrange.'

Shepreth told the others what Vaughan had told him.

'We could go through the tunnel,' Marysa said.

They all looked at her.

'Angel was boasting about his escape from the island,' she said quietly, 'and his friend – the pig you shot – he told him about a tunnel he has built under the border, right under the Rio Grande.'

'Did he say where it was?' Docherty asked.

'Not exactly. But he has a bottling plant – for Mexican beer, yes? – and he said the noise of the machinery covered up the noise of the digging.'

Docherty reached for the telephone directories on the washstand. As far as he could work out there were only four bottling plants in Ciudad Juárez, and only one of them – according to the city map they had already borrowed from the girl in reception – was within stone-throwing distance of the river.

'Now?' Shepreth asked him.

'Why not?' the Scot said.

They all climbed back into the car, and Docherty drove them towards the centre of the town. It was a quarter to one in the morning, but small groups of men seemed to be loitering on every corner of the ugly modern streets, looking like they'd been hired by some spendthrift movie mogul to create a restless, almost ominous atmosphere. The main square showed more activity, but the hustlers were too busy to notice them and the whores turned away when they noticed the women in the back seat.

Payán's bottling plant was another kilometre to the west, one of several industrial premises which lay between the wide road and the glorified concrete drainage channel which went by the name of the Rio Grande. There was a light shining through the open door in the loading dock as they went past, but no sign of a night shift in progress. The high wire gates were closed.

A few hundred metres further up the road Docherty turned the Nissan round and stopped for a moment. There was probably a way in from one of the adjoining premises, but he was still wondering what to do with the other three while he investigated when a Toyota Land Cruiser purred by.

He watched as it slowed and came to a halt, either at the gates of the bottling plant or somewhere very close by. He turned off his own lights and moved the Nissan forward, pulling up behind the other vehicle just as the gates swung open.

'Ready?' he asked Shepreth, and followed the Toyota in.

As he drew up behind it a man on the loading dock glanced in their direction, then gave the men in the Toyota an enquiring look. They obviously had no idea what he was asking them, because neither of them looked round until their questioner's hands shot up in the air, and by that time Docherty's Browning was waiting to invite them out of the cab and into the factory.

Once everyone was inside, the loading-dock door shut behind them, Shepreth and Carmen held guns on the three men while Docherty went to make sure that the rest of the building was empty. He came back a few minutes later with a ball of wire and the news that it was.

The sight of the wire made the Mexican night guard talkative. 'Do you know who you are messing with?' he asked them contemptuously. 'Payán – that is who. He will roast your balls over a slow fire for this.'

'I doubt it,' Docherty told him mildly. 'We killed him yesterday.'

The man started to laugh, but the look on his companions' faces put a stop to that. They were now frightened.

'Where is the tunnel?' Docherty asked them briskly.

'We don't know,' one of them said. 'We have just come from Chihuahua. He will know,' he added, indicating the night guard.

'Well?' Docherty asked.

'I know nothing about a tunnel,' the man said sullenly.

Docherty walked over to him, grabbed his belt with one hand and thrust the barrel of the Browning down inside it with the other. 'Where is the tunnel?' he asked again.

'I show you,' the man said breathlessly.

It was under one of the storage rooms which lined one wall of the main building. A concrete slab floor on steel rollers slid aside to reveal a shaft about thirty metres deep. Aluminium ladder-like stairs were provided for humans, winches for the bundles of cocaine, heroin and whatever other contraband came this way.

The night guard obligingly turned on the lights and Docherty went down. In the chamber at the bottom there was a neatly stacked mountain of plastic bags containing enough drugs to relaunch the American 60s. Facing this yet-to-be-realized fortune was a large opening in the wall. Docherty flicked one of the switches beside it and the lights came on, illuminating a concrete-reinforced tunnel some two metres high and one metre wide which stretched away into the distance. He flicked the other and heard the hum of air-conditioning. Well, he thought, you couldn't expect smugglers to raise a sweat.

'Send 'em down,' he shouted up to Shepreth, and the three Mexicans descended the stairs. Once Shepreth had joined him Docherty fastened the three men's wrists and ankles with wire. They wouldn't have much trouble getting free once their captors were gone, but by then it wouldn't matter. As the other three started down the tunnel he cast a wistful look back at the hoard of drugs, thinking that it would have been nice to wash them down a drain. Unfortunately it would also have taken most of the night.

The tunnel, which proved to be about a kilometre in length, ended in another chamber at the bottom of another shaft. Docherty climbed the metal stairs and listened for signs of life above. Hearing none, he pulled the switch which rolled back the concrete slab and climbed out into a warehouse full of shoeboxes. He called down the all-clear and went in search of the outside world.

A single bolted door led him out on to one of El Paso's darker streets.

The other three emerged, and all four of them started walking towards the better-lit street in the distance. The neon signs of several hotels appeared above the rooftops, and they were just nearing the crossroads when a police car cruised into view. Docherty instinctively put his arm around Marysa's neck, knowing without looking that Shepreth had done the same with Carmen. Marysa flinched and then stiffened at his touch, but she didn't pull away, and after one lingering stare at the late-night revellers the cop drove on. Two minutes later they were bribing a night receptionist to give them rooms.

Docherty was woken by the sun streaming in through the crack which he had deliberately left in the curtains. Shepreth was still asleep in the other bed, snoring slightly.

The Scot lay there for a moment, then got up and gently prised open the connecting door. In the adjoining room the two sisters were sleeping like spoons, Carmen's left arm wrapped protectively around Marysa's waist. They looked like young girls, a picture of innocence.

He had heard Carmen and Shepreth on the balcony in the middle of the night. They had been whispering at first, but then there had been silence for a while, and finally the ecstatic breathing of lovemaking, her muted cry, his muted groan. Docherty could remember a handful of occasions in his adult life when he had been an unseen witness to others' pleasure, but this time he had taken a strange delight in the sounds. This was love he was listening to, not just sex.

He had no idea what would happen to the two of them. They came from different worlds – Shep had the worst job in the world for relationships, Carmen a sister who would be needing more attention than most children. Maybe he was turning into a romantic in his old age, or maybe he was just seeing his younger self and Isabel reflected in their mirror, but Docherty found himself believing that they would a find a way to be together.

It was almost seven-thirty. He took a shower and then woke Shepreth, who looked groggily up at him. 'You're on guard,' he told the MI6 man, picking up Bazua's ledger from the top of the TV and letting himself out of the room.

The hotel still seemed half asleep, but the rest of El Paso was already well into its stride. Docherty walked across the palm-lined square thinking that the town looked more Mexican than American, and nothing like the place described in the Marty Robbins record he'd bought in 1959.

The office supply store was just opening as he reached it, allowing him the choice of the six copier machines in the window. There were almost five hundred sheets in Bazua's ledger, which meant that he would be turning them for the best part of two hours.

As the copier whirred and the bright light slid to and fro he stood there, turning the pages on automatic, thinking about Guillermo Macías, whose name he had found under the date of his arrest. Toscono had not lied about the reason for that – the boy had been picked up with a group of others and charged with 'spreading malicious propaganda'. For five weeks he had been repeatedly hung by the wrists and given high-voltage shocks with electric cattle prods, for no other reason than the warped pleasure of his captors. On Christmas Eve he had been one of seven dropped from a helicopter into the River Plate, his wrists bound with wire.

To judge from many of the other entries he had been one of the luckier ones, but Docherty didn't imagine the boy's parents would see it like that.

He thought about the five young women who had been kidnapped into slavery more than a year before. Marysa had told them that Rosalita had killed herself after only a few weeks on the island, but had so far refused to say anything more about the long ordeal. Placida and Irma were also dead, Victoria and Marysa damaged in ways he couldn't begin to comprehend. He asked himself how his fellow-men could behave in such a way and got no answer.

The machine whirred on, and eventually the entire ledger had been copied. He packed it into a box provided by the store and then made three additional copies of the two pages which detailed the involvement of two named American Intelligence operatives – there was no mention of which agency they worked for – in the extended torture and gang-raping of four female student prisoners at the Rosario army base in early 1977.

After making three copies of the covering letter he had composed in the early hours of the morning he gathered everything together and headed for the post office. Half an hour later the box was on its way to his own address in

Chile and the three envelopes were travelling express to the *New York Times*, the *Guardian* and the German magazine *Der Spiegel*.

He re-emerged into the sunlight with the original ledger and dodged his way through the busy traffic to the centre of the square. It was still only ten o'clock, and on impulse he bought a coffee from the kiosk and sat in the shade to drink it. The people, like the town, were mostly Mexican, and he sat there watching as they went about their daily business. Maybe it was the sunshine, the riot of colours, but now, as in 1977, he found these people so full of life.

Maybe that was why they needed their Days of the Dead – yearly reminders that life was also hard and cruel.

Docherty didn't think he needed the health warning any more. Maybe this time the good guys had emerged relatively unscathed, but there had been enough times in the past when that hadn't been the case, and he had his doubts whether either of the surviving women would ever be the same again.

But then even the bad guys had souls.

Docherty looked up at the pure blue sky, sighed and got back to his feet. He had seen enough days of the dead. He was ready to write the fucking memoirs.